THE COMPLEXITIES
OF LOVE

BY

M.A. QUIGLEY

Published by Fourlegged Pty Ltd

ISBN (paperback): 978-1-7640154-2-4
ISBN (ebook): 978-1-7640154-3-1

Author: M.A. Quigley
Cover design: Mary Schmidt

Second edition (this edition) released on 30 May 2025.

'It's not who we meet in life that defines us.
It's how we respond to them.'

– M.A. Quigley

For Ben, thank you for believing in me.

CHAPTER ONE

What would you be if you were an animal? I am a homosexual like the Guianan cock-of-the-rock, a gay bird, albeit stuck in the confines of a cage. Pigeon-holed because of society's beliefs about who I am meant to be, how I'm supposed to live my life, and who I should marry. My secret was forever steeped in my fears and fantasies. I couldn't tell anyone because I envisioned being rejected. Instead, I walked a line of loneliness and misguided guilt.

Ten years ago, Dave Ogilvy disappeared in the Spring of 1966. That day left an indelible mark on my heart like a shirt stain that refused to budge, no matter how many times I tried to remove it. The first day I met him was in primary school. He'd kissed me behind the shelter sheds during recess when we were in Grade 2. Dave had run towards me smiling and his lips grazed mine. His fingers lightly touched my hands, and a tingling sensation erupted through my body. He'd walked away in a hurry. I mouthed for him to wait, but Bradley ran around the corner chasing him. I was eager to know if anyone had seen what had happened. Girls nearby were skipping rope and none of them looked my way.

Other children were talking, but they didn't say or do anything. It was like I'd imagined everything, but I knew the entire scene was real. Dave used to come over to my house and we'd play football in winter and cricket in summer in my back garden or his after school. Other times, we'd play with my marbles or his toy cars. On weekends, we'd go to the oval and watch the local team play football or cricket. We were inseparable.

During our first year in high school, Dave didn't want to know me anymore and I couldn't understand why. He'd moved on and I mourned the loss of our friendship, always asking myself what I'd done to him to make him not want to be my friend anymore. Anyone who knew us would've thought we'd had an argument and had fallen out as friends. Dave didn't speak to me, but I believed the prying eyes of the schoolyard kept him away from me. I never dared to ask him. My mind would be in turmoil, going wondering why. I likened it to a death and found it hard to cope, aggrieved that he'd found other boys to hang out with instead of me. If anyone looked at us, they'd think we had nothing in common.

He was unlike any other boy I'd ever known. He appeared more refined and had a better sense of me, more so than Laura or any of the other children in our school year. Dave had a certain air about him, not snobbish or regal. It was a confidence that everyone seemed drawn to. He never had a girlfriend, but Beth and another girl, Amy, always hung around with him and his gang.

During my first year of high school, I was a loner out of necessity more than anything else until Laura came along. She felt sorry for children on their own and tried to be friends with everyone. I pushed her in the deep end during swimming lessons, knowing she couldn't swim. I hoped that she'd hate me for it and our so-called friendship would end. Instead, she thanked me later because her favourite teacher dived in and saved her. My habitual fear of being found out wasn't subverted because I was still worried, Nora would discover I was gay and laugh at me and run around telling everyone.

Laura loved to gossip, and if she ever suspected anything, she never asked me. We studied in the library after school together or at her house. I used to listen to her talk about other girls, her family, and school. She was strong-minded and hardly ever asked for my opinion.

Laura picked me to be on her swimming team. I was always last to be picked, but she flattered me by telling me they were imbeciles, and she believed what her mother said, an old cliché, that they save the best 'til last. Other kids would ask her why she'd chosen me, but she'd shrug her shoulders and have her usual reply ready before walking away 'Why does anyone do anything?' She didn't have a boyfriend, and I often wondered if she was waiting for me to ask her out. If she was, she never said. The other kids at school thought she was my girlfriend, but I never confirmed nor denied it. As far as I knew, neither did she. I let her have her way because I didn't care. I'm sure other girls would've tired of me because I never retaliated. Laura helped me escape from the negative mindset I had of myself by focusing on her never-ending problems: pimples, dresses, shoes, make-up, and how to wear her hair.

I blamed liking sweets, not puberty, for the assault of pimples on my chin and thought that Laura would take an instant dislike to me, but she didn't. I couldn't help but notice how her skinny body turned shapely. Her breast grew bigger, and her nipples were erect under her school shirt, none of which turned me on. It was Dave in the locker room that interested me.

The structure of his face changed. His cheekbones became more pronounced, and his eyelashes grew longer. Hair grew on his upper lip and around his chin while I remained bald in comparison. In our first year in high school in the showers, I noticed the hair growing in his pubic area and his penis appeared slightly larger. He was developing, and I felt there was something wrong with me. One moment we were the same height, and the next morning he appeared taller. His Adam's apple protruded more from his slightly longer neck.

He was becoming a man, and I was still a gangly pimple-faced boy. Even his voice changed: instead of a high-pitched tone, it deepened while mine came out monotone and low. Even though other boys surrounded me, I didn't notice if their bodies were any different. Perving on men was something I was encouraged not to do. Dad had taken me to the toilet on an outing when I was five and I'd pointed at a man's penis. The man said if I was older, he would've hit me for being so brazen. It was an unspoken rule that men knew not to do. I had to be discreet when I thought someone else was watching and pretended, I'd dropped something or walk away.

At night-time after dinner, I'd squeeze my pimples. When I did it before school, it made my face inflamed and sometimes bleed. I worried I'd have scars from removing pustules and tried abstaining from eating anything sweet, but they still appeared. I held my head up high around Laura because she had pimples, too, but around Dave and his gang, I'd look at the ground feeling inadequate because they had clear complexions.

Stan called me pox head and syphilis, which made me angry. Heat rushed to my face and I'm sure it made me look worse. He laughed at me, and I wanted to hit him. Instead, I would put my arm around Laura and speak to her. If I were on my own, I'd walk in the opposite direction and pretend I hadn't heard him. As far as I was aware, neither Stan nor the rest of Dave's gang had a girlfriend, and I knew it must've irked them because they always looked at me with contempt whenever I was with her. I wondered if Laura saw anything in me, but I was too frightened to ask.

All of them vied for her attention and she'd smile and stick her chest out, accentuating the curve on her back. It was like they wanted to take her away from me and despised me because she'd chosen to be with me. If she wanted to, she could've walked away from me and gone out with anyone, but she stayed by my side.

One afternoon, we had an argument on the way home from school and I let her know we were seeing too much of one another. I needed space. Laura was never one to sulk, and unlike me, she made acquaintances easily. On the way to school the next morning, I saw her walking with two other girls on the other side of the road. They giggled when I walked past them. We spent two weeks apart. Laura came up to me one lunchtime and said she'd missed me and needed help with her history assignment.

No one was home at her house after school, so we sat in her bedroom and listened to the radio while we did our homework. Afterwards, she insisted we practice kissing. I hung back, not wanting to do anything. She let out a frustrated sigh, but I appeased her to stop her continuous chatter.

Laura ran her fingers through my hair while I held her close to me. My hands touched her lightly as though she were a fragile package. I'd overheard other boys talk about how aroused they felt at kissing a girl, but I never did. Whether it was because it was Laura, I'll never know because she's the only girl I've ever done it with. My sweaty palms and the buzzing sensation in my head I likened to anxiety because I wanted to get it right. I wouldn't have said I enjoyed the experience.

⁂

Laura spoke to anyone who would listen, and I'm sure she never knew what it was like to sit in silence. Whenever she had other kids from school at her house, I stayed away, happy to be by myself. Laura used to tell me her friends couldn't understand what she saw in me but never let me know what she'd replied. I never asked her. Laura never questioned why I preferred to be alone, even though she was the exact opposite and loved to spread herself around drawing people to her like bees to honey and supplying the same unsurpassed kindness to everyone.

I felt the blood draining from my face the first time she kissed me and closed my eyes. She guided my hand between her bare skin and knickers. I opened my eyes, and hers were open too, watching me. She moved my fingers between her flaps and let out a moan. I thought I'd hurt her and pulled my hand away and whispered I had to go. She pleaded with me to stay, but I ran over to my bike and picked it up off her front lawn. I heard her laughing as I rode away.

'Come back,' she yelled, but I ignored her. She made me feel like a clumsy, awkward fool. I wasn't brazen or confident. In truth, I was more like a girl than a boy.

On her fourteenth birthday, Laura asked me to have sex with her. She wanted to know what it felt like and how to do it 'properly,' her words, not mine. She remarked we could call it 'research.' My parents seldom went out, so I said it was safer to do it at her house. Her parents weren't going out for the next two weeks, but the Saturday after that they were going to a dinner party in Dandenong.

At school, Laura would put notes in my locker with the same sentence: Looking forward to research. She signed her name with a L.' Mum thought I wasn't feeling well because I looked pale. My skin was clammy to the touch. She insisted on putting a thermometer in my mouth, but my temperature was just above normal. When we went to visit the doctor, he said there was nothing physically wrong with me.

Each night, I had a recurring nightmare. Not about having sex with Laura, I feared buying condoms. A year ago, Dad double-parked his car near the supermarket, so I could buy menstruation pads for Mum. She was in the toilet and had run out of them. I cursed Nora for being at a sleepover with her girlfriends and pleaded with Dad to park somewhere, so he could purchase them instead of me, but he wouldn't listen. It was Thursday evening peak hour when most families had been paid and were doing their grocery shopping. I found the offending item and went to pay for it, but the lines at each cash register were full of trollies. I saw a boy I knew from school and went and waited in the aisle furthermost away from him. A woman entered behind me with two children - one of which was Dave's friend Dillon and his sister.

I looked around me, wondering where I could hide the package, but there was nowhere. Three sets of eyes penetrated me from behind when I put the item on the conveyor belt. A woman said, 'Look what a good son he is, helping his mum.' I ignored her and concentrated on paying the cashier, a schoolgirl in her last year at my high school. My heart pounded, and an electric shock went through my body, making me break out into a sweat. I strode away with my head down.

'Excuse me,' said the cashier. She held up her hand with my change. I wanted to run away and hide. Dillon locked eyes with me and had a sly look on his face. I had a deep urge to scream. I could've killed her for calling me back despite the change. My stomach churned, and I knew I'd be laughed at and teased once word got around school.

⚬⚬⚬

When Dillon saw me in the schoolyard during recess, I knew he'd spoken to Dave and his friends about what had happened the previous evening. One of them asked me if I was a boy or a girl. Another said I was queer.

'Drop your trousers. Let's get him,' they all chanted and chased me around the building and onto the oval where the landscape appeared hazy. My heart leaped into my throat, and I knocked over a rubbish tin in the quadrangle. They cornered me at the far end of the property behind a tree.

'Drop 'em, or we'll do it for you,' shouted Stan.

Anger and humiliation were like cactus thorns stuck in my body that I couldn't remove. There were too many boys to take on.

'Come on, let's go,' said Dave, but no one moved.

I had nowhere to run, so I undid my trousers and dropped my jocks and the rest of them laughed at me. Dave was standing behind them and mouthed, 'Sorry.' They ran back to class while I got dressed.

They called me a dork and made ugly faces at me. I never understood how Dave could be friends with the other five. He always stood back and watched them, never joining in unless they spoke to him. I'd never seen him hit anyone, but I'd seen the other boys fight many unsuspecting victims.

On the way to school, I mentioned to Laura that I didn't have any condoms. She said it wouldn't be a problem because her dad had some. I left my house after I'd eaten dinner. Mum and Dad were sitting in the living room and Mum insisted on knowing where I was going. I mumbled I was visiting a friend. I never mentioned Laura. Certain things stayed in my memory, and I could remember Mum saying what a lovely girl Laura was and that any mother would be happy to have her as a daughter-in-law.

When I arrived at her house, her parents had already left for the evening. I insisted on turning the living room lights off and let her undress first. Laura acted carefree, like I wasn't there, and I wondered if she'd be any different if the lights were on. A family portrait sat on the mantelpiece, and I turned it around to face the brick feature wall.

Laura pulled her long auburn wavy tresses out of her ponytail, and they framed her small face. She moved her jumper up over her head, unzipped her jeans, and took her runners off without untying the laces. Within minutes, she stood in front of me, naked. I'm sure I appeared awkward in comparison, taking my time undressing while she lay curled up on cowhide in front of an old oil heater. The flames illuminated her skin and made her eyes change to maple. We kissed, and our hands explored each other's bodies.

Her breasts were small and soft, and her nipples became erect when my tongue lingered on them. Her mouth enveloped my erection, and I sucked her nipples and orgasmed straight away; grateful she wouldn't be able to see how embarrassed I was. She wanted me to have another erection, but my body refused to respond to her advances. No one had ever spoken to me about sex, and I thought I was abnormal. I stated I wasn't feeling well and went home. Mum sat bent over a tapestry in the living room with her glasses resting on the bridge of her nose. She paused when she saw me, the threaded needle in her hand.

'You're back early. Is everything okay?'

'Yep. Goodnight.'

Dad slept in a lounge chair with his head back, and his mouth opened, snoring. Mum wanted me to stay and talk, but I wanted to be alone.

On the way to school, Laura ran up to me and tapped me on the shoulder. She'd spoken to one of her girlfriends who'd explained the male anatomy to Laura and advised her I was normal. She laughed, but I didn't think it was funny. I was more relieved than anything else. She wanted to do it again, and I broke out in a sweat. I didn't know which was worse, that she'd spoken about what we'd done in private or that everyone would laugh behind my back because I'd failed her.

Three weeks later, her parents were going to a mid-year ball for her dad's work in the city and wouldn't be home until around midnight. Laura insisted I come over for dinner. Her mum had made a chicken casserole. Mum teased me before I left. She thought things must be serious if Laura was having me over for dinner. I wished I'd told Mum I was going to a mate's place and cursed myself for telling her.

Laura's front door was open despite the coolness of the evening. I yelled, 'Hello,' and she called out for me to come in. I walked through the house and found her setting the kitchen table. The meal her mum had cooked smelt delicious. She didn't ask me what I wanted to drink but produced two wineglasses from the kitchen cupboard and a bottle of wine from her dad's cabinet in his study.

Laura handed me the bottle to open, and I poured the wine. Her glass clinked against mine, and we toasted our research. I had a swig of the yellow bubbly liquid. It tasted sweet like honey and tickled my throat. Laura drank some more and appeared deep in thought over dinner. I asked her what was wrong. She replied her dad didn't have any condoms, and she'd forgotten to go to the chemist to buy them.

I glanced at my watch. They wouldn't be open now. I suggested we could have sex at another time, but she insisted we do it. Laura clasped her glass and had a few gulps. She moved towards me and spilled wine over my jumper and tried to wipe it off with a tea towel, pushing her face into mine with a silly smile. Her swaying made me feel sick, and I drank the rest of my drink. The wine took the edge off my anxiety, and I smiled and shrugged my shoulders. She kissed me hard on my mouth and poured us both another glass. While we ate our meal, Laura spoke about a friend of hers that had sex and what her experience was like. On the third glass, my face and body felt warm, my eyelids closed, and I found it hard to stay awake and listen to her. She picked up our plates to clear the table and laughed at me.

'Hey, don't go to sleep.'

My eyes opened, the glare of the overhead lights blinded me, and I asked Laura to turn them off. She grabbed my hand and pulled me out of my chair. I gripped her waist and broke out into a slow trot behind her. She quickened her pace, and I propped making her turn around. Laura's middle finger traced the centre of my face, stopped at my mouth, and she whispered, 'Shh.' She said something else, but I couldn't recall what. Her hands shook either side of my waist, gently rousing me. Laura held onto my arm and guided me into her parents' bedroom and pushed me backwards, making me free fall onto the bed.

'You'll just have to remember to pull your penis out before you ejaculate.'

Laura sat beside me, leaned into me, and we kissed. Laura moved away from me and stood up to take her clothes off and closed the blinds while I got undressed. She straddled me and tried to force my penis into her vagina. Her body moved against mine, and I felt an explosion of lightness and fluttering through my whole body. She rolled off me and let out a small sigh.

I yawned and closed my eyes, waiting for her to yell at me because I'd come inside her. In my dream, it was a school day, and I'd slept in. Dad yelled at me to get up and pulled my arm, but I ignored him and rolled over. His yelling intensified, and I heard Mum wailing in the background, commanding me to wake up. I ignored them. My arm felt like it had been yanked out of its socket and my body jerked. I opened my eyes, and an angry face beamed at me. It was Laura's dad.

'What do you think you're doing in our bed, you stupid idiots? Get out!'

'We were only sleeping,' said Laura, stifling a yawn.

'Don't lie and don't answer back,' yelled her mum and slapped her across the shoulder. 'Get to your bedroom and put some clothes on.'

Laura's mum glared at me. Her blood-red face filled with scorn. I heard her mutter that she couldn't believe this was happening, and I could tell she blamed me. Laura's dad shook me and yelled at me to stay away from his daughter while her mum walked out of the room after Laura. I picked my jeans up off the floor and dressed in a hurry, and her dad escorted me to the front door.

He slammed the door behind me. My hands shook, grabbing my bike up off the front lawn. I stood on the pavement with it and buttoned my shirt before riding home. The house was in darkness when I returned. I lay on the couch and turned on the television. I was too restless to sleep, worried Laura's parents would phone my parents or come around to see them.

·◦✖◦·

Laura was in the schoolyard at lunchtime talking to her friends, so I waited until after my last class to approach her. She stood at her locker, putting books into her bag, and said, 'Hello.' Another girl who I didn't know was hovering around. My eyes locked with hers to buzz off, but she stayed. Laura nodded at me to come with her into an empty classroom.

She spoke in a matter-of-fact tone, but then again, she always did. 'My period came early. Mum went on a rant and insinuated I could've got pregnant. As if! Anyway, they think it's all your fault... They think you're too forward. Sorry, I'm banned from having anything to do with you ever again. You better go. Mum's coming to pick me up. If she sees me with you, she'll smack the shit out of me.'

·◦✖◦·

On the way to school the next day, I expected Laura to yell out to me to wait up or come from behind and tap me on the opposite shoulder from the side she was walking on, like she usually did. I was halfway to school when her mum drove past, with Laura sitting beside her. They both looked straight ahead. I said, 'Hi' to Laura on my way to class, and the three girls she was with giggled, but I didn't care because they were always laughing at someone or something. Laura's reaction interested me the most. She smiled and turned around like I hadn't uttered a word and walked past me towards Stan.

Stan appeared smug, holding hands with Laura while they walked around the school grounds together. The sight of them agitated me. He always wanted what everyone else had. When he saw me, he whispered something to her, and they both laughed. I put my head down and walked back to class.

'Loser. Tosser,' he shouted.

The acne on my chin and cheeks I picked had scabbed overnight. More pimples came after the wound had healed, and I was self-conscious of how I looked. In each class, I sat in the front row, so no one would have to turn around and see my face when I answered a question. It didn't worry me what the teacher thought of me.

⁘

I ate my breakfast and went to school earlier than usual. Mum asked me where I was going. I said I wanted to study in the library before class. She shook her head and smiled in disbelief. I waited for Laura at the school entrance. She stepped out of her mum's car and acted like I wasn't there. Laura saw Stan and walked over to him. He smirked at me when he saw me, and I watched them go to class together. My fingers touched the mess on my chin, and I took a longer route to class to avoid them.

During recess, I sat on a seat in the schoolyard and watched her talk to Marjorie and Melanie, her two friends. They bantered back and forth, laughing. I ignored them. Having Laura with me allowed me to spy on Dave without seeming conspicuous. Now, I had to be more discreet.

At school, I'd waited many times for an opportunity to see Dave on his own, but he was always with someone. Laura hung out with him because of Stan, and I hoped she never spoke to them about me. A week later, I saw her with Dillon on my way to the library. He walked close beside her and whispered something in her ear. My face felt like it was sunburnt. I heard a rumour that Laura had stopped dating Stan and that her family was moving to Edithvale. I walked over to the lockers and viewed the linoleum floor. Dillon shoved me in the shoulder as they moved past.

The week before Dave disappeared, I noticed him watching me several times during our math's exam. I wanted to know if he was going out with anyone. By some coincidence, Dave and I were the last two boys left in the showers after playing football. I reached across for the soap, and it landed on the floor. Dave bent over to pick it up and his hand gently brushed my penis, which had a mind of its own, and moved upwards.

He handed me the soap and smiled before kissing me gently on my forehead. My cheeks grew warm, and I turned around to face the wall when I heard footsteps approaching. The physical education teacher walked in and advised us to hurry, or we'd be late for the next class. My fingers reached for the cold tap, and I stood there while Dave dried himself and walked into the adjoining room, where the rest of the team were changing back into their school uniform. When I came out of the shower, he was gone.

I kept playing every detail over and over, knowing it was real, but doubt crept in, and I didn't know if he was making fun of me or if he felt the same way that I did. I longed for him to pursue me and waited in hope, too scared to make the first move and frightened his friends would find out and bully me. Fear of rejection burned inside of me and made me keep to myself.

At recess, I sat on the oval and waited behind a group of trees for him to appear with his mates. The damp grass was chilly underneath me. The bell sounded, and I watched everyone return to class. I couldn't see Dave anywhere. On the way home, the winter sun shone through the pale grey clouds, but I still felt cold.

On the weekend, my parents were out. I was bored and took some money out of my piggy bank and went to the milk bar to buy something to eat. The bell over the door signalled another customer. I turned around to leave and was surprised to find Dave entering alone and could only assume his friends had already gone somewhere for their holidays.

He surprised me when he asked me to wait. This was it. Finally, we were alone together, and I could talk to him. My fingers fumbled with the icy pole wrapper. I licked the frozen lemonade several times, thinking about what I could say. I had a lightness in my step and took a deep breath to compose myself. A tingling sensation whirled through my stomach. Everything seemed surreal. I opened my mouth to speak, but no words came out. Dave mentioned that his family was going to his aunt's house several kilometres outside of the city. They were leaving in a couple of days. I wished I had somewhere exciting to go, but we were staying home.

I invited him over to my house. The words blurted out, and then I had internal chatter asking why. When we arrived at my house, it was like when we used to play together in primary school. We climbed the side fence and hoisted our bodies up onto Dad's garage and dangled our bare feet over the front of it. The sun shone through our next-door neighbour's gumtree and made Dave's curly locks shine like gold falling around his face.

I popped a chewing gum in my mouth, and it was sweeter than any candy I'd ever tasted. We watched the Greek lady across the road water her concrete. No one knew why she watered it. Dad said she was a looney and to stay away from her. She looked up and flicked her hose in our direction, missing us, before disappearing around the back of her property. Dave moved closer to me. I'd never noticed the pale freckles on the tip of his nose. His eyes were luminescent jade. Tiny gold hairs outlined his top lip and chin. For a moment, I felt self-conscious being so close to him. My chin was covered in pimples, and I shut my eyes and looked away. His hand touched my cheek, and he turned my head to face him. I'm sure I felt his lips on mine.

Dad's car approaching up the driveway made me move away from Dave. We lay down, our bodies like snakes slithering along the hot rooftop towards the fence. We climbed down, unaware if my parents had seen us. I could hear them talking when they stepped out of the car, but didn't know what they were saying. Dave waited until we heard them go inside before he held my hand and kissed me firmly on the tip of my nose and lips.

A tingling sensation swept through my groin, but before I could say anything, Mum stood at the back door and called my name. Dave opened his mouth to say something and stopped. The sound of high heels on the concrete path made us let go of each other's hands and we came around the corner to greet her. Mum said hello to him, and he nodded his head in her direction.

'It's time for dinner. You can stay if you like.'

He declined and left through the side gate. His kiss lingered on my lips, and I could still taste the sweetness of his breath as I walked inside with Mum. She served the evening meal, and I sat and watched my parents eat. Their spoons clinking against the ceramic bowl competed with the ticking of the clock on the kitchen wall. I wasn't hungry and said I was going over to visit Laura to do my homework.

Telling lies wasn't something I did, and I said it so easily that it surprised me. Dad made me sit at the table until I'd finished eating my pumpkin soup. When he and Mum left the room, I browsed through the paper he'd left folded on the table and read a story while I ate. Someone had acted with courage and the story buoyed my confidence, and I knew what I had to do.

When I arrived at Dave's house and knocked on the door, his mum answered. I asked her if Dave was home. She replied he wasn't feeling well. He was asleep, and she'd tell him I came to see him. My thumbnail bled from chewing it. I hopped on my bike and rode up and down the street. I should've asked her if he had a cold or if it was something worse. Part of me didn't believe her because he seemed fine when I'd seen him earlier. For all I knew, he could've had a migraine like the ones Mum used to get. In the library, I opened my books to do my homework but couldn't concentrate. My mind conjured up many illnesses and told me Dave was going to die.

Each day, I arrived at school early and waited on a seat near the front gate for Dave to walk through, but he never did. I phoned his house and pinched my nose, so my voice sounded different. When his mum asked who was calling, I changed my name to Edward, but she told me the same thing: Dave was sleeping. Another time, she stated he was at the doctor's with his dad. Dave being sick made me moody and anxious. It was over a week, and he still hadn't come back. I hoped it was nothing serious. In the playground, Dave's sister, Sue, was talking to four girls, and I hovered close and waited until she was alone before I approached her. She disclosed Dave had a virus and should be back soon. There were no tablets to cure it, and it would go of its own accord.

I went to his house and knocked on the door, but no one answered. For a few days, I thought I must've imagined our encounter, but Mum commented over dinner one night how nice it was to see him the previous Saturday. She asked me why he didn't come around anymore. I ignored her question because I didn't have an answer.

When I sat in my English class, I couldn't concentrate. My teacher flicked a piece of chalk. It hit me in my chest, and he asked me to answer a question. I hadn't heard what he'd asked and replied I didn't know. Someone else put their hand up, and my teacher nodded at them. They said T.S. Elliot wrote the poem The Naming of Cats and recited it word for word.

Later that evening, I lost my appetite and asked to be excused from the kitchen table.

'You can stay there until you've finished eating. It's not a cafeteria,' Dad said. 'Those nig nogs overseas would give anything to trade places with you.'

He was referring to an advertisement on television about donating money to starving children in Ethiopia.

'I don't care.'

'You'll care in a minute. You're never too old to hit, you know.'

I swear he was angry about something else but took it out on me. His nostrils flared, and he yelled at me to go into the living room. He stood up from the kitchen table and took his belt off and stormed after me.

'I've done nothing wrong. I'm not hungry.'

'Bend over.'

I can still hear the resounding whack across my buttocks and remember the stinging feeling on my soft flesh. He didn't stop there. He struck me two more times.

'Do it again, and I'll whip you from here to the next suburb.'

It hurt to sit down and only added to my sadness.

⸻◈⸻

I sat alone in the playground at recess eating an apple. Laura and her friends, Marjorie, and Melanie, walked over to some children standing in a small group. I thought nothing of it until the three girls stood in front of me and stared at me intently.

'Let me do it,' said Marjorie.

'No, I will,' said Laura and asked me if I already knew.

'Know what?'

'Dave Ogilvy was at the station two nights ago, boarding a train with his dad. My dad saw them, and Dave's dad stated Dave's not coming back.'

They watched me like they were waiting for me to say something. I don't know what sort of face I made, but the three of them laughed at me and walked away. I hoped what Laura said wasn't true, and that they were teasing me. Dave had said something different, and I didn't know what to believe. My apple had lost its sweetness, and I threw it in a nearby bin. The last bite I'd taken was stuck in my throat. I looked away and coughed. I wanted to know why and ran over and asked them. The three of them turned around.

'Nobody knows,' replied Marjorie.

'How do I know you're not lying?' I asked, looking through them like they were invisible.

'My dad doesn't lie,' Laura replied with an angry face.

They turned and walked away from me. The bell sounded, ending recess, and my body felt like it was bolted down on the seat. I sat there for a while longer, letting her words sink in.

The sky outside was dark, not because it was night. A storm descended across the sky and the colour of the clouds depicted my mood. I imagined Dave viewing the skyline. Why had he left suddenly without saying goodbye to anyone? Was he thinking about me all the time, like I was thinking about him?

⚬◦✦◦⚬

Dave wrote to me once during the first year he'd disappeared and then nothing after that. He said he was visiting an aunt in Ballarat. We were both thirteen and his letter gave me hope he felt the same way I did, even though neither of us had ever said anything. There was no forwarding address for me to write to him, so Sue gave me her aunt's address and I wrote Dave a letter.

I was obsessed with the mailbox each day after school, sifting through envelopes for my parents, looking for the upright letters of the alphabet that I'd recognize at once if I saw them again. I always felt depressed if there was nothing for me. Everything appeared typed and there was one bill after the other. Several weeks later, my envelope arrived with a return to sender in handwriting I didn't recognize. I couldn't understand why he never wrote again. My letter was general, in case anyone else opened it. I mentioned I was looking forward to catching up when he returned and that the high school football team lost on the weekend.

In the weeks that followed, I tried to put Dave out of my mind, something which proved impossible. I immersed myself in my school-work and playing football, all the while wondering when he'd return. Each morning, I'd jump out of bed believing Laura and her friends had lied. I'd eat my breakfast quickly, envision seeing him on my way to school, running up to me and telling me how sorry he was for playing such a cruel joke. Months dragged by and my hope turned to doubt, and as time passed, I knew I'd been fooling myself and that he didn't feel the same way about me.

⁂

After that, no one ever mentioned Dave again until ten years later when I bumped into Sue, in Coles' car park, in the Autumn of 1976. Mum wasn't feeling well, and I went to get the groceries early, before breakfast. I mentioned to Sue that Nora had arrived a week and a half ago for two weeks' vacation with her husband Alfonso and their daughter, Isabelle.

'What a coincidence. Dave's coming back. Mum and Dad are having a party for him on Saturday night the week after next. We're not sending invitations, but you're all welcome to come. I'm sure Dave would love to see you.'

'Is he bringing anyone with him?'

'No, just him.'

I could tell by the look in Sue's eyes and her tone that she was excited about her brother's return. Their family was part Scottish and English like us.

If I saw Dave again, what would I say to him? Over the years, I'd had many imaginary conversations with him. One thing was for sure: I wanted him to like me. He was at an age when he could be married or divorced.

My mind slipped away into a world only I could imagine where Dave and I were married with three children. Even if no one else in my family wanted to go to the party, I knew I'd be there. Each night since he'd left, I yearned for him. Not having him around anymore had left me feeling frustrated. Hearing he was coming home filled me with a new promise.

⁓◦❧◦⁓

I walked along the shopping strip on the way back to my car, glimpsing at the shop windows. Despite the rain, everything seemed brighter. I felt happy, eager to see what Dave would be like after all these years. After I'd unpacked the groceries, I lifted the top end of my mattress, pulled out Dave's creased and dirty envelope from all the times I'd opened it over the years. I knew what was written in the letter because I'd read it many times. His words held hope in my heart. I couldn't help but open it again to see his writing, which was the only thing that seemed familiar about him to me. His words stood out like he did, commanding attention.

Dave's letter was brief. He said he had something he wanted to ask me face-to-face and that he'd be home in two weeks. For years, I'd dreamt the same dream. Dave faced me and held my hand. He looked me in the eye, opened his mouth to speak, and I woke up. I couldn't remember how many times I'd had that dream. It was always the thirteen-year-old Dave that I saw. Now we were both 23. No matter how many times I tried, my mind refused to create an older Dave. Instead, he was locked in the past where I last saw him.

CHAPTER TWO

Throughout my life, shame and guilt had been my two best friends. I'd carried them around with me like a favourite jacket that I was loathed to get rid of. Some people would say, think, or even argue that I should've been born a female because I loved to cook.

We lived in Noble Park, which was 25 kilometres out of the city where many families didn't speak to one another mainly because of cultural differences. I had a sister, Nora, three years older than me. Lots of single-level cream brick veneer houses, like the one we lived in, dotted the streets and weatherboard homes. In summer, we would run through the sprinkler to cool down while it watered the lawn and the garden beds, and at night, we would open the windows to let in a cool breeze.

Some immigrants lived in big two-storey houses surrounded by concrete instead of gardens. If you drove through Noble Park, you'd think it was just like any other suburb with a church, a football oval, a technical school, and a primary and high school. Mum used to go to church with her parents, but Dad didn't believe in God, so he refused to let her or us go.

We weren't poor or rich. Ours was a middle-class family. Dad drove an old Holden, and every week he'd clean the car in the driveway, making the chrome on the bumper bar sparkle even on a dull day. Nora and I used to stare at ourselves in it and giggle at how it distorted us like mirrors at the circus that made our bodies appear smaller and our heads bigger.

She never wanted to play with my model cars or farm set. My toys were left aside, and I embraced her world of make-believe, where the cubby house became our home. Nora would hand me one of her naked dolls and tell me to dress it. That was her favourite game. Whenever our parents were out, she would make me play it with her. I was Nora's husband, and she always bossed me around. Her teddy bears and dolls were our children, and she'd light a fire in the brick barbeque, and I'd cook sliced lemons from our lemon tree and pretend they were steak. Other times, I'd make mud pies. Nora would half fill a saucepan with water, put the doll's bottle in it, heat it, and feed our children.

We seldom argued. Nora was more like the husband, and I was more like the mother. Sometimes we'd fight. I never won. She was on the school debating team. If Dad caught us arguing, he'd punish us, so we tried not to be caught. If Mum heard us, she'd tell us to be quiet. Our fights were usually over who was going to wash or dry the dishes. We were supposed to take it in turns, but she loved getting her hands wet and refused to let me. That was why I loved to soak in a bubble bath. There's something about soapy water and watching the froth slide over the dishes and my skin and the sound it makes as it evaporates.

Ever since I left high school, Mum insisted I started dating girls. She always asked me if I'd met anyone nice or if I was seeing anyone.

'Don't be shy. You can bring them home to meet us. We don't bite.'

'There's no one yet. I'll let you know when I do, Mum,' I'd replied, knowing I never would.

Nora met Alfonso soon after she'd left school. He'd worked at the local greengrocers for Alfonso's uncle, Vince. Dad couldn't stand the fact that Nora was dating an Italian. To him, they were wogs and ate stinky stuff. Mum wanted lots of grandchildren and was disappointed Nora only had one child. Her biggest fear was dying before she got to see who I'd married.

Our neighbour, Mrs Appleby, scolded me the last time I saw her. She thought I was too fussy, and no one would want me.

'Who do you think you are?' she'd said. 'You'd better find someone fast. The older you are, the harder it gets. All the nice ladies will be snapped up.'

Mum told me to pay no attention to Mrs Appleby, even though Mum married when she was 21.

'You're a male, so you can take your time. Just don't get anyone pregnant without being married. If you do that, you're not welcome back.'

I'd often heard snippets of my parents' conversations in their bedroom while I lay in my bed. Mum wanted Nora and me to be happy, but Dad wanted us to marry someone who spoke English. I didn't care what he thought. It was none of his business how I wanted to live my life. No one interested me. I'd heard of other boys and girls I'd gone to school with whom had married young. Some were separated and would never marry again. They were on welfare with children to feed. Others had children and were miserable, stuck at home while their husbands went to work.

Dad didn't know what Nora was thinking when she announced she was getting married. He worried that Alfonso's parents would want to stay with us when they came to Australia a week before the wedding. He was relieved when Nora stated they were staying with Vince and his wife, Loretta. We were all invited to their house for dinner to meet them. Alfonso's mum, unlike her son, was a short, solid woman whose rough hands pulled at either side of my face. She gave me a bear hug and kissed both my cheeks and voiced something in Italian. Nora smirked.

'She thinks you're handsome, but you're way too thin.'

At our house, we never said a prayer before we ate, but that night we bowed our heads and listened to Alfonso's dad and waited for him to pick up his knife and fork and start eating before we did the same.

We presumed the first meal, lasagna, was all we were eating. I liked their food and had a big serving only to discover cannelloni next, then spaghetti bolognese and pizza. I lost count after that. Nora nudged me and motioned for me to keep eating. Otherwise, I'd offend them. My parents had the same amount as I did, but Nora had smaller portions protesting she wouldn't fit into her wedding dress if she ate anymore. Vince's vino made me cough before it reached my lips. One small glass made me feel like I'd taken a sleeping pill. I excused myself and yawned to hint that I was tired. But Alfonso's parents wouldn't let me leave until I'd had dessert with the strongest coffee I've ever tasted in the smallest of cups.

Nora invited them to our house for dinner, and Dad's eyes rolled back in his head. He opened his mouth to speak. Mum nudged him and he stopped.

'Gracias,' said Alfonso's mum, smiling.

His father nodded.

⁕

'What the hell are we going to feed them?' Mum had asked on the way home.

'How the hell would I know?' Dad had replied under his breath. 'You'll have to get Nora to knock somethin' up for them.'

The following weekend, Dad sat at the kitchen table while I set it. He argued with Nora about what Alfonso's family would like to drink.

'You can buy your alcohol. Vince will probably bring some more of that petrol shit anyway,' Dad stated, referring to Vince's wine.

Vince had invited us to his house last summer to pick grapes growing over his carport. We'd placed them in a wooden barrel. When the barrel was half full, Vince stomped up and down on the grapes with his bare feet to make his wine, or vino, as he called it. Vince had handed Dad a bottle from his cellar, and Dad folded his arms. Mum took it and thanked Alfonso's uncle. Her advice was never to reject what someone wanted to give you, but Dad had other ideas. He'd tried it before and thought it tasted like cat's wee.

'Don't be such a racist, Dad. They won't be here for long anyway,' Nora had exclaimed as she checked the oven.

'I'll say what I like. Don't think you can answer me back just because you're getting married. You're still my daughter.'

'I'm glad I am. If it weren't for Mum, I couldn't stand living here anymore.'

Nora turned to Dad. 'You should try going to church sometime. You might enjoy it. I know Mum would if you let her go.'

I'd left them to argue and drove down to the local liquor shop and bought a cask of Riesling. The only thing our family agreed upon was that none of us liked Vince's wine.

When I'd arrived home, Mum had a headache and went to bed. Alfonso's parents wanted to see her, but Nora told them Mum wasn't feeling well. Our dinner of vegetable soup, roast beef and apple pie seemed meagre compared to all the food we'd eaten the previous evening, but they seemed happy with what they were given. I wished I could understand their banter across the table. Dad usually held the conversation over dinner, but that night he didn't speak and nodded now and again.

When they were leaving, Dad and I stood on the veranda and waved goodbye to them. Alfonso's parents and Vince and Loretta walked ahead while Alfonso stopped and kissed Nora good night in full view of us in the driveway.

'On your way, you two,' said Dad.

'Leave them alone,' I said.

'That'll be enough out of you.'

When Nora married Alfonso, it was more like a funeral than a wedding. Parents were usually overjoyed when their children were wed, but both sides looked glum. It was obvious his family wanted him to marry an Italian. They'd only known us for a short while and had already taken a dislike to us. Dad whinged through the whole wedding ceremony, a full Catholic mass, and stayed seated while everyone else had communion. Mum went to stand up, but he pulled her back beside him.

'The house will fall down if we eat any of that rubbish,' he insinuated.

Nora and I weren't baptized, and Alfonso had insisted Nora become a Catholic. The priest said he would teach her in private, but Dad rebelled. He'd disown her if she did.

I was jealous when she married. Every time they came over to visit us, I would shy away, feeling bitter because she had what I wanted, someone who was attractive and loved her. When Isabelle was born, I envied Nora because she had her own family, and I still had no one. Alfonso was a quiet man when Nora first met him, but after he married Nora, he would answer Dad back. Neither knew how to apologize, and Nora would phone Mum or me and ask us if Dad was home. Whenever he wasn't here, she would visit us with her family, but if Dad were home, she would come alone or with Isabelle.

Nora learned Italian at the local TAFE College before she went to Italy, and we'd mind Isabelle. If they'd stayed in Australia, she wouldn't have bothered, but she didn't want to sit around not knowing what everyone was saying.

Dad walked in on us one afternoon when Isabelle was playing with her toys in the living room and Nora was having a cup of tea before she went home. He said he wasn't feeling well. Dad was too proud to tell us he'd been made redundant. Isabelle ran over to greet him and seemed to be the only person who could make him smile.

'Don't you go speaking any garlic muncher talk if you ever come back here,' he blurted. 'The English language is universal. You should teach your grandparents to speak English.'

I don't think Isabelle understood what he was saying, but she nodded in agreement with him.

'That's my girl,' Dad murmured, but he never hugged or kissed her. He handed her a dollar note instead.

Nora chided him for putting ideas into Issy's head. Nora rummaged in her handbag for her car keys and motioned for Issy to get her toys because they were going home. She found it difficult staying home and going to playgroup, talking to other mothers who thought their child or children were better than hers, asking her why she had one child and not more. She used to come home and complain about it and Mum would tell her to ignore them. The thing was, Nora couldn't let it go. Someone was always buying the bigger house or a newer model car. I thought Nora turned out to be one up on all of them moving to Italy and still being married because living anywhere else other than Noble Park was more exciting.

Nora's move to Italy was hard on me. Alfonso thought Isabelle would have a better life in Italy, surrounded by his family. He was one of eight children. I missed the three of them, especially Isabelle. In a way, I used to feel like she was my daughter because I'd mind her on weekends and the occasional weeknight while Nora and Alfonso went out with their friends.

Since she'd moved to Italy, I didn't envy her anymore. I guess it was because she was no longer on my mind. When Nora initially left with her family, it was like she'd never existed in our lives apart from photos that adorned the sideboard in the living room. We heard nothing from her for several months. She'd given Mum her new address and phone number, and Mum had put it somewhere safe but couldn't find it.

'It's no use contacting the I-talians. We wouldn't be able to understand them. Besides, it would be too expensive anyway,' said Dad.

'I could ask Alfonso's uncle,' I said.

'To hell, you will.'

'She'll contact us when she's ready,' said Mum.

Mum would rush to the phone every time it rang, hoping it was Nora. One month later, she phoned, and Mum acted nonchalant on the phone like she wasn't expecting to hear from her, but then Dad took the receiver from Mum and spoke to Nora.

'Why haven't you rung us sooner?' asked Dad. 'You're living over the other side of the world, and for all we know, you could've been murdered. Your mother has been worried sick about you.'

CHAPTER THREE

Mum's migraines started two years ago when Nora announced she was moving to Italy with Alfonso and Isabelle. Issy was in Grade 1 at the local primary school. Sometimes Mum's vision would blur, or she saw double and thought she needed new prescription glasses, but the doctor advised her it was psychosomatic. Mum worked as a typist for a tobacco company. She had a seizure at work and went to the hospital in an ambulance. I'd caught her several times, staring at nothing like she was deep in thought. The neurologist informed Mum she had a brain tumour. We asked Mum why she never mentioned her headaches until after her diagnosis. She believed she'd complained enough about her eyesight and didn't want to bother anyone.

She didn't want anyone to see her 'fake' hair and insisted I drove her to the city for all her medical appointments instead of catching the train. Every weekend she'd put her hair in rollers and tie a scarf around them, but when her hair fell out, she opted for a wig the same colour and length as her straight hair.

Most nights, she didn't feel hungry and went to bed early. Dad and I would sit in the living room and a few minutes later, his eyes would close, and he breathed deep with his head back and his mouth open. Soon after that, his snoring competed with the television.

Each day he commuted to the city by train and worked in an office job. Our paths crossed in the kitchen. I made my breakfast, and he'd just finished eating his. It was the only meal he ever made for himself because he believed cooking was women's work and couldn't understand why I wanted to cook. Ever since I started working at the bakery on the main street of Noble Park after school, I'd dreamed of being a chef. Conjuring up meals that people had never tried like a duck with mango and chocolate, but I'd have to wait until I'd worked in a restaurant to try making it because my family wasn't into fine dining.

·~⁊⁊~·

A girl who worked at the bakery asked me why I was smiling so much. One of our regular customers said I looked like I'd won something. For the past week, I'd pulled everything out of my wardrobe thinking about what I was going to wear to the party and picked fault with each item I tried on. I contemplated having my haircut or putting product in it to control my unruly curls. I had a trim, and to my dismay, the barber had talked too much.

Now my ears appeared bigger on my narrow head. I tied a scarf around my neck, but my earlobes rested on the bulky mass of the scarf, making them more pronounced. As I served the customers, I imagined Dave's reaction when he saw me. He commented on me being like the big bad wolf in *Little Red Riding Hood*. Laughing. Teasing. We sat on the couch together, oblivious to all his other guests, and he let me know where he'd been and what he'd done. None of my clothes had seemed good enough, and I invested in a new pair of jeans and a polo shirt and jumper the week before he was due to arrive home.

·~⁊⁊~·

This morning, Mum seemed agitated on the way to the city for her check-up with the specialist. It had been three months since her operation, and she hated any medical appointments. Mum always made excuses about why she should not go. The wig made her scalp itchy, and her hair had grown, but it was finer, and to her dismay, the colour had turned grey. I told her to dye her hair when it grew longer, but she was superstitious it would make the cancer return.

Nora, Alfonso, and Issy were staying at Alfonso's uncle's house because Dad didn't want an I-talian staying with us. He used the excuse that there wasn't enough room. Nora wanted to see as much of Mum as she could and had been around every day to visit. She wanted to come with us to Mum's appointment, but Mum thought it was no place for Issy. Alfonso was helping his uncle out at the greengrocers and there was no one to mind Issy, so Nora stayed home with her.

⁓∾⁓

A train strike created more traffic on the roads, and we came to a standstill when we were halfway there. Nerves got the better of Mum and I topped up my petrol tank so she could use the toilet at the service station. Mum complained she had a tension headache, but I put it down to being on edge about visiting the specialist. I said she shouldn't worry so much.

'You'll be fine.'

Her voice sounded irritable. 'Don't tell me that. How would you know? I wonder what your dad will do without me. Promise me you'll be kind to him if anything happens to me. I know he can sound blunt. and offhand, but he is a gentle soul underneath that rough exterior.'

'Stop talking negatively, Mum. You look good.' Our family always thought negatively. My positive words never showed how I felt.

'You're not in my body. Besides, how would you like to have hardly any hair?'

'It'd be cool in summer.'

'Trust you to say something like that, Mr. Positivity. How do I know how many days I've got left? No one does. Hell Mark, Nora will be back in Italy soon. It's a shame you aren't there instead. You're single. I won't get to see my only grandchild grow up. Life is so unfair.'

I knew not to reply. Each time I drove her to an appointment; the conversation was always the same. The first time I argued with her, and it brought her to tears. She was vulnerable and scared, so I ignored her and kept driving.

31

On her first visit after the operation, the specialist said she'd recovered well. He believed he'd got all cancer and was pleased with her results. He placed the images up to the light. Her brain was a walnut with a grey splotch on the right-hand side corner. The next image had the splotch removed. I could tell by his face that he was pleased with his handy work. This time, Mum complained about her hair colour, and he eyed her with a stern expression on his face and stated it was better to have hair than no hair.

We walked past the newsagents in Collins Street, and I bought her a lottery ticket and told her to keep it somewhere safe.

'I often wonder how you'll all cope if I get a bad report.' Mum's right hand went to her head whenever she spoke about herself, touching the area where the scar was ever so lightly, even though I don't think she would've been able to feel it.

'It won't come back. You've already beaten it.'

'That's easy for you to say.'

'Try not to pre-empt it,' I replied, trying to sound more convincing than I felt.

I hated it when we had these conversations. I could only guess what it was like for her to lose her dignity and self-esteem with her hair falling out. She felt like a semi-trailer had squashed her brain each time she had a headache. Whenever I had a cold or my head hurt, I never complained. I pitied her frustration and fear. It unnerved me, and I hoped she couldn't see that.

We walked along the street and waited at the traffic lights until we could cross the road. We always had a look in the shops and something to eat before we went home.

Mum stopped when she got to the other side, contemplating which way to go. We passed Myers Department Store, and she retraced her steps, lured in by a sales sign, and viewed a dress in the window. I walked inside with her. She hadn't bought clothes since she'd stopped working. The shop assistant's eyes centred on Mum's hair.

Mum held her head up high and outward appearances showed a woman of confidence, which was true, but since she'd had cancer, it had proven otherwise. If she noticed the girl looking at her, she didn't show it and found the dress in her size on the rack and went into the dressing room.

Mum came up to me and twirled around. Her hands ran down the front of the fabric. The maroon jersey clung to her petite figure, and she smiled for the first time in ages.

'It's very flattering on you,' said the sales assistant.

'I'll take it,' Mum replied.

The young sales lady looked at me, making me feel self-conscious while Mum changed back into her clothes and paid for the dress. I was sure the sales lady was trying to work out who I was: a young man with an older woman, lover, son. We walked down the street in silence for a few minutes, and Mum peered in another window and kept walking until we came to a cafe, with the menu stuck on the window near the door. We went inside, and I already knew what she would order. She had a cup of tea and a slice of cake like she did every other time after her appointment, and I had a toasted ham and cheese sandwich on rye bread and a cup of coffee. To me, everyone's cooking was different, no matter if the contents were the same. She liked to buy me something to take her to see the specialist and would pick a different cafe each time.

Dad annoyed me. He didn't like to eat out because he thought the best meals were at home and couldn't understand why we went to a cafe. I'd argued with him several times, saying it was good for Mum to go out and try different cafes.

'You don't know what's in it, but you know what's in the food you eat at home. What if they haven't washed their hands or they've coughed all over what they're preparing for you? It's unhygienic, and you could get sick. There was an article in the paper about a restaurant in the city having rats in their kitchen. They were closed and fined by the council,' he'd admonished.

From what I could tell, Mum loved eating out, trying a slice of cake with her cup of tea, and if it made her feel better, I was all for it. What harm could it do, anyway? Some cafes even had magazines for us to flick through. Heaven forbid, if we bought a magazine home because Dad thought magazines were full of rubbish. According to him, the paper had everything anyone needed to know.

'Where's your mother?' asked Dad when he returned from work.

'She's in your bedroom. Dinner's almost ready. Nora, Alfonso, and Issy will be here soon,' I said and set the kitchen table.

The shadow of fear on his face lifted to reveal concern.

'Is she alright?'

'Yeah, you don't have to worry. The specialist said her brain looks healthy, and the cancer hasn't come back.'

The back door opened, and Nora and Alfonso walked in with Issy. Dad went to see Mum and came back into the kitchen. Issy ran over to him. He picked her up in his arms and she wriggled her way free, so I could hug her and say hello.

'I'm glad you're here,' I said. 'Dinner's ready.'

'What is it?' asked Issy.

'Chicken Masala. Grandma bought a new dress. Ask her to show you.'

Mum appeared in the doorway. Her eyes widened, and she moved her hand across her mouth, telling me to zip mine. I took the plates I'd warmed out of the oven, placed the casserole dish on the sink, and served dinner.

Dad's brow furrowed. 'And where were you thinking of wearing it?'

She hesitated.

'I saw Sue the other day while I was getting the groceries. She invited all of us to her house for a party next Saturday. Dave's coming home,' I said, trying to change the subject.

'I wish I could see him and his brother, John,' said Nora. 'Can we stay a while longer, so we can go to the party too?' She looked at Alfonso, and he shook his head for no.

'I hope Issy finds someone like John or Dave when she's older. Those boys have good manners and good looks as well. I'd be delighted for her to marry someone like that.'

'Usually, a man has one or the other. It's hard to find both,' said Mum.

'What about Sue? Have you been on a date with her?' asked Nora.

'No, she's not my type.'

Dad turned to Mum. 'You could wear something you've already got.'

I ate a piece of chicken and listened to Nora saying something to Alfonso in Italian.

Dad waved his finger at Nora. 'Stop talking I-talian when you're with us. You're in our country now. Have some respect.'

'For God's sake, Dad, calm down. We'll be gone soon,' said Nora.

'Well, it's my house.'

Mum's voice sounded strained. 'I haven't treated myself to anything new in ages. Anyway, Mark bought it for me.'

The chicken was stuck in my throat, and I coughed. I didn't care about the dress. Seeing Dave again was at the top of my mind.

Nora scowled at Dad.

'You want to see nana's new dress? Don't you, Issy?' asked Nora.

Issy nodded.

'Now look what you've done,' said Mum. She hated being the centre of attention.

Mum finished her dinner, and Nora and Issy left the table with her while I cleared the plates before serving the trifle I'd made. Dad walked into the living room with a bottle of port and motioned Alfonso to come with him. Mum and Nora came back into the kitchen talking about dresses and sat back at the table.

⤜⧉⤛

Thunder clapped, and I lay in bed and buttoned my pyjama top, listening to the rain drumming on the window. I thought about Dave and what he was doing and slowly drifted off to sleep. In my dream, I was a chef in a city restaurant called Art on a Plate, because everything I created was an art form. My meals were my creations like Titanic, an open beef burger with the lot. I cut the beef into the shape of a ship and placed it on one side of a round bread roll. On the other side, I put cheese, beetroot, tomato, and lettuce and topped it with mango chutney made from real mango and fresh coriander to garnish. I made thick chips seasoned with salt, chilli powder, paprika, and curry powder served with mayonnaise and sweet chilli sauce. My restaurant was highly regarded and had rave reviews in the newspapers.

Nora came around after breakfast before she left the next morning. Dad had to pry Mum's arms away from her so she could leave. Alfonso's uncle was driving them to the airport.

'It's always his bloody way,' Dad uttered.

I whispered to Mum that they'd be back again, but I shouldn't have opened my mouth because it didn't make any difference.

Dad put his arm around Mum's shoulder and led her back inside while I stayed on the curb and waved Nora goodbye, wondering if I'd ever find the happiness that she had. An electrode of emotion welled up inside of me, but until now, I'd never dared to let it. Instead, I would clam up, fearful I'd be laughed at or frowned upon if I showed my true self to anyone. I'm sure if my parents knew, they would tell me to leave and never come back, especially Dad.

Ever since Sue mentioned Dave was coming home, I'd walked past his house several times, hoping he'd arrived and would be outside, but he never did. I wanted to knock on his front door and say, 'Hello, I heard you're back,' but feared rejection. Despite the sun beaming down on me now, I felt frigid and kept moving. Everything at his house appeared the same: mowed lawn, weeded garden beds, and the blinds drawn like no one was home. Down the street, I heard the clatter of lawnmowers and smelt freshly cut grass mingled with leaves burning in incinerators and gutters.

The entire day inched along in millimetres. No sooner had I arrived home from the bakery than there were chores for me to do. With Nora back in Italy and Mum not feeling well, I'd been given the responsibility of doing the housework. Other men would've balked, but I quite enjoyed it. Dad always chided that I should've been born a girl.

I baked a black forest cake to take with us to the party. Mum had a headache, and it got worse as the day progressed. She kept asking me now and then who we were going to see, like she had short-term memory loss.

'You remember Harry and Grace's son, Dave, Mum? He went away.'

'That's right.'

The vague expression on her face made me realise she didn't have a clue about whom I was talking about. She vomited in the laundry after lunch, and I convinced her to take an afternoon nap.

In my bedroom, I played with my hair, hoping it would magically grow. Feeling content, I went into the bathroom and sprayed it with Mum's hairspray. If my parents noticed anything different about me or knew the way I felt about Dave, they never uttered a word. I was grateful Nora wasn't around in case she did.

In the bathroom, I gazed at my reflection in the mirror. I could've stood there all night and never been good enough. I checked my appearance one more time.

'Hello,' I said. My complexion turned red, and I left the room to see if everyone was ready.

Dad took a bottle of wine out of the pantry cupboard. It was one that Alfonso's uncle, Vince, had given us. On the way to the party, I walked with nervous energy, listening to my parents talking. I didn't know where Dave had been living. If I were in the street, would he recognize me, stop, say hello, or walk past me? Would I approach him or pretend not to notice?

I'd rather meet him in the street and go somewhere quiet where we could talk, not a party because there were too many prying eyes. I'd thought of Dave with a moustache, a beard, and both. Dave with long hair, a crew cut, and with an earring in his ear. Did he wear glasses as I did for reading? Were his hands soft like mine, or had they formed callouses from working on the land? Would he recognize me and think that I'd changed? Would he smile and say, 'Mark, is that you?' I would widen my eyes and say, 'Of course, it's me. How are you?' Or would I say, 'Sorry, you've got the wrong person,' and shy away from him?

CHAPTER FOUR

On Dave's veranda, I stood behind my parents. My throat tightened, and I tried to compose myself and chewed my thumbnail and made it bleed. Mrs Ogilvy answered the door and ushered us inside. She asked Sue to find Dave and to tell him we'd arrived. The living room had a table set up with desserts, and I placed the cake on the corner of the table. Dad handed her the bottle of wine and there was Dave coming to greet us. Five other people looked up when we entered, none of whom I recognized. I presumed they were relatives, but I didn't care. He was there with me, and he was home.

I felt lightheaded when I saw him. His body, sexy in tailored pants that showed off his slim figure and well-defined buttocks. I wanted to hug and kiss him in front of everyone, so they'd know he was mine, unaware of how he'd respond. He strolled toward us. His clean, trimmed nails brushed my skin as he drew his hand away from mine. My hand pulsated with electricity, and I shivered with excitement. His voice sounded deeper. His thick, wavy hair was devoid of curls, but his eyes were the same, graced with long lashes.

For a moment, I couldn't move. It was as if I was hypnotized seeing Dave in the same room standing in front of me. My dream had become a reality, and I felt like I was viewing a prized piece of art. The candour in his voice made me lightheaded and giddy.

'Mark, how are you? It's nice to see you again.'

I hesitated; fearful I'd come across as too revealing. My voice sounded high pitched like a pubescent schoolboy. 'Welcome back.'

'How are you?' he asked, smiling at me.

He didn't appear to notice how astonished I was at seeing him, or, if he did, he said nothing.

'I'm great. Thanks. You remember my parents?' I asked. He shook Dad's hand and said hello to him and Mum.

Sue came and excused herself. Dave had other people to meet. He walked away with her. I didn't realize that I had been holding my breath until I started breathing again.

Throughout the evening, I stole a glance at him, wishing I could have him all to myself, wondering if it would happen tonight or some other time. A woman walked into the room whom I saw earlier. At first, I thought it was Laura. Hesitant one to make the first move, I stood back and watched her. I put it down to shyness. I'd been that way ever since I could remember. Dad had chastised me in high school and said, 'Girls won't come to you, son. If you want a girlfriend, you're going to have to approach them and try to get to know them,' but I was glad to watch people mingle. If someone wanted to find me to talk to, they would. Dave came over to her and kissed her on the cheek. She leaned into him and whispered something, and he shook hands with the man beside her. It wasn't Laura.

I drifted in amongst the strangers with a glass of Riesling I picked up from a waiter. Sue came up to me with a tray of mini sausage rolls, and I took one and ate it. People nodded my way as if they knew me, but they were faces I couldn't recognize. I nodded back politely, keeping my eyes on Dave.

John and Sue were also good-looking and could've modelled, but it was the mischievous look in Dave's eyes that made him stand out from his siblings. John was the eldest by one year to Dave and three years to Sue. The first time I saw them, I knew they were related. They smiled and nodded their heads the same way. If you had your back to John and Dave, you couldn't tell who was laughing.

That evening, Dave and his siblings appeared differently. John had filled out more, but Sue was still the same, albeit taller than her brothers. Small lines adorned Dave's face, showing a history of smiling and worry. His stance was no longer like his siblings. His frame was still lithe, but he walked with purpose and appeared different somehow that I couldn't put into words.

John's wife Yvette was at the house with their two children. His chin and cheeks were covered in stubble, and his curly hair hung over his forehead and framed his face. His waist protruded over his belt from good home cooking.

I averted my eyes, frightened they'd noticed me scrutinizing them, and walked into the dining room and stood with Mum at a trestle table while Dad went to say hello to Mr Ogilvy. We placed some carrots, potatoes, and green beans on our plates and waited in line for some meat. Dave came over to us and put his arm around Mum's shoulder. She looked away, unwilling to meet his gaze. I knew she was self-conscious because of her wig.

'Would you like a drink, Mrs C?' asked Dave.

'No, I'm fine.'

John interrupted, wanting to know who was next to be fed. She ignored him and declared Dave had grown tall and handsome.

'He's already got a big head,' said John, wiping his brow with his forearm. Mum smirked.

We moved forward in line and held out our paper plates for John to put slices of meat on, and Mum complimented John on his cooking. I wanted to tell Dave how good he looked.

Instead, I said, 'I heard Beth's getting married to a guy she works with.'

Dave shifted his stance, and I noticed a slight agitation across his face.

'Is she still the same? I can't remember the last time I saw her.'

'Her son turned ten not so long ago,' I replied.

'A son, wow!'

Dave shook his head in disbelief and came with us into the sunroom. Dad was there having a beer, talking to Dave's dad. Mum walked over to them. Dave took a piece of meat from my plate with his fingers.

'That tastes better than army grub.'

'Are you back for good?' I felt like an uncle asking questions, but I wanted to know firsthand, not hearsay.

'I'm not sure.'

'Where have you been since you left?'

'New Guinea and then Vietnam for a while.'

'Noble Park must seem ordinary after travelling.'

'It's good to be back. Are you married?'

'Still single. And you?'

'Same.'

I wanted to ask him why he'd just got up and left. Did his dad make him leave, or did he want to go? But I considered it prying too deep and kept my mouth shut. I believed if someone wanted me to know something like that, they'd tell me.

His eyes searched mine and I could feel my face growing warmer and viewed the burnt orange carpet. A tingling sensation swept through my body. The only person who had scrutinized me closely was the dentist when I was having a routine check-up. His mum came towards us and excused herself before asking Dave to come with her. I eased my way through the crowded sunroom to a makeshift bar and the person behind it poured me a glass of wine. The room reminded me of a seedy bar with its thick haze from men smoking pipe tobacco and people smoking cigarettes. A man came in and ushered everyone into the living room.

Dave stood beside his parents, smiling. His dad held a small piece of paper in front of him and said that on behalf of the family, he was grateful to have Dave back home after his many travels and how good it was to be a family again. He recalled fond family memories of Dave and thanked everyone for coming before reading out all his relatives' names so as not to miss anyone. His mum had made a cake and handed Dave a knife to cut it with and everyone yelled out, 'Speech!'

A man of few words, Dave said it was good to see his family again and thanked his parents for having the party. He looked forward to catching up with what we'd all been doing before, mentioning other guests whom I didn't know. I watched him and caught his eye while I listened to the sound of his voice, not what he was saying.

His tone and mannerisms were full of the usual charm he'd had ever since I'd known him, but there was something different about him I couldn't understand. His face appeared strained, and his voice faltered, like he didn't mean what he said. It was like he was standing in front of all of us because his parents had made him make a speech. His face softened when it was over. Hands pounced on a nearby tray one of his aunts produced, and I managed to snavel a club sandwich before cheering Dave. I looked around me to see if I could recognize anyone. People had their backs to me, moving into other rooms. My eyes stopped on Dave's lush penis, sitting to the left of his trousers, commanding attention.

'This is my partner, Madeleine.'

I wolfed the last mouthful of my club sandwich, and it caught in my throat. I had a sip of wine and turned around. It was Daniel, a boy from high school.

A tall, skinny girl dressed in black trousers and a white shirt shook my hand.

'Pleased to meet you,' I said, holding her limp hand.

'Come on, let's dance,' she said to Daniel, and they headed to a room off the hall where loud music was playing.

Her voice trailed after her. 'It was nice meeting you, too.'

I imagined tonight to be different, and an intense sadness fell over me like a tidal wave drowning me. The students I knew still hung out with the same people. A girl walked past me laughing, and a man strode up to her towards the music. John came around with glasses of beer on a tray on his way back to the bar, and I took one from him and drank three quarters like I couldn't quench my thirst.

Dave's family and friends were talking or dancing, but I didn't want to do either.

Sue stood in amongst a group of women and called out to me. They all turned around, and I kept walking. I leaned against a wall near the kitchen and overheard someone talking to Dave's mum.

'It's nice to see Dave is still as popular as he used to be. At least he won't have any trouble fitting back in here after being away.'

'As long as he takes his medication,' said his mum.

I wondered if Dave was coming down with a cold or if it was something more sinister. I waited for the other person to reply, but they didn't. People spilled out of the room where the music played, and they danced in the hall. I eased my way through them and noticed Dave talking while he danced with Marjorie. Despite being at the party, I felt disassociated. The room smelt of finger food mingled with alcohol, perfume, aftershave, cigarette smoke, and body odour. Three girls had their backs up against the wall near where I stood.

'Wow, look at Dave,' said one girl, her eyes fixated on him.

'He's better looking than when he was in school,' said another girl. I noticed a hint of bitterness in her tone. 'What's she doing dancing with him?'

'I don't know,' said someone else.

Dave turned around, and I wondered if he knew we were all viewing him from across the room. I wanted to approach him, but I was a coward and walked over to a woman carrying a tray of party pies. I had one and downed the rest of the beer. Dave played with Marjorie's hair and pulled her away from him and then close, making me simmer with jealousy. It was obvious they were ensconced in each other, oblivious to everyone else around them. The song ended, and I went to move away, but Sue came over to me. She took hold of my hand and insisted that I dance with her.

'Come on, it'll be fun,' she said.

'But I don't dance.'

A slow song started, and she pulled me closer to her and swayed back and forth with the music.

'See, it's easy.' Sue placed her arms around my upper back. 'Just move your hips.'

Dave distracted me while I moved around the room, not listening to what Sue said. Her head rested in the crook of my shoulder. There were only a handful of people dancing, and it made me feel self- conscious even though it was dark.

Sue raised her voice. 'How are your parents?'

I explained about Mum.

'Sorry I didn't know.' I could feel the warmth of her breath on my neck and cheek. Her voice was tender in my ear. 'She'll be alright.'

The song ended, and I went to move away.

She spoke with a sense of teasing. 'Just one more,' she insisted. 'You're good at this.'

I was thankful that the tempo of the next song was more upbeat, and I copied her movements, jerking my body back and forth like a battery-operated doll. More people joined us.

When the song ended, I said I was thirsty and moved away despite Sue protesting. At the bar, I asked for a scotch and coke and had a swig while I walked outside, eager to be alone. No one was in the back garden. I watched people talking and eating in the sunroom. The silence cleared my mind, and the alcohol warmed me in the cool night air. I felt foolish about coming and wished Sue had never invited me.

The sunroom door clicked open, and Sue walked towards me.

'I wondered where you'd got to. Come on, let's dance.'

'I'd rather stay out here for a while. It's stuffy in there.'

'I'm so glad you came.'

She reached out and stroked my arm. Her eyes searched my face and focused on my mouth. She leaned into me, and I gulped my drink.

'There's no need to be shy.'

She took the glass out of my hand and put it on the ground. Her feet faltered when she stood up and I held onto her, swaying slightly from all the drinks I'd consumed. Our noses touched, and then the unspeakable happened.

'I'm sorry, I don't know what came over me,' she said.

I coughed and looked at the ground, unwilling to make eye contact or say anything. Sue's dad opened the door and said she was wanted in the kitchen. She hesitated, said she was coming and walked towards him.

I picked up my glass, drank the remaining liquid, and walked around the side of the house. I cursed under my breath, kicked the wall, and fell backwards onto my bum. The glass fell and smashed over the concrete, and I swore under my breath. My body shook, and I turned slightly and held onto the fence railing to pull myself up and pat my backside.

I walked around to the side gate and pulled the latch up to release the lock to go home. I couldn't bear going inside again and saying goodbye to anyone. A man walked into the garden with a woman.

'Well, I'll be. If it isn't Mark Cooney,' she said.

I knew that voice anywhere. It was Laura. I'd never seen her again until now. She waddled towards me, her girth heavily pregnant.

'How did you know it was me?'

'I'd know you anywhere. You haven't changed a bit except you're taller.'

Laura hugged me and introduced me to her husband. He took a packet of cigarettes out of his trouser pocket and offered me one. I declined. He lit one. His eyes swallowed me, making me self-conscious. I focused my attention on Laura and ignored him.

'Are you married?' Her eyes flitted around the back garden like she expected my wife to appear.

I hated being asked that question. It seemed like I was the only person at the party who wasn't going out with anyone, let alone married.

'No.'

'Tony and I have been married for a year now,' she said, smiling at her husband. He whispered something in her ear and walked away.

'Do you have a girlfriend?'

'No.'

'Maybe there's hope for you, now that Dave's back,' she whispered, nudging me and waving to Dave through the window.

Dave smiled and came outside to join us, eating a piece of the cake I'd made. He put his arm around her.

'Laura, I see you haven't been wasting any time,' he said. His eyes fixated on her bump.

'You were always the cheeky one,' Laura replied. 'I'm due in eight weeks. My husband is over there getting us both a drink. I don't think you've met him.'

'Congratulations,' I said, though it belied how I felt.

She smiled and introduced her husband to Dave. Her husband handed Laura her drink and butted his cigarette under his shoe.

'What sort of cake is it?' asked Laura, patting her belly. 'I've had the biggest, sweet tooth.'

'Black forest. It's the nicest cake I've ever tasted,' said Dave.

The door opened and the boys who Dave hung out with at school walked towards us, drinking. Dad called out to me from behind them, and I excused myself and went back inside.

Mum wasn't feeling well after she'd eaten, so Dad walked her home. I surprised myself and stayed for a while longer. A man near the bar handed me a can of beer, and I held onto it but didn't drink from it and listened to him and someone else talk about their wives and their concerns about drugs and alcohol when their children grew up. I walked away from them and overheard pieces of conversation as I moved through the house, watching everyone.

The evening was like a reunion seeing Laura, Dave, and all his mates. I shied away from everyone whom I recognized. It was like I was a younger version of myself, and my insecurities and aloofness were with me once again, and I couldn't let go of them or the past. Many people I knew had moved away from Noble Park. After tonight, I wouldn't see them anymore, so I didn't care if they thought I was rude. The sound of chatter in the sunroom competed with a John Denver record Dave's mum insisted on playing.

'There you are,' said Dave. 'You remember the gang?'

I eyed them with trepidation. Dave's aunt came over to us and spoke to him. He walked away from us. Each member of the gang nodded and shook my hand. Sue held out a tray of sandwiches cut into triangles, and I took one. My eyes focused on the far corner of the room where the ceiling meets the walls, and I put the sandwich in my mouth and woofed it down. I didn't realize I was holding my breath until Edward asked me a question.

'Are you married?'

The weight of his belly made the seams on his shirt pucker and the buttons pop out like they were about to burst. I could see his hairy chest, and his trousers hung off his frame, making his backside appear bigger.

'No.'

'I'm divorced,' he said, even though I hadn't asked him. 'In fact, we all are.' His face pinched as though he regretted what had happened.

'Any children?' asked Stan.

'Heavens no.'

'I'm on my second marriage,' said Stan. 'I'm paying maintenance, and I've got two kids.' He smiled as he divulged this information.

That explained his shock of grey hair, his scuffed shoes, and the hole in his jeans. They each spoke through a haze of cigarette smoke, but I didn't pay any attention to what they were saying. I viewed Dad on the other side of the room talking to a neighbour. What Mum saw in him, I didn't know. He never had a kind word to say about her or anyone else, which often made me wonder why she stayed with him. I couldn't understand why everyone wanted to know if I was married. There were other things to discuss, like work and hobbies.

Since Dave had gone away, he remained a fantasy I liked to engage in. It took me away from the real world, where I was a bored actor walking solo through life. All of them made me feel uncomfortable, and I pretended to see someone I knew in the crowded room and excused myself.

Before the party, my life was going along fine, but after being around so many familiar faces and hearing fragments of their lives, it felt like something was missing. Would I ever travel or find a life partner and have children like the rest of them? I didn't like my chances. I was 23, and this was the first party I'd been to in a long while. How was I going to meet anyone if all I saw was the inside of my parents' house and the local supermarket?

Dad walked through the sunroom and went outside with John Ogilvy and his dad. One of Dave's relatives standing nearby said something was a tragic loss. In the kitchen, Mrs Ogilvy stood at the kitchen sink, washing dishes and talking to Sue. I overheard her call me a nice young man. I kept walking, not caring what Sue replied, because I didn't want to use her to get to Dave. He might rebuke me if I mistreated his sister and never want to see me again.

Whenever there was an article in the newspaper about someone being gay, Dad referred to them as queer and pansies. At dinner, he'd ask Mum and me what we thought. I muttered people should be able to be who they wanted to be, which always led to an argument. Mum murmured that if our family was okay, she didn't care what the rest of the world did.

On nights like that, I'd question my beliefs. Is that why no one wanted to be friends with me? Did people find me odd? I'd scrutinize myself, and sometimes I'd become full of self-loathing. Other times I'd have a shower and find pleasure with my body to relax before I fell asleep. Otherwise, I'd stay awake for hours staring at the ceiling.

I'd overheard Mum telling Nora once that if you haven't found someone to marry by the time you're 20, people will think there's something wrong with you. My job at the bakery and learning to cook in a city school were the only two things I'd achieved. Everyone else around me had grown up, but I still felt like a young boy in high school. I scanned the area around me and couldn't see Dave anywhere. A gust of wind swept over me when I opened the front door and let myself out. Dave was out the front saying goodbye to Laura and her husband.

'Hey, Mark, wait up,' said Dave.

Their car tooted and pulled away from the curb. Laura wound down her window and blew us a kiss. Dave's hand brushed my arm, sending tingles through it.

'Is everything all right?'

'Fine. Thanks for inviting me.'

'Wait, come with me,' said Dave.

My heart raced, eager to see where we were going. We went to the oval near where he lived and stood behind the shed. He put his hands under my shirt and ran his fingers over my chest and kissed me hard on my lips.

'I've wanted to do that all night,' he said. 'I thought you'd forgotten me and that you'd be married.'

For a moment, I stood there in a trance. A warm fuzzy sensation ripped through my whole body.

'I'd better go before they wonder where I am,' he said and hugged me. 'We'll have to catch up.'

He ran back towards the house.

'It's good to see you again,' I said.

My footsteps were light on the way to my house and my stomach felt queasy. I opened the front door and walked hurriedly into the bathroom and vomited everything I'd eaten that night into the sink. My forehead was hot and clammy, and I wondered if I had food poisoning or if I'd caught something. I downed a nausea tablet with a glass of water and had a shower. I called out to Mum and Dad to see if they were feeling like I did, and there was no answer.

Their bedroom was like the scene from a movie where a person arrives home, and everything is different. The light in my parents' bedroom was on, but they weren't there. I expected them to have a cup of tea in the kitchen or living room, talking about the night and what was said and commenting on how everyone had aged since they'd last seen them. The rest of the house was in darkness. I called out to them again, but no one answered.

CHAPTER FIVE

Mum died in hospital three days later of a brain haemorrhage. Dad and I didn't move from her hospital ward, held together by our aloneness yet unable to reach out to each other.

'Who are you ringing?' he asked when he saw me dial the phone.

'Nora. She'll have to stay said here if she comes back with Alfonso and Issy for the funeral.'

'Oh no they're not.'

'Well, what am I gonna say? I'm sorry, we've got a spare room, but you're not welcome. You'll have to book a hotel. She is family.'

'If you're too weak to tell her, you can give the phone to me. This is my house, not yours.'

'Fine, have it your way; you always do.'

⁂

Issy answered the phone when I telephoned, saying something I couldn't understand.

'Issy, it's me, Uncle Mark.' She put the phone down and I could hear her calling her mum.

Nora spoke in a matter-of-fact tone, like she was half expecting something to happen. None of us ever showed emotion. Our parents believed it was a sign of weakness.

'I'll be there as soon as I can.'

'Are you bringing Alfonso and Issy with you?'
'I'll discuss it with him and let you know.'
'But...'
She hung up.

CHAPTER SIX

Dave and I hadn't exchanged a word since the party. I was sure he had lost interest in me. Otherwise, he would've contacted me by now. I didn't have time to see or phone him because Dad asked me to help him organize the funeral. We argued about Nora constantly. He wanted to have the funeral without her.

'Nora will never forgive you.'

He stood with his feet wide apart and pulled his braces out so far, I thought they'd snap off his trousers.

'If that bitch of a sister of yours doesn't have the respect to turn up to bury your mother, I'll have to do it without her. We've already waited a week.'

'I'll phone her again.'

'Don't bother. The phone bill will be too high, and I'm the one who has to pay it.'

'Well, Nora said she's coming. Give her another couple of days.'

'My arse, I will. Wait 'til I see her.'

Two days later, the doorbell rang. I went to see who was there, knowing he wouldn't answer it. Floral arrangements covered the mantlepiece in the living room, and I half expected it to be the florist with more flowers. Nora stood at the door like a bargepole with a harried expression on her face. An overnight bag sat at her feet. I poked my head out the door, expecting Alfonso and Issy to be somewhere close, and noticed a taxi pulling away from the curb.

'You could've let me know when you were coming, and I would've picked you up at the airport.'

'You've got enough to worry about without having to do that,' said Nora, hugging me.

'I'm glad you could come,' I said, picking up her bag and putting it in her bedroom. We walked into the kitchen together.

Dad sat at the kitchen table, holding his knife and fork. His face twisted, and he snivelled like a child, but his appetite never faltered. The smoke alarm went off because the sausages were burning, and Dad acted like nothing had happened. I wanted to yell at him but dropped the bag, turned off the griller, and banged the pots full of vegetables on the sink in frustration before taking the batteries out of the alarm.

Nora gave Dad a pitiful look.

'How are you?' she asked him.

'Oh, you're here. Where's that husband of yours and Issy?' asked Dad.

'They're not coming.'

'Well, it's just as well. There's no room for him here, anyway.'

Nora shook her head at Dad, and her voice tightened. 'Don't be so rude. If Alfonso changes his mind, we can put the foldup bed in my room or go to a hotel. If you must know, Alfonso wanted to come, but he's busy at work and wanted me to tell you how sorry he is to you and Mark.'

'Go to a hotel would be more like it. Can my granddaughter still speak English, or have you filled her head with all that I-ti gibberish? Why didn't you bring her?'

She raised her eyebrow. 'You know she speaks Italian well. She was only here a while ago. Besides, I didn't want to take her out of school.'

'That'd be right. What took you so long to get here?'

'I had to organize the funds.'

I admired Nora for being able to stand up to Dad. She used to hide behind her thoughts and wouldn't speak, but since she met and married Alfonso, she was a different person. She used to wear her hair straight, but now she wore it in a bun which showed off her facial features. Her nails were always painted and matched her lipstick and the colour of whatever she wore.

Dad liked to tell things as he saw them. He didn't care if he offended anyone. Mum always apologized for his behaviour. He ignored Nora, buttered a piece of bread, and ate it. She served dinner while I rummaged around the laundry cupboard looking for new batteries for the alarm.

He didn't wait for us and started eating. Mum had caused him to be like that. She'd pandered to him for as long as I could remember, warming the plates in the oven before she placed food on them. He liked to eat his dinner before it went cold, while the rest of us didn't want to burn our mouth.

We sat in silence. I swirled my mashed potato around and pushed my plate aside. Dad finished eating and wiped his mouth with his serviette and left it on the table.

'Give it here. If you don't want it, I'll eat it,' said Dad. 'You don't know what it's like to be hungry.'

'The meal is ruined,' I said.

He stretched his hands out.

'My arse. You wouldn't know what ruined is.'

I handed it to him, and he bent his head and didn't look until he'd finished eating. I made a pot of tea and filled three mugs.

'What are you going to do?' asked Nora.

'Stay here and keep workin',' Dad replied.

'You could always move into a unit or a flat.'

'What the bloody hell would I want to do that for?'

'Isn't this place too big now?'

'I don't think so.'

'Have it your way,' said Nora. Her cheeks flushed, and she raised an eyebrow.

'I was only thinking of you having to look after the house on your own.'

'I'll manage fine. Besides, I've got Mark here. You know I've loved your mum since the day I met her. There will never be anyone else for me.'

'I'm only saying it because I care,' she said.

Nora came over and took the mugs to the table while I cut the apple pie I'd baked and put a slice into each bowl and set them on the table. Dad poured cream from the jug over his and started eating.

'Mark, what about you?' asked Nora. 'Are you still going to live here?'

'I guess so.' Everything had happened so fast I hadn't had time to think.

Dad pushed his chair back and stood up.

'It's been a long day,' he said. 'I'll see you both in the morning.'

Nora and I sat in the living room, and I turned on the television and changed the channels to see if I could find something we'd both like. She walked out of the room, and I waited for her. She smiled inwardly when she re-entered the room and motioned for me to turn down the volume.

'What are you smiling for?'

'Some things never change. He's already snoring. Mark, you need to leave here as quick as you can.'

'And why is that? I don't know what I'll do yet. I'll probably stay around here,' I said, all the while knowing I lacked conviction.

'You won't meet anyone if you stay here with him. Don't you want to meet a girl and get married?'

'What about you? Will you come back?'

'I don't know. I don't think so. Alfonso's enmeshed with his family, and Issy's made new friends. I can't see us moving anytime soon. Don't change the subject. I care about you.'

'You don't need to worry about me. I'll be fine.'

'Have it your way, but you'll be sorry,' she said, walking out of the room.

'Where are you going?'

'To phone Alfonso.'

⁂

I drove down the street to stock up on groceries while Nora took Dad to the funeral parlour with the maroon jersey dress for Mum to wear. Rain pelted me when I stepped out of my car, and I ran across the road wiping my brow with my jumper sleeve. Dave walked along the strip holding several shopping bags.

'Mark, you look like you've seen a ghost. How are you?'

I looked at the wet leaves stuck to the bitumen unwilling to make eye contact with him and blurted that Mum had died. He'd caught me unaware. It was strange, but it made it feel real telling someone. Dave put his arm around me with his free hand, and my body tensed.

'I'm sorry.'

He let go of me. Dave insisted on buying me a coffee, but I said I had to be back at the house.

'I won't keep you long.'

We went to a cafe just down from the supermarket. I found an empty table at the back of the cafe, away from everyone, and ordered two cappuccinos.

'So, what are you going to do with yourself now that you're back?'

'Wouldn't you like to know?'

'Well, I am asking, so I guess I do.' I could feel my cheeks growing warmer.

'I thought I might try to get a job.'

'What doing?'

'I'm not sure.'

The waiter placed our coffees in front of us, and Dave had a mouthful of his.

'I thought I might see if I can work as a motor mechanic in Dandenong. I don't mind getting my hands dirty. If it doesn't work out, I might go travelling for a while.'

'Where to?'

'Maybe I'll travel to Africa.' 'Africa... Why there?'

'Why not?'

'I've only been to Sydney and Melbourne. I don't know what it's like anywhere else.'

'You can come with me if you like.'

I drank some of my coffee, wondering how Dad would react if I left suddenly. I didn't have the cash to spend on holidays. We'd gone to the beach on day trips but never ventured any further. I'd invested all the money I'd earned at the bakery into my cookery course.

I was like a conversation starved old person who wanted to tell him my every thought and feeling. He listened attentively and had a way of valuing what I said. He never interrupted me.

'Why did you leave without telling anyone the first time?'

'Before I left, Beth got pregnant, and her parents thought it was mine. They wanted me to marry her when we turned eighteen, but my parents sent me away. Mum and dad thought it was someone else's child she was carrying. How would I know if it's mine, anyway? I contemplated going to see Beth but decided to leave the past alone.'

'What will you do if it is yours?'

'I don't know, I haven't thought about it.'

I slurped some of my coffee. The hot liquid burnt my mouth and throat. I'd enjoyed his receptiveness, but the thought of him having Beth's child left me feeling hollow inside. Dave didn't stop me when I said I had to go.

·❧·

Nora held onto a small, battered suitcase when I arrived home.

'Are you leaving?'

'No, silly. I was looking through mum's personal effects for the funeral and found this in her wardrobe. It's full of old pictures and love letters from her courting days. Look.'

She placed the suitcase on the kitchen table, and we sat beside one another and browsed through a handmade album full of black and white photos. Nora held up a photo of Mum smiling and sitting on a blanket amongst trees and looked at the back of it. Dec' 50. I picked up a card with two birds kissing. Inside it read:

Marry me. I want to be yours forever. Love Joe xxxx.

'Let's see what he looks like,' I said, handing the card to Nora.

Three male faces smiled back at us on different pages, and we flicked each photo over to reveal dates but no names.

Dad let himself in the back door and entered the kitchen. His pallid skin had hints of grey stubble over his chin and cheeks. The wrinkles on his brow were deeper.

'What have you got there?' asked Dad.

'Photos of mum,' Nora replied.

'Give that to me. You should've asked before prying.'

'For God's sake, I was looking for some photos for the funeral.'

'Put those things back in the case and give the suitcase to me. You had no right.'

He linked his thumbs in his braces and moved them in and out while he waited.

'You've only been in the country for a couple of minutes and you're already taking over.'

'Keep it up and I'll go home.'

'Geez, Dad, she's only trying to help.'

'Don't worry, Mark. He's nothing but an ungrateful pig.'

'Can we just get through this without arguing?' I asked. She rolled her eyes at me, and Dad stormed off with the suitcase under his armpit. The doorbell rang, and I left her to unpack the groceries while I'd see who was at the front door.

A man held a huge heart-shaped wreath filled with red carnations nailed to a wooden easel. He propped it in the doorway and Dad came over to me.

'Here, give that to me,' said Dad, taking it from the man.

I closed the door behind us.

'Who the hell would send such a thing?' Dad exclaimed. 'It's ridiculous.'

'What's going on?' asked Nora.

She peered at the tiny card that was taped to the back of the easel and pulled it off.

Her face crumpled. 'It says: Please accept our sincere condolences. Sorry, we can't be with you on this sad occasion. Love from the Caviano family.'

'What sort of man are you married to when he can't even make it to his mother-in-law's funeral?' asked Dad. 'Doesn't he understand wreaths go to the chapel, not to the house? How the bloody hell are we going to get the damned thing out of here?'

'They're beautiful,' she said. 'Leave them where they are. They don't have to go to the chapel. You may as well know I've changed my flight. I'm flying back to Italy the morning after the funeral.'

'Why?' asked Dad. 'I thought you'd stay a while longer.'

'When are you going back to work?' asked Nora.

'The day after the funeral.'

'Well, there's no point hanging around here then, is there? Besides, my family needs me back home.'

'And what are we?' asked Dad.

·⌘·

At the funeral, I focused on the floral arrangement at the altar and bowed my head as the celebrant began his prayer.

> *'God our Father,*
> *Your power brings us to birth,*
> *Your providence guides our lives,*
> *and by Your command, we return to dust.'*

Dad pulled a handkerchief out of his trouser pocket and wiped his eyes. His hands clenched it, and I noticed him gazing at a tall man with black curly hair standing near a pew on the other side of the church flicking through the pages of the order of service. Words flew out of the celebrant's mouth, but I couldn't catch them. My physical body was there, but part of me was elsewhere, like watching all the characters in a movie. Everything blurred, and my mind kept telling me that this wasn't real. Mum was on holiday and coming home soon. Afterwards, I stood beside Dad and Nora and shook people's hands while each person offered condolences.

'Who is that?' I asked Nora. It was the man with black curly hair with a streak of grey through the front whom I'd seen earlier. He stood away from everyone else and didn't approach us.

'I don't know. I'm going to find Vince and Loretta.'

The man weaved in and out of people, making it hard for me to reach him. I raised my voice slightly, not wanting to draw attention from everyone.

'Excuse me,' I said.

People peered at me, and an elderly man asked me if I was alright. I ignored him and kept walking, but the distance was getting further. Someone touched my arm. It was Dave.

'Hey mate, sorry for your loss. I let mum and dad know, and they insisted we all come.'

His hand squeezed my shoulder, and his parents came over and offered their condolences. Sue walked behind them, kissed me on the cheek, and hugged me tightly to her. She smelt like a bouquet of roses.

'We'll have to catch up,' said Dave.

Mr Ogilvy asked if we were having a wake, and I said Dad didn't want one. Nora came up to us and said we were leaving. I excused myself and had a quick look around. The man had gone.

⁂

When we arrived home, a casserole dish sat on the mat at the front door. Nora picked it up and took the lid off.

'Who left that?' asked Dad. 'We don't need anyone's charity.'

'It looks like eggplant,' said Nora. 'Maybe Vince and Loretta dropped it around before going to the funeral. I'll put it in the kitchen.'

A piece of paper fluttered in the wind in the garden bed near the veranda and I picked it up.

'It's from the Greek lady,' I said. The note looked like it was in a child's handwriting. All it said was 'from no. 23.'

'She's trying to poison us,' said Dad.

Nora let out a heavy sigh. 'That's nonsense and you know it, Dad. Someone's probably let her know about Mum, and that's her way of saying she knows and she's sorry. Why do you have to think everyone's against you all the time?'

'Because she's always sneering at everyone.'

Nora opened the lid again and smelt the contents. 'We can have it for dinner.'

'Oh no, we won't,' exclaimed Dad.

Mum always had a saying for everything, especially death. She used to tell us that rain was a sign of a release when someone died. If it was sunny, they died in torment. It rained the night she died, and it was overcast the day she was buried. It didn't feel like a release. Dad said it was bullshit, and when you're dead, you're dead regardless of any old wives' tales.

I helped Nora peel the spuds to make mashed potatoes, glad to have company. I envied the way she cooked. She never measured ingredients. Everything was done in a slapdash way. The fat hissed in the pan and Dad walked over to turn it down.

'Don't touch it. I'm cooking, not you. Go sit at the table. Dinner won't be long,' she said.

'But you're getting fat everywhere.'

'Since when did you care? You do nothing around here.'

He placed his thumbs around his braces and pulled them out, expanding the black-and-white striped elastic, and walked out of the room muttering with indignation.

'Bitch. You've only been here for a short while and think you know everything. Bossing us both around and expecting us to adhere to everything that you say.'

Nora turned the radio on. A popular soft rock song played, and she sang while she prepared fried chicken. Dad walked into the kitchen and turned the radio off.

'What did you do that for? Turn it back on,' said Nora.

'I can't hear myself think. It's too loud.'

She walked past him and flicked the switch. The song ended, and the commentator spoke, so she lowered the volume a notch.

CHAPTER SEVEN

The smell of something burning woke me, and I wondered if Dad had left for work. In the kitchen, a haze had formed around the room. He moved his knife up and down a slice of toast until it turned white.

'Bugger it,' he said.

He threw the toast in the bin, and I turned off the kettle boiling on the stove and made us both a mug of tea. He sat at the kitchen table and read the newspaper while I prepared my breakfast.

'Now that your sister's gone back to Italy, you can get rid of those flowers. They're half dead and starting to pong, so is the vase of flowers work sent me as well as the ones the baker sent you.'

'What the hell are you making at this hour?'

'French toast.'

'Well, you can make me some too.'

I stood at the stove wishing Nora, Alfonso, and Issy still lived in Australia. Dad finished drinking his tea. I walked over to the table and put the toast in front of him.

'You'll have to eat it. I've got to get out of here.'

'See you tonight,' I said.

Through the living room blinds, I watched him step into his car and drive down the street. When I finished eating, I fossicked through Dad's wardrobe for Mum's suitcase. A black-and-white picture of them on their wedding day sat on the dresser. I picked it up and gazed at it but found nothing unusual other than the solemn expression on their faces. On mum's side of the bed, I lay on the bedspread, closed my eyes, said her name, and asked her where Dad had put the suitcase. My mind was a blank page. In her wardrobe, my face brushed against a dress she used to wear, and I could smell a faint hint of her favourite lavender perfume.

I put Mum's navy mohair jumper on and kicked my shoes off. Her slippers were too small for my feet, but I stood in them anyway, squashing the circumference. My eyes closed, and I hugged my body, imagining she was hugging me. The phone rang, bringing me back to reality. I picked it up only to discover it was the wrong number.

I took her jumper and slippers off and wiped the kitchen bench down. Despite Dad's rantings, Nora and I had eaten the casserole, and we both enjoyed it. I picked up the clean casserole dish from the kitchen bench. Outside, the autumn sun shone, but it didn't warm me. I felt chilled to my core despite wearing my jeans and jumper.

Next door's cat came to greet me. Normally I'd stop to pat it, but I walked across the road and left the dish on the veranda. I needed to clear my head and went for a walk to a nearby oval that Laura and I used to go to sometimes after school. Someone was running around the oval. As I moved closer, I realized it was Dave dressed in shorts, a long-sleeved t-shirt, and expensive runners with sports socks. I shuddered just looking at him. His well-toned legs were as white as his socks. He jogged over to me.

'Are you trying out for a triathlon?' I asked.

'We exercised every day in the army and when I stayed in the hospital. It's ingrained in me now to keep fit.'

'Hospital? I don't understand. Did you have an accident?' I asked, while climbing over the metal fence. He walked beside me.

'No, my parents sent me there. They caught me with a boy from the technical college. We were kissing and mucking around in my house while my parents were out. They came home unexpectedly and took me to the doctor's that week, and she recommended psychotherapy. I tried to avoid appointments in the evening. Dillon and the other boys kept asking me why I couldn't hang out with them, and I kept making excuses.'

'The sessions were crap. The therapist informed my parents that because of my age, I may grow out of liking boys. I said I never would. It's not like I've got a switch inside me and can turn off my feelings. They don't understand love the way I do. Just because I'm a male, they think I should be in a relationship with a female and that males are forbidden. In the end, they recommended aversion therapy because I said that I'd never change.'

'What is that?'

'A perverted form of shock treatment. I stayed at my aunt's house, and she took me to the mental hospital each week.'

'Shock treatment?' I stopped walking and leaned up against the metal fence, trying to understand what he'd just said.

'I tried to make everyone believe I was heterosexual. That's why I dated Beth. Don't get me wrong, she's a nice girl, but there's something about women. I don't feel the same way about them as I do about men.'

We walked over to the swings and sat down on a nearby wooden seat.

'You can tell me more if you want to.'

He kicked the moist dirt.

'What about the gang: Edward, Daniel, Stan, Michael, Brad, and Dillon?'

'My life is a farce. I hid behind who I was by hanging around with them. They're the exact opposite of what I believe in.'

'No, it's not.' I could relate to everything he said.

We sat for the longest time in silence. No one was around, and I put my arm around him, frightened he'd rebuke me, but he rested his head on the crook of my shoulder, and I stifled a sigh of relief and positioned my head closer to him. His hair was soft on my skin.

There was a lot about Dave's past I still didn't understand, and I wanted to tell him how I felt about him, but now wasn't the right time.

The sun disappeared. Rain drops sprinkled us as we walked home together. When we got to his house, I hoped he'd ask me to come in, but he said he'd catch up with me.

I waited for him to phone me or come over, but I heard nothing. My mind replayed our conversation repeatedly, trying to fathom if I'd said or done anything wrong, but I couldn't tell. Three days later, I phoned his house, and his mum answered the phone. Dave was out. She didn't know where. I could've sworn I heard him in the background, or it was the television. I left a message for him to phone me.

The calm in the house unnerved me. I opened the blinds and looked out the window. The lights went on in the house across the road and someone closed the curtains, shutting out the world. People were arriving home from work or wherever else they'd been. Outside, the frigid evening air made me tremble. I walked up our street, expecting his car to turn the corner at any minute. In my mind, I played the scene out. I would pretend I was late and arrive after him. In truth, I never felt close to him. We were like two odd socks that had been thrown together.

The streetlights came on. I imagined my earlier life with my parents. Mum prepared dinner while Dad changed out of his work clothes. I sat in my bedroom or the kitchen, reading a recipe book or talking with Mum about her day and what she was cooking. Everything was different now, waiting for Dad to phone, constantly wondering if he'd had an accident or working back. Would he be home soon? Was he okay? Was his train delayed? He parked his car at the station every morning and caught the train to the city. I walked back inside and phoned his work number. It rang out.

We used to sit at the kitchen table each night for dinner and weren't allowed to move until we'd finished everything on our plate, but now food doesn't interest me. I sat in front of the television. The noise of someone else doing and saying something made me feel like people were in the house with me. I closed the blinds in all the rooms and drifted around the house in a zombie-like state, doing nothing. At 2am, I woke up on the couch. I checked Dad's bed on the way to my bedroom. His bed was still made. Bile rose in my throat, and I swallowed it.

The next morning, I gnawed at my thumbnail and bit the quick while I waited for him to answer the phone, eager to see if he'd gone to work. My call went to the switchboard. The woman cut me off, and I phoned again. She put me through to his desk, and a man answered and said Dad was in a meeting. He asked me if I'd like to leave a message.

'Tell him his son called and ask him to phone me.'

I contemplated not going to work, but anything was better than being alone. I stood under a cold shower to wake myself up and walked to the bakery. A woman complained that she didn't order wholegrain bread and someone else complained I'd given them the wrong change.

A customer whom I hadn't seen for a while said they were sorry to hear about Mum's passing. Another customer asked how I was coping. It was like a mantra that I didn't know how to respond to, and I said nothing. I continued cutting loaves of bread for toast or sandwiches and imagined Dave turning up unexpectedly to buy a Cinnamon Loaf for his mum. Mrs Mackie, the owner's wife, asked if anything was wrong, and I said I wasn't feeling well, so she said to go home. I walked past the oval, expecting Dave to appear. A woman walked a dog near the swings, and two boys kicked a football near the goalposts.

Nora phoned, wanting to speak to Dad. She'd spoken to me on the previous evening and couldn't believe he still hadn't returned home.

Her voice sounded terse. 'Have you rung the police?'

'No, I've rung him at work. A man answered and said Dad was in a meeting.'

'I wonder why he hasn't rung you back?'

'I don't know. There's got to be a reason. It's totally unlike him not to come home. Maybe he doesn't want to because it's too painful and reminds him of Mum.'

'Nonsense. And what about you? What have you been doing?'

'Going to the bakery.' I'd forgotten when I'd last eaten and hadn't gone to my cooking class.

'Mark, are you still there? Listen to me. Don't stay at home. Mum wouldn't want you to mope around. You need to get out and do things and make her proud. Understand?'

'Alright.'

'Promise me you'll do that.'

'I already said I would.'

'And don't worry about him anymore. Worry about yourself.'

'That's easy for you to say.'

'No, it's not. He's getting on with his life, so you should get on with yours.'

CHAPTER EIGHT

At the bakery, my other colleague stopped talking to a customer when Mrs Mackie asked how I was coping. Two people came in and I served one of them and she served the other one. If someone pricked me with a pin, I wouldn't feel it. My whole being was numb, my actions robotic. At the end of my shift, she spoke to me again.

'You know you are too thin. I'll bet your dad is, too. Here, take these,' she said, handing me a bag of leftovers.

Mr Mackie insisted on driving me home, but I reneged. It was still daylight when I left the bakery. I forced my feet to keep moving. At home, I poured a glass of Vince's wine and gulped it. It no longer burnt my throat. I shuddered and downed the remaining liquid and went to bed. In my dreams, Dave and I were on holiday and having a massage in the same room. The woman flicked her hands back and forth on my back and shoulders.

'Wake up.'

I wanted to stay with Dave and kept my eyes closed.

'Wake up, damn you!'

I opened my eyes and saw Dad peering at me.

'It's the afternoon. What are you still doing in bed?'

'It's the weekend. I'm allowed to do what I want to do. Where have you been? I phoned the office.'

'Jesus, Mark. Anyone would think you were my wife the way you carry on. It'll do you good to mind your beeswax and not act like that sister of yours. I don't ask you where you've been, so don't ask me if you know what's good for you.'

I let out a heavy sigh. 'Fair enough. I only phoned because I was worried.'

'Well, take it from me. There's no need. I'm fine.'

He walked out of my bedroom and whistled as he walked along the hallway. I went to answer the phone, hoping it would be Dave, but Dad motioned for me to move and picked up the receiver. He hooked his left thumb in his braces and moved it away from his chest. I turned on the tap and poured some water into the kettle, listening in on his conversation.

'Oh, here we go. Concerned?' He let out a small laugh. 'I'm getting clothes to take to a friend's house. Never you mind. Now don't be like that. No one's after my money.'

Dad's voice raised an octave. 'Fair go. I'm not rich… That's where you're wrong. What are you insinuating? An affair? I would never do that to your mother. It's none of your bloody business. Keep it up and I'll hang up on you. You've got no right to talk to me in that tone. What's wrong? Can't you hear? That's enough out of you.' He slammed the phone down into the receiver. 'Your sister is an ungrateful bitch.' He walked into his bedroom and came out carrying a pile of clothes with him and said he had to go.

'When will you be back?'

'I'll be back when I get back.'

One month later, Dad cleaned out the detritus of old clothes that had accumulated in his wardrobe and disposed of Mum's clothing. Apart from the photo of them both on their wedding day, everything was placed in bags for charity. It was like she'd never existed. He arrived home early the next evening carrying several shopping bags filled with new casual clothes and shoes and took his time placing them in his wardrobe.

'What are you lookin' at?'

'Nothing. Are you staying?'

'I'll be off in a minute as soon as I get this mess sorted out.'

In the kitchen, I ate the pizza I'd made in my cooking class, trying to appear like nothing had changed since he'd last been here. I wanted to know what he'd been doing but decided not to ask him.

'Well, how do I look?' asked Dad.

He'd trimmed his nose hairs and his eyebrows. The hair on his head wasn't as grey anymore. When I was seven, he used to race me around the block or time me with his stopwatch when I ran the length of our street and back. It took a lot to make him angry. He adored Nora and me until we started high school, but why had he changed towards us?

I placed my knife and fork down in the middle of my plate. Dad's presence caused me to stare, speechless.

'Well?' he asked.

I croaked. 'Okay.'

He patted the side of his head.

'Just, okay. I would've expected better from you, Mark.'

He walked out of the room, and I heard the hum of his car's motor. The clock on the kitchen wall ticked louder. I luxuriated in a bubble bath and changed into my pyjamas and dressing gown. My fingers hovered over the phone. I wanted to talk to Dave, but I decided against it. In Dad's bedroom, I opened his wardrobe door to search for Mum's suitcase. Nothing. A thick layer of dust covered the carpet under the bed: nothing. The linen cupboard was filled with towels, sheets, doilies, and the vacuum cleaner. Nora's wardrobe was empty. It was too dark to search outside. When I was five, I walked into a web in the dark and a spider ran down my face. The creepy sensation of its legs was something I'd never forget. I've had a phobia of spiders ever since. I'd have to wait until daylight to look outside.

CHAPTER NINE

There were 12 of us in my class. Chef Inglesman, our teacher, paced the room. He was a short man with a rotund belly, beady eyes, and a moustache that hung down on either side of his mouth. Chef wore a white coat that hugged his body and a hairnet so that none of his thick, black, wavy hair fell onto the food. He couldn't stand dirt under anyone's fingernails and made us clean our hands before we began preparing the food. We all wore the same attire that he did.

'Today you are making crème brûlée, which means burnt cream.' Chef laughed to himself. His eyes widened, and he eyed us individually. 'You don't want to burn it. The trick is that it should be tender and jiggle in the middle.'

We stood around and watched him make it first. It seemed easy. Chef gave us a spoon each, and we sampled his cooking as he did ours at the end of the lesson. His dessert was rich and creamy, and the texture was firm.

Chef walked around the room, watching us, and peered into my mixture as he passed. He used to make me nervous, but now I was used to him and acted like he wasn't there. It was at the end of each class that his presence worried me.

I placed the mixture into a ramekin and cooked it. At the end of the lesson, he started in the back row, asked a student for a spoon, admonished him about cleaning, and said that it wasn't cleaned properly.

The student washed the spoon again and Chef tasted the crème brûlée and said it was too watery. I liked to feel I was improving, but he was a harsh critic and never had a kind word to say to any of us. Today was no different. By the time he arrived at my desk, the hot water had splashed over the side of the ramekin. The consistency was ruined and created a pebbled surface and soggy interior.

'It's clear that none of you have been paying attention. You must measure the ingredients properly.'

He pronounced it 'ingrediunce.'

'If you don't have the right amount of each one, it won't taste right. You need to have patience.'

He pronounced it 'patieunce.'

'You've been too slapdash. I insist you make it again at home, remembering to take your time.'

We all ate what we'd made after the lesson. I tasted my crème brûlée, and he was right. It was soggy, but I didn't mind the taste. At the end of the lesson, he made us clean all the equipment we'd used. He liked the stovetop to shine and inspected everything before we left. I gathered my belongings to leave, and he asked me to wait.

'You've been missing too many classes.'

'I haven't been feeling well.'

His eyes narrowed. 'If you think a person is a genius at anything just by giving something one go, you're mistaken. You won't be any good at anything unless you practice. The same applies to cooking. Half of it is in the setting up. Remember that.'

I never argued with him and nodded in agreement, but I was annoyed because I wanted to be good at it now. The truth was, I hated cooking for myself and would rather cook for other people. Now I only had myself to feed.

·❧·

Crumpled leaves blew around the front door, and inside the house, it was quiet. I walked outside into the back garden, peered through the garage window, and saw my reflection. No car. A thin-faced, skinnier version of me stared back. Inside, my hand gripped tight to the phone, my fingers dialled Nora's number, and I hung up.

I laid awake reading a recipe book until I fell asleep because I couldn't stop thinking about Dave and why he hadn't contacted me. The next morning, the front door opened, waking me. It was Dad. I found him in his bedroom. He was in the same clothes he'd left for work when I last saw him.

'Where have you been?'

He glared at me.

'Mark, how many times do I have to tell you? It's none of your business where I go or what I do.'

He smelt like a mixture of aftershave and alcohol.

'You can make me some breakfast if you want to make yourself useful.'

My voice raised an octave. 'Don't worry, I won't ask again. You can make your breakfast.'

My body shook, half expecting him to give me a slap for answering him back. I walked into the bathroom and turned on the taps in the shower. The warm water soothed me, and I dressed and left the house to go to class.

I heard the rhythmic motion of the train slowing down before it got to Noble Park Station. The man in front of me opened the door, and I sat in a two-seater alone. The train jolted and screeched back in motion. It was express, from Caulfield to South Yarra and the scenery blurred. I leaned my head against the window and closed my eyes. Just outside of Richmond Station, the train jolted to a halt, waking me. It felt like the train wasn't going any further because it sat there for the longest time. Walking would be faster. Chef was a stickler for being on time and didn't like anyone making excuses. I tried once, and he said to catch an earlier train.

When I disembarked at Flinders Street Station, the air was chilly, and I pulled my scarf out of my bag and wrapped it around my neck. On Swanston Street, I waited for a tram to take me to the TAFE

College. By the time I opened my locker and put my apron and hairnet on, I noticed Chef was already seated on a stool near the blackboard.

I had five minutes to spare and went to the toilet. Anything was better than sitting in the classroom waiting for our lesson to begin. We each made a sponge cake. I'd watched Mum make sponges effortlessly. Hers always turned out light and fluffy. Each time I'd made one at home, mine sagged in the middle, and the texture was rubbery. I felt like Mum was beside me, guiding me as I made two cakes, beating the eggs, and slowly adding sugar.

Chef came past me as I folded in flour and peered at the mixture in the bowl before leaving to see someone else. When the cakes came out of the oven, I allowed them to cool on a metal rack while I cleaned up my mess. Once cooled, I spread the top of one with strawberry jam and whipped cream and placed the other cake on top. I covered it with pink icing like Mum used to do. I was pleased with my result and wished she could have a slice with me as well as a cup of tea like we used to after she visited the specialist. The cake looked like something out of a cake shop and I waited for Chef to cut it and try a slice.

'Mmm ... It's delicious, and the icing is not thick and gloopy like your neighbour,' he said, peering at a classmate. 'I'm glad that you have been paying attention.'

After I'd finished cleaning, Chef saw me go to throw the cake in the bin and came rushing over.

'Stop! What are you doing? I can understand if the cake didn't turn out right, but this is good.'

'There's no one to eat it.'

His eyes widened. 'I'll take it.'

I handed it to him and couldn't help but smile. It was the only good thing that had happened.

That evening, Nora phoned. She was disappointed Dad had forgotten Issy's birthday.

'Where's Dad?'

'He's out.'

'Out where? He never goes out.'

'He didn't tell me.'

'What's going on?'

'Ask him, don't ask me. He's changed, that's all.'

She sighed. 'Well, tell him to phone Issy when he gets home.'

I spoke to Issy, and she thanked me for the doll I'd sent her.

'Mum said she'll phone back in half an hour.'

Dad arrived home two nights later and came into the living room. 'What are you doing sitting in the dark? We can afford the electricity bill, you know.'

He walked over to the television and turned it down. In the kitchen, his eyes searched the bench and stove.

'Have you eaten?' he said.

'I'm not hungry.'

He sat at the table and opened the mail. 'Well, you can make me something. A man must eat. You can cook something for yourself while you're at it. You're the one who wants to be a chef.'

I could feel his eyes penetrating the back of my head, and I opened the fridge door.

'There's nothing in here. See for yourself. All the meat's in the freezer. If you want me to cook for you, you'll have to let me know when you're coming home. Have a biscuit.' I placed the biscuit barrel on the table in front of him. He took the lid off it and surveyed the contents before pulling out a shortbread cream.

'Nora's rung twice. Issy's disappointed you've forgotten her birthday.' His tone turned sharp, and he placed his glasses on the bridge of his nose and held a piece of paper up to the light.

'That'd be right. I rely on you to tell me now your mother's gone.'

'You'd better phone her.'

'Just hearin' my voice on the other end of the phone will be enough of a present. What's the number?'

He went into the hallway and picked up the phone.

I poked my head through the doorway and said the numbers aloud and waited. A few moments later, his face softened.

'Happy birthday, sweetheart. Uncle Mark forgot to send you my birthday card. I've put ten dollars in it for you, so you can buy something nice. You should receive it next week. How's Mum and Dad? That's good. Put her on.' His left thumb hooked into his braces.

It was pointless arguing with Dad. He always had the last word. I took the chops from the freezer and left them in the sink to thaw. I placed the kettle on the stove and lit it. Dad stood in the doorway. He took his thumb out of his braces and waved at me to be quiet. He must've had a poor connection. His eyes narrowed, and his face grew redder.

'No, you're not having any money. Is that why you've made all your phone calls reverse charges to here? Tell me the I-talian you're married to is working and can pay his bills.'

'Well, why are your phone calls being charged to here? Your point of view! I can't believe I'm having this conversation. I don't care. After all your mother and I have done for you, you have the audacity to speak to me like this. We gave you everything we could. You should've stayed in Australia if things are too expensive over there. It's not my problem if you're renting. You should've thought about that earlier.'

'You owe me eighty quid for all the reverse phone calls you've made and fifty for all the calls you made to Italy while you were here. What? Your mother's inheritance all went to me. You'll get yours when I'm dead and buried. Not before. And if you want to know, I don't plan to die soon, so you'll be waiting a bloody long time.'

I took two mugs out of the cupboard and placed some loose tea leaves in the pot. The kettle let out a shrill whistle and Dad waved at me to take it off the stove. He yelled at Nora. The phone cord stretched, and he stood in the doorway, pulling his left brace out with his free hand.

'Look, Nora, I've just about had enough of your small talk. He'll just have to get another job. I had to when your mother had you and Mark. We couldn't afford much either.' He paused. 'Well, you married him. What is he, a mummy's boy? What? Jewellery? There was only your mother's wedding and engagement rings and a brooch I gave her on our wedding day. They're in the bank for safekeeping. No, I'm not sending them to you. What do you want to do, pawn them to pay some bills?'

I poured the tea and set the plate down, and he dropped the phone into the receiver. It took him several minutes to stop shaking. His thumbs forced his braces out so wide I thought they'd break. He paced back and forth between the kitchen and the living room like a caged beast, stopping to speak, but nothing came out. His mouth opened and closed, and he'd pace again.

He strode into the kitchen, and I turned around, holding onto the bench, frightened my legs wouldn't support me, knowing he'd try to pick a fight with me to vent his anger.

'Don't look at me like that,' he said.

He slurped the hot liquid, took another biscuit, and ate it ferociously like he was eating Nora and trying to get rid of her.

'What happened?'

'I've given her everything and never asked for anything in return. Now Nora thinks she's entitled to one-third of the estate. She thinks I should sell the house and divvy up the money. To hell with that. She speaks to me a lot worse than you do. Why didn't you cook me something?'

I picked up the bag of meat. 'It'll take hours to thaw.'

I leaned against the bench and listened to him ranting about Nora. He ate another biscuit and looked like his mind was elsewhere. I was sick of him always ostracizing everyone. Nora would never come back now after that outburst.

Issy would be an adult the next time I saw her. I wouldn't be able to watch her grow into a woman. We'd have nothing in common except her mum. I'd have to save to visit them.

Alfonso's uncle, Vince, saw me pick up a zucchini at his greengrocer shop and came over to say hello. His smile was wide, and his eyes shone despite the overcast day.

'Nora is,' he said, moving his hand in an arch over his stomach.

'Yes,' I lied. 'When is it?' I asked, as though I'd forgotten. He shocked me with his announcement.

'February.'

'That's right.' I paid for the zucchini, cauliflower, and a bag of carrots in a hurry, eager to get away from him, all the while wondering why Nora didn't tell me. She hadn't rung since she'd spoken to Dad. I swore I'd call her on Sunday evening, but I became distracted by preparing meals for the week to freeze, and then it was too late.

Nora phoned three weeks later. I didn't want to ask her if she was pregnant. I wanted her to tell me.

'Has he calmed down yet?'

'I think so.'

'Is he there?'

'No.'

'You mean he doesn't come home anymore of an evening?'

'No.'

'When are you expecting him?'

'I've got no idea.' I didn't want her to worry, but I needed to tell her. 'Sometimes he doesn't come home for several days at a time.'

There was a long silence at the other end of the phone.

'Is he seeing someone? I bet he is the bastard.'

'If I knew, I'd tell you.'

'You know I've tried to phone him at work, thinking he'd be more civil in front of his work colleagues, but as soon as he hears my voice, he puts the receiver down.'

Someone said something to her in the background.

'I've gotta go,' she said and hung up before I could say anything.

CHAPTER TEN

On the odd occasion, when Dad ranted about someone at his office who acted like a poofter, my body would automatically stiffen. My hands sweated like I was standing trial, and it was me he was accusing. I'd swallow hard and find an excuse to leave the room, paranoid he'd accuse me. I've been cautious and mindful to show no sign of preferring the same sex. He still made jibes whenever I cooked, but I'd smile at him and tell him if the food I made wasn't good enough, he could do it or find someone to do it for him. My latter comment I wished I'd never said because he found a woman named Irene.

I opened my wardrobe and contemplated what to wear for dinner at Dave's house. He apologized on the phone and said he'd been busy. I didn't question him about what he'd been doing. His parents were having a family dinner for his birthday and invited me. In the afternoon, I did something I've never done before. I bought a face mask from the chemist. It was new on the market for people with acne. The woman serving gave me a strange look when I placed it on the counter, and I said it was a present for my mother.

At home, I put the egg timer on in the bathroom for five minutes and waited for the mask to dry before I washed it off. I'd never heard the house creaking and groaning when everyone was home, but now it sounded like a human. Water intermittently dripping in the laundry annoyed me, and I tried to tighten the tap when I thought I heard a female laughing. Dad stood in the hallway dressed in a new suit, a tie loose around his neck, and with his arms around a woman trying to hold her up.

'Oopsy,' she said.

She laughed and tried to regain her balance. Dad rolled his eyes when he saw me.

'You'll be right,' he said. 'This is Mark, the one that I was telling you about.'

His eyes narrowed and his jaw grinded. 'What's that cocky poo you've got on your face?'

'It's a mask,' I said.

The woman stumbled forward and held out her hand to me and I shook it.

'Hell-oo, Irene,' she said in a high-pitched, slurry tone.

Irene's smile showed a set of straight white teeth. She stared at me with long eyelashes. Blue and grey shimmering eyeshadow accentuated her blue eyes. Red wavy hair hung around her rouged cheeks, which matched her lipstick. Short in stature, her strappy high heels made her shorter than Dad. A woollen dress with a belt showed her tiny flat frame, like a young girl who hadn't developed yet, but the wrinkles on her forehead and her laughter lines proved otherwise. A strong smell of jasmine perfume floated off her. She took a step back away from me and fell into Dad's chest.

His speech slurred and his eyes moved from Irene to me. 'We're not staying. I forgot something.'

'When will you be back?'

'Tomorrow.'

I darted into the bathroom and shut the door. The man staring back at me in the mirror had cracks around his jawline and forehead. I washed my face in the basin and patted it dry with a towel, amazed at how smooth and supple my skin felt. The pimples on my face weren't as angry looking as before. Dad's voice sounded muffled, talking to Irene in his bedroom. I turned my radio on in the bathroom to drown them out and had a shower. I squeezed some shampoo into my hand

and washed my hair. Seeing Dad drunk and with another woman made me realize the stop button had been put on my family life as I knew it. Anger seethed through my belly like a raging bushfire because of how he'd treated Mum. I dried myself in a hurry and wrapped the towel around my body, eager to tell him how I felt. Dad and Irene were staggering out the front door, and Irene turned around.

'Nigh-ight,' she said and wiggled her hand at me in what was a wave. Dad ushered her out and pulled the door behind him without looking up.

Something made me hold back. I turned the radio off and sat on my bed. How could someone be in a relationship and act one way and then completely differently when someone else came into their life? Was that how my parent's relationship started, the softness of rose petals and light-hearted fun, only to realize the thorns along the way but to stay married because of their vows or because they had children? Did it happen in any relationship, like Laura and me at school, because I didn't love her anyway, despite our age? My only guides were my sister, my parents, and Laura. I wondered if it would be any different with Dave.

I changed into the clothes I'd laid out on my bed earlier. Outside, the temperature had dropped lower during the evening and the smell of burning wood from people's chimneys permeated the air. I climbed the step onto the veranda and rang the doorbell. Even though I'd been to Dave's house many times before during my childhood, my palms grew sweaty. I took my jumper off and tied it around my waist.

His mum opened the front door and ushered me inside with no pleasantries, her face pale with no makeup. Her eyes were red and her cheeks puffy like she'd been crying. In the living room, Dave and his dad were watching television. Sue came in and sat beside me on the couch. Her knee touched mine, and I was conscious of the proximity of the two of us. She turned and kissed my cheek to greet me and rested her hand on my shoulder.

'How have you been?' she said. 'It must be hard for you with your mum gone.' She pulled her hair back behind her ears and I could feel her eyeing me.

I felt awkward and mumbled that I was okay.

'Dave, get Mark something to drink,' said his dad before leaving the room.

'Sue, Mark's my friend. Do you mind?'

She made a face at him. 'I'm going out soon, anyway.'

Sue left the room, and Dave jumped up off his chair. He had a seriousness about him, his stance rigid, and he seemed preoccupied. He walked out of the room and came back with two beers, handed me one, and sat beside me on the couch. I watched his Adam's apple move when he took a mouthful of beer and swallowed.

'Is everything alright?' I asked.

'I heard from Beth.'

'Where's she livin' these days?'

'In the city.'

'Is she married?'

'I didn't ask her, and she didn't say.'

I rolled my eyes at him and pursed my lips together. 'Is this about the child?'

He shrugged his shoulders.

'I don't believe you. You must know, otherwise why bother?' I asked.

'You just don't get it, do you?'

'I guess I don't.'

The smell of roast lamb made my stomach growl. Mrs Ogilvy came into the room and said dinner was ready. In the dining room, Dave slid into the seat beside me and his hand reached out for mine under the table. My body tensed. He made me feel self-conscious in front of his family. I went to pull my hand away, but he held it tighter. His dad extracted a bottle of champagne from an ice bucket on the table and he took the paper off, twisted the wire, and popped the cork.

The champagne spewed over the sides, and he poured some into each flute on his side of the table. When he came towards us, I let go of Dave's hand. His mum carried a soup terrine, and Sue placed the bowls on the table. Mrs Ogilvy ladled pumpkin soup into each one. His dad said cheers for Dave's birthday. We raised our glasses, clinked them against one another and said, 'to Dave' before drinking from them. We all bowed our heads, and Dave's dad said grace. I murmured, 'Amen,' and waited for them to eat before I picked up my silver spoon.

'I heard you're learning to cook,' said his mum. 'You might be able to teach Sue and me a few new dishes.'

Sue turned towards me and grinned.

'I'd love to,' I said.

'And how's your dad coping now that your mum's gone? May God rest her soul,' his mum said, crossing her chest.

'I don't see him. He's out most of the time.'

'Mark wants to be a chef,' said Dave.

'I'm sure you'll make some girl happy cooking all the family meals for her,' said his dad.

'Oh yes. Wouldn't I love that?' said his mum.

'Me too,' said Sue. 'If you'll excuse me, I've got to get ready to go out.'

'Aren't you going to eat the rest of your dinner?'

'No, I'll be fine, mum,' she said before sliding out of her seat.

'Sue's staying at a girlfriend's house for a sleepover,' said Mrs Ogilvy as if I'd asked her.

My knee pressed against Dave's knee as I reached for my glass of champagne and electricity pulsated through my leg, making it jolt up and down.

'You look flushed, Mark. Are you hot?' said Mrs Ogilvy. She didn't wait for me to answer and asked her husband to turn the heater down.

'It's a good meal, mum, you've done yourself proud,' said Dave.

His dad's face piqued, and he moved in his chair. 'That'll be enough out of you.'

'I was only complementing her on the food.'

'It's the way you do it.'

'Leave him be, Harry,' said Mrs Ogilvy.

'I wasn't doing anything wrong,' said Dave.

'Thank you for having me over,' I said. 'You sure make a nice soup, Mrs O.'

'See, Mark thinks so too,' said Dave.

An uncomfortable silence ensued, and I gulped down the rest of my champagne.

Dave pulled his chair back and stood up. 'I'll be back in a minute,' he said.

His dad's voice turned to a whisper.

'You know, we couldn't help but send Dave away all those years ago. We didn't want to, but we had to for his own sake.'

'You look like you don't understand what I'm talking about, Mark. I thought he would've confided in you.'

My eyes penetrated him, not knowing what he was talking about.

'Let's just say if you know what's good for you, you'll stay away from Dave.'

'Harry, please,' said Mrs Ogilvy. Her eyes averted to the door.

Dave came back and sat beside me and rested his hand on my knee.

His dad pushed his chair back and came around and filled my glass, and Dave moved his hand away.

'Jesus Dave. I thought we'd cured you of all that,' he said.

'What?' said Dave.

My face burned like I'd been sunbathing for too long.

His dad let out a resentful sigh, his face livid. He coughed to clear his throat and spat into a crumpled handkerchief he'd pulled out of his trouser pocket.

'That bloody vulgar stuff. I swear you've got the devil in you. You're my son, for Christ's sake, and I'm ashamed to know you.'

'Is that right?' said Dave.

'You know the Bible doesn't agree with what you're doing. Haven't we taught you anything? I don't think so. Yet you still defy us after all we've done for you.'

'You're one to talk. What about you? You don't even love mum. You left her, remember?'

'That's enough. What I choose to do is none of your business.'

'So, what? I'm supposed to adhere to your bullshit. I'm an adult and can do what I like.'

His dad ignored him and turned towards me. His tone was flat. 'Surely you knew what he was like, Mark? You should've stayed away from here. If he didn't see you again, maybe none of this would've happened. It's obvious you're just like the rest of them.'

'Rest of who?' I asked.

'All his other queers.'

His answer shook me.

'You weren't the only one. Didn't he tell you about them?'

'Don't listen to him. He's talking shit,' said Dave.

'What he did in the past is no concern of mine,' I stammered, hoping my words didn't betray how I felt.

'It's all because of you coming here that this has happened. Get out!' said his dad.

'What would you know? Don't blame, Mark. You're so fucking rigid with your ideas of how you want things,' said Dave. 'The way you treated mum was appalling. Why she had you back, I'll never know. What part of the Bible allowed you to treat mum like you did? I haven't read that section.'

Mrs Ogilvy's face crumpled.

Mr Ogilvy placed the bottle on the table and hit Dave in the back.

'You leave your mother out of this.'

Dave jumped up, knocking her chair backward onto the carpet, and punched him in the face.

'Stop it, both of you,' said Mrs Ogilvy. She stood up and darted towards them, trying to split them up.

'Calm down, Harry. We have a guest. You're only making matters worse.'

Mr Ogilvy lunged at Dave and hit Mrs Ogilvy in the shoulder, and she squealed.

Sue strode into the dining room. Her mouth opened wide when she saw the commotion.

'What the hell is going on?'

Mrs Ogilvy held onto the top of the chair to regain her balance and Sue ran over to her.

'Dad, why are you doing this?' said Sue. Her voice sounded shrill.

'I can't live in the same house as some doughnut puncher for a son. I won't have it. It's him or me.'

A car tooted, and Sue asked her mum if she was alright.

Mrs Ogilvy viewed the chocolate brown carpet and said, 'You go, honey, and have a nice time.'

'I'd better be leaving too,' I said. My legs vacillated, and I walked to the front door and opened it. Dave ran after me.

'Please stay.' His dad grabbed him by the shirt collar and hurled him backwards.

The cool night air smacked me in the face.

His dad's voice raised an octave. 'Stay away and don't come back,' he said and slammed the door shut.

Dave shouted, 'For fuck's sake, how am I meant to have any friends with you carrying on like this? Now you know why I've stayed away all these years.'

I unravelled my jumper from around my waist and put it on.

His mum's shrill voice echoed. 'Stop it, both of you.'

I didn't want to go inside when I arrived home and drove to Brighton Beach. Two dogs chased one another along the shoreline. The sun had already set, and two men dangled fishing lines over the side of the pier. The halyards beating the masts in the breeze made an eerie sound, and waves swept over the rocks and up onto the path in front of me.

At the end of the pier, I walked along the rocks and climbed down them. I sat for a while and dangled my feet in the ocean. The waves were black like the skyline. City lights came on, on the other side of the sea. In my mind, I always thought only our family had problems. I was wrong and naïve. What was I expecting everyone else's family to be better than mine? On the outside, Dave's family appeared perfect.

At home, Dad snored in his bedroom. In the kitchen, dirty dishes littered the table and bench, and the smell of tobacco hung in the air. The ashtray was full of cigarette butts. Fish and chip paper covered in oil stains and salt granules sat beside two empty wine bottles on the bench. Fuelled by anger, I was tempted to wash the dishes and make a lot of noise but decided against it. I filled the kettle with water and took it off the gas before it whistled and made myself a cup of tea. A piece of rhubarb pie with cream I found in the fridge would have to satisfy my hunger. I sat in the kitchen, biding my time before bed, hoping that Dave would turn up on our doorstep.

'Oh, my head,' said someone.

It was Irene. She rubbed her forehead and pushed her hair off her face. Her mascara had bled around her eyes, making her look like she'd been punched in the face.

'Oh my, I think I've got a hangover. My head won't stop throbbing.'

I ate a mouthful of pie.

'Mark, isn't it?'

She stood there searching my face for a comment. I didn't answer and walked into the living room and turned the television on low.

She stood in the doorway. 'Do you have any nausea or headache tablets?'

'They're in the laundry. Help yourself.'

She stood in front of me and clasped her hands around her stomach. 'Where?'

'Through the kitchen on your left.'

She sauntered past me and smelt like nicotine and alcohol. My fork stabbed the pie, and I had another bite, listening to her fossicking through the cupboard. I walked into the kitchen. She stood at the sink, turned the tap on, picked up an empty wineglass off the bench, and filled it with water. She threw her head back and swallowed a tablet before leaving the box of painkillers on the table in front of me. Her breasts heaved like they were about to fall out of her lace nightie.

She sighed, turned to face me, and said goodnight before ambling out of the room and down the hallway back to my parents' bedroom. I felt like she was trying to flirt with me. What was she after from Dad? Our inheritance? It would have to be lust on his part. Shame on him. Irene repulsed me. In the living room, I drank my tea and peered through the blinds at the empty street. I ate the last mouthful of pie and turned the television off.

In my bedroom, I lay awake on my back under a cold sheet and two blankets, unable to sleep. I thought about Dave's well-defined muscles and my penis grew erect in my hand. My body turned to its side, and I imagined Dave and I were living together and having sex. I ejaculated over the sheets and the tension of the evening dissipated, and I fell into a dreamless sleep.

The next morning, I turned the radio on and washed the dishes. I opened a cupboard to put the plates away that I'd dried and banged the door shut. Dad closed the flywire screen door and sat at the kitchen table.

'I heard Irene spoke to you.'

'You could've cleaned up your mess,' I said and picked up a plastic bag to put the rubbish in.

'You want to work in a restaurant, so you must clean up afterward. It's good practice.'

My hands gripped the bag tighter. 'Where is she?'

'At her house.'

'This is your rubbish from last night. You can put it outside.'

I threw the bag at Dad. He caught it and stood there for a moment before opening the back door while I made breakfast. He came back inside and sat at the kitchen table.

Someone knocked on the front door and yelled, 'Mark, are you there?'

'Who the hell is that so early in the morning?' said Dad.

'Maybe Irene left something behind,' I said, hoping he'd look, but he didn't move.

'She doesn't drive, smarty pants.'

My eyes widened. It was Dave. He had a black eye and a sullen expression on his face.

'What happened?'

'Can I come in? I need to explain...'

I placed my index finger on my lips and whispered, 'Dad's here.'

He opened the flywire door and walked behind me down the hallway into the kitchen.

'Where did you get that shiner from?' said Dad.

'Just a little family argument.'

'Have you eaten?' I asked.

'No, I'm not hungry.'

'Nonsense. A growing man like you needs to eat,' said Dad. 'Sit down.'

Dave pulled out a chair and slid into it. Dad placed his knife and fork down on either side of his plate and I served him his French toast and juice and set another place for Dave and gave him mine before pouring them both a mug of tea. Butter bubbled in the pan, and I wished Dad would eat faster and leave.

'I've never had this before,' said Dave. 'You'll make an excellent chef, Mark.'

I waited for Dad to say something derogatory, but he kept quiet and put three sugars in his mug and stirred the spoon around and around. He licked his lips before bringing the mug up to his mouth and drinking from it.

'It's quick and easy,' I said, unwilling to look at him in case Dad scrutinized me.

'Do you mind if I stay here for a few days?' said Dave. 'Just 'til I find somewhere else.'

Dad slurped on his tea before placing his mug on the table. His voice raised, and his thumbs locked around his braces.

'Well, I'll tell you one thing and hear me good. There's no room for you here. You'll have to find somewhere else.'

Dave sat back in his chair.

'Why can't he stay here?' I asked. 'Irene slept here last night.'

A look of disdain crossed Dad's face.

'It's my house and I'll do what I like. If you don't like it, you can get out.' Dad slurped the rest of his tea and slid out of his chair. He turned to face Dave.

'You need to go home and make amends with your family, son. We're not buying into other people's arguments. If you don't want to do that, there are plenty of hostels around here. I'm sure one of those will take you in.'

I drank my juice and started eating. Apart from the sound of my cutlery connecting with my plate, the kitchen was silent. I waited until he left the room and suggested to Dave that we go for a drive.

At Edithvale beach, we sat in front of one of the brightly painted bathing boxes. Lightning pierced through the morning sky across the sea. We huddled together in the icy wind, and I put my sweater on.

'I'm sorry about the other night,' said Dave.

'What happened?'

He stood up and kicked the sand.

'The aversion therapy didn't work, and my aunt complained I was unruly. She didn't want me to stay with her any longer, so my dad came to visit. He said he'd take me fishing. Just the two of us. We set out early in his car the next morning. He said he'd left mum and was living with another lady who worked with him. I asked him if I could live with them, and he said it would be too complicated. He said he had no alternative but to send me to an orphanage where they'd care for me until I turned eighteen. He gave mum an allowance, but she couldn't afford to keep us. I thought he'd pick me up and bring me back home.'

'I sent a letter to you at your aunt's house, but it came back to me with 'return to sender' written across the front of it.'

His eyes widened. 'I never knew you wrote to me.' I could tell by the look on his face he was telling the truth.

'We didn't go fishing. The bastard drove me straight to the orphanage. It's obvious he's got no time for me. I haven't seen my parents until two days before the party.'

'You weren't disruptive. Why did they take you away and not Sue or John?'

'Rumours were flying around about Beth and my parents decided I should leave because I was considered a troublemaker. Mum could cope with Sue and John.'

'Are the rumours true?'

He shrugged his shoulders.

'I don't know. I only saw her, not her child. We had a drink at a bar in town. I didn't ask her anything about him. She said Toby was waiting for her and that she had to go. I presumed she meant her child.'

'Why didn't you ask her?'

'What's the point? It was so long ago. Besides, it would only complicate things.'

'I don't understand. If your dad left your mum, how come he's with her now?'

'The woman he was seeing had cancer and died, so dad pleaded with mum, and she let him come back. I kept in contact with Sue, and she let me know what was happening. If it weren't for her, I wouldn't have bothered returning. Now I don't know where I belong. I feel like moving somewhere no one knows me.'

I opened my mouth to speak, but didn't know what to say. His shoulders hunched forward and there was a vulnerability in his demeanour that I'd never seen before. He screwed his face up and looked at the sand.

'But you can't leave. You're home now. You can always move out and rent.'

'I don't know. There are too many bad memories around here. I'd rather go.'

'You can't keep running away all the time.'

'That's easy for you to say. You haven't been through what I have.'

'Tell me.'

He hesitated. 'You can come with me if you like,' said Dave. 'You can open a restaurant.'

'Where?'

'I dunno. Anywhere but here.' He stood up and walked towards the shoreline.

'I don't have enough money for a restaurant.'

'We can get a loan.'

'Dave–.'

A man and a woman walked past, and I didn't want to create a scene. They glared at us, and I could hear them whispering and the word 'pansies' uttered under the man's breath. Dave acted like I wasn't there. I ran after him. My hand reached for his and he brushed it away with his fingertips. His eyes darted this way and that across the sea, anywhere, instead of me.

A strong sense of guilt and shame vibrated through my core, and I felt like I was the underlying problem. I internalized his pain and blamed myself. The ease of our earlier conversation turned to awkwardness. Dave picked up a shell and threw it into the water. A seagull landed near him, looking for scraps. I didn't know what to do and gazed at the horizon. It started to rain.

'I waited for your return, searched the school ground for you, reading and re-reading your letter. Every day I hoped that you'd return.'

Dave flinched. 'I need to go.'

He walked along the shore. His soggy footprints disappeared as the waves swept over them and retreated into the sea. My hand reached out for him again.

'Don't. For fuck's sake. Why the inquisition? You've got a nerve.'

'Well, what am I supposed to think? All this talk about Beth. You touch my arse and caress my back. Are you trying to seduce me? Tell me to walk away now and I will.'

'Shouldn't I be asking you the same thing? You were always with Laura at school.'

I let out a heavy sigh and realized I'd been holding my breath. 'She meant nothing to me.'

It felt surreal having him back here again, but I was frightened I was just another card in his deck to play with until something better came along.

'I'm going,' I said, hoping he'd tell me to stay and confide in me.

He seemed disinterested, consumed by a myriad of thoughts, and picked up a stick. A wave sprayed us, thundering down onto the shore. I walked past a row of bathing boxes on the way to my car. Dave walked silently beside me with his head down. Except for our footsteps on the pavement and the sound of a car in the distance, the silence between us was overwhelming.

When I reached my car, Dave turned around, walked towards me, and waited for me to unlock the door. I opened it and he stood for a moment as though he was contemplating saying something before stepping in. He shut the door and strode away. I called after him, but he kept moving away from me.

I stepped into my car and turned the heater on. In the rear vision mirror, I glimpsed myself and pushed my wet fringe off my face. Water streamed down the windows, and he looked like he was melting with his shoulders hunched and his hands in his pockets.

My mind was reflective on the sluice of the wipers. I stopped at the traffic lights, and he jogged along the main road. I turned the radio on and did a U-turn and headed towards him. The traffic was too heavy to drive beside him, so I turned left two blocks away and stepped out of my car and ran down the street towards him.

'Why are you doing this?' I asked. 'Come home with me. You're soaking wet. We can talk about it when we get to my house. I'll cook you something.'

Dave focused on the pavement, and he turned around.

'What about your dad, won't he be there?'

'Who cares? He hardly lives there anymore. We can go somewhere else if he is.'

My arm linked in his and we ran to my car.

A car tooted, and the driver wound down his window and yelled, 'Poofters!'

I stuck my index finger up at him. We didn't speak. I could see Dave out of the corner of my eye, sitting beside me like a brooding hen. He turned his body away from mine and looked out the window. The commentator on the radio played one song after the other about love and loss. I turned it off and listened to the rain tapping on the roof.

A resounding mantra rolled around in my head, 'Please be out, Dad.' I asked Dave to wait at the front door and I walked inside. No one was home. I yelled out to him to come in and he had a shower while I put his clothes on the clotheshorse. I opened a bottle of Vince's wine and found two wineglasses at the back of the kitchen cupboard and ordered a pizza. When the pizza arrived, we sat on the floor in the living room in front of the gas heater and I poured him a glass of wine.

The anguish had vanished from his face, but he seemed distant. My glass clinked against his and he had a swig of wine. I expected him to say something about the potency of the liquid, but he had another taste and said nothing. His cheeks were like fairy floss. He put his glass on the carpet, took a slice of pizza from the box and ate it while watching the flames move up and down.

'You know I've been meaning to ask you something?' he said.

I ate some of my slice of pizza.

'Ask me anything you want.'

'Remember the letter I sent you?'

I nodded.

'Do you know what I was referring to when I wrote it?'

His intense gaze made me feel hot.

'No,' I replied and ate the rest of my slice.

For as long as I could remember, I'd wanted him to say that he was gay too and that he wanted to be my partner, but I didn't have enough guts to say it in case he rejected me.

'I used to think there was something wrong with me until you came along. All the boys I hung around with were always gazing at girls, but I had no interest in them. All I could think about was you. I liked you the moment I met you and thought you felt the same way until you started hanging around with Laura.'

'Why didn't you want to know me when primary school was over?'

'I knew it would be harder to hide my feelings in front of my peers once we went to high school. It was better to go my way. Mum used to say I was an open book, and she could tell what I was up to no matter how much I tried to convince her otherwise.'

'You could've said something. I didn't know what I'd done to you.'

'Thinking about it, I guess I should have. I thought you would've understood. Stan and Daniel always challenged everyone in the group, so we had to prove we were men, even though we were boys. Daniel used to bring one of his dad's pipes and some tobacco down by the creek. He'd light it and we'd each have a puff. I could never understand why they all wanted to smoke. Stan said we'd look like adults if we smoked a pipe or cigarettes and that it was fashionable.'

'He believed girls would want us if we did it. I thought it was a disgusting habit. We used to put mud on each other's faces, drink Stan's dad's whiskey, and tried to light each other's farts. They were always laughing over nothing and commenting on girls at school. I only hung out with them and joined in on the conversation so they wouldn't suspect anything. Stan was jealous of your relationship with Laura. He thought you were a dork, and he wanted a girlfriend. Part of me always felt frightened they'd find out that I was, well you know...'

His laugh spluttered with anger.

'That's why I started dating Beth. She'd hung around with us and I knew she liked me. I could've dated her a year earlier if I'd wanted to. Why did you date Laura?'

'For the same reason.'

'I used to feel sorry for myself and hated my family because no one else I knew went to an orphanage.'

'But what has that got to do with the letter?'

He gulped his wine. A car turned into our driveway, and I stood up too quickly and felt lightheaded. I peered through the side of the blind. The car reversed and turned in the opposite direction. I sat down next to him on the floor and had another piece of pizza.

'Do you remember when our football team won the grand final?'

I nodded.

'The team was excited because our coach invited us back to his house to celebrate with a beer mixed with lemonade. A shandy, I think he called it. Anyway, we asked if we could have a beer, but he wouldn't let us. When he went to answer the phone in the other room, we all took it in turns to drink straight from the bottle until he returned. We finished one bottle, and Stan put it behind the television unit and opened two more while Daniel waited by the door in case the coach came back. We laughed so much, my jaw ached, but the pain from getting short-winded in the last quarter wasn't as intense as what I felt for you. You had too much to drink, and the coach asked me to walk home with you.'

'I remember winning.'

'It was early evening, and the streetlights came on when we left. You said you felt tired and queasy when we were halfway home, so we stopped and sat on the curb. Tears welled in your eyes, and you were blubbering. You wouldn't look at me. Your whole body flung forward, and I thought you were going to vomit, but you cried and wouldn't stop. Your tears left me questioning whether you were happily drunk from our victory or distressed about something else. I asked you if anything was wrong and you cried louder. I wanted to put my arm around you but worried someone was watching us.'

He finished his glass of wine, and I poured him another one.

'Go on,' I said. 'I can't recall anything.'

He took a deep breath and let out a heavy sigh.

'Come on, let's go,' I said, but you wouldn't budge. You turned and leaned your forehead into my shoulder and your body shook. I moved back, thinking you were going to spew on me.

'He, hee, hee...,' you said.

I looked at him, disbelieving what he was saying.

'And you expect me to believe you?'

'It's true. Your body heaved, and your face puffed. You gulped several times and put your hands on either side of your head. I attempted to pull you up by your arms; however, you wouldn't budge.'

'I must've been drunk,' I said, though I had no recollection.

'Your voice came out in a quivering stuttering whisper.'

'What did I say?'

'You said your dad played with you. I don't mean toys either. You couldn't recall how old you were when it started happening. All you could remember was him coming into your bedroom late at night and lying beside you naked under the covers. He gave you a lecture about never mentioning it to anyone. He said if your mum knew, she would send you away. Does that make any sense to you now?'

A memory of Dad entering my bedroom with his finger to his mouth flashed, and I tried to block it. My body shuddered.

My voice raised an octave, and my heartbeat thundered like a drum. 'Why are you doing this to me? Is it because you're hurting, and you want me to do the same too?'

Dave's knees moved up and down.

'No. I've always had too many people overly concerned about me and felt no compassion towards anyone until I sat there with you. You seemed helpless. At first, I thought you were acting, trying to humour me, lying to get a reaction, but you thrashed your hands around and wailed and I could see the pain and mental torment in your face when you looked up at me.'

'That's not me. I don't act like that,' I said.

'Right, but you were drunk, and I asked you what happened. You don't recall any of this, do you?'

My lips moved, but no sound came out.

'It was like the alcohol freed you so you could let it out. Your dad used to work in a factory before you started primary school and whenever he was working the night shift, he'd visit you when he arrived home. Everyone else in the house was asleep. He wanted you to know that you were his special boy.'

'That's enough.'

'So, you remember?'

I ran my hand through my hair. 'What if I do? What if I don't?'

His words were torturing me, and I couldn't stand it. I drank the rest of my wine, and he made an impatient face.

'All I wanted to do was protect you because I felt sorry for you. I insisted on confronting your dad, but you wouldn't let me. You refused to go home and wanted to stay on the curb. Despite my wishes for you to come to my house, you remained where you were. I was worried the other boys would leave the coach's house and see us. I panicked and left you there. After dinner, my dad said we were going on a vacation, just the two of us for school holidays. Dad said we were leaving early the next morning. I kept thinking you were still sitting in the gutter and when everyone was asleep, I left the house and walked to where I'd left you. You were gone. Did you ever say anything to your dad?'

I stood up and Dave jumped up.

'Why are you bringing all this up for now?'

'I didn't mean to upset you. Mark. You said you were going to confront him and that's what I wanted to ask you face-to-face when I saw you again. I wanted to know what he said.'

'If that's true, why did he pull me under the car and tell me I'm a boy and should be a mechanic instead of making cakes?'

'I don't know. Was your mum or sister there?'

'Yes, Dad mocked me and insisted I didn't want to be a member of a sausage factory. Mum stuck up for me. She asked him to stop taunting me and leave me alone. I don't think she cared who I liked because she just wanted me to be happy. He said I'd turn into a poof if I kept wanting to be in the kitchen. I remember her slicing a turnip slowly with precision. The more he spoke, the deeper the indents became on the chopping board. She took her time placing eight chops under the griller. I could tell Mum was thinking. Dad provoked her, and she turned around. A small frown appeared on her face, and she eyeballed him. She said her son could do whatever he liked. Dad sighed and called her a stupid woman and walked out of the room.'

'Maybe he wanted to exert his authority in front of them in case they were suspicious.'

A vague memory came to mind of someone using the toilet when Dad lay beside me. He whispered in my ear to be quiet and warned me that if I told anyone, no one would believe me. Either Mum or Nora came up to my door and opened it slightly, waited a few seconds, and went back to bed.

My door was open when I slept because the dark frightened me. The kitchen light shone into my bedroom. I trembled involuntarily. He must've closed my door when he entered my bedroom. One night I woke Mum and said I'd had a bad dream. I knew Dad would be home soon and wanted her to find out, but she sat with me for a while and went back to bed. I don't know why, but Dad didn't come to visit me that night.

'Why is he dating Irene and not a man?' I asked.

'I don't know. Love is complex. He could be bi-sexual or like little boys. Has he ever touched Nora?'

I shrugged my shoulders.

'Could you ask her?'

'Are you serious? How could I do that without giving away what happened to me?'

'That's something only you'd know.'

I sat in silent amazement, trying to process everything.

'You'll have to leave,' I said. 'This is all a bit too much for me. Jesus, and to think that I thought...'

He stood up and made a poker face like a child who'd been lying and expected me to believe it. He appeared regretful, reached out his hand, and patted my arm as a gesture of comfort. I drew away. I didn't want him to pity me. He was hiding something he didn't want me to know, not about me, about him. In a way, I felt like he was hurting me to make himself feel better. I turned to face him and asked him to leave again.

'If that's the way you feel, then that's fine. I never said it to hurt you.' He let himself out, and I closed the door behind him and walked back into the living room and drank the remaining dregs of wine. I went into the bathroom, lifted the toilet lid, and vomited. I washed my face with cold water and wiped it with the hand towel. My eyes narrowed at my reflection.

'What were you thinking? You idiot.'

In the shower, I turned on the hot water tap and scrubbed my body with soap and a nail brush until my skin felt sore. As I drove down the street, I concentrated on what the commentator said, but my mind was unabated. I screamed at it to stop, hating what I'd become. In the bottle shop, I placed a cask of wine on the counter before I realized I didn't have my wallet. I walked out of there.

At home, I was worried I wouldn't sleep and searched the cupboard for a bottle of wine, but I'd drunk the cupboard dry. In the bathroom, I looked for Mum's sleeping pills, but I couldn't find them. I lay in bed and stared at the ceiling. My thoughts were like filthy clothes spinning around in a washing machine. I must've eventually dosed and woke early. My teeth were furry, and my eyes were sore and crusty. My head felt like someone had thumped me several times with a hammer. A voice in my head kept telling me to stop hanging around with Dave, but I knew I wouldn't. I tried to sleep and thought about what had made me fall for him. What was wrong with me? Why didn't I prefer girls? Life would be so much easier.

CHAPTER ELEVEN

The winter sun shone through the branches of the cotoneaster tree, making the berries glow. I went for a run and put on my tracksuit and runners. I broke into a sweat while jogging to the oval conscious of my body, unfit and panting. No one was there, so I sat on a swing to rest, and my mind moved to Dad. I likened him to an actor in a movie playing someone younger and richer. The week before, he'd arrived home in the latest model, Holden.

When Nora phoned, she was livid and accused him of spending her inheritance. I couldn't imagine him in a bar buying Irene a drink and making conversation. Dad hated going out to dinner with Mum because, according to him, no one cooked as well as she did. I thought he said it to appease her. Is that what all men did once they got married? He said drinks were too expensive, and it was cheaper to drink at home. They only had the odd tipple, anyway.

I never envisaged him dating another woman and wondered if he had loved Mum as much as he said he did. He always said there was no one else for him but her and that his love for her was eternal. Now, he was a liberated man. Who was he trying to kid? He never loved her. From now on, if he spoke about his love for anything, I wouldn't believe him.

⁂

I'd hardly slept and walked through each day like a zombie, feeling exhausted. If I could stay between the sheets, I would have, but

I forced my body out and into the shower. I'd been drinking most nights to sleep. At first, I had a few swigs of wine. When that did not work, I had a glass and now I'd resorted to having several glasses. The trouble was when I woke up two or three hours later, thoughts would churn around in my mind and make me anxious about everything. I didn't want to go to class because I hadn't practised cooking anything since my last lesson a week ago, but I knew Chef wouldn't like it if I didn't show.

My teeth chattered. It was freezing while I stood at the station. The train screeched as it stopped at the platform. When people finished getting off, I walked towards a window seat and leaned my head against the glass and closed my eyes, unwilling to face anyone. In my cooking class, we made lemon chicken. Chef complimented me on the way I'd placed the chicken thigh and vegetables on the plate. I remember him saying food had to look and taste good. He took a bite out of the meat and asked me what I'd been thinking about while I'd been preparing and cooking the meal. I couldn't reply quickly enough. He flung the thigh back on the plate.

'Your mind is elsewhere. You need to concentrate. The chicken is dry, and the sauce is too lemony. Your cooking is getting worse, not better. If you want to be a chef, you need to have patience and practice. What part don't you understand?'

'Believe me, I do. You're right. I'll try harder next time.'

The truth was, I couldn't focus on anything after Dave's revelation. I tried to stop thinking about what he'd said, but flashes of the past kept screening on my mind no matter where I was or what I was doing. At home, I turned the television on, watched a movie, and immersed myself in the characters' lives to pause mine. No sooner had the movie ended and my mind would replay an event from my childhood. I read a few recipes and drove to the supermarket with the radio on and sang along with each song. If the radio announcer came on, I changed the channel to another song to drown my thoughts. I needed to occupy my mind. Find a hobby or something.

In the supermarket, I repeated the ingredients I had to buy to make filet mignon. I stopped at the liquor shop and bought a cask of wine. At home, I focused on preparing the meal and took my time. When it was ready, I didn't want to eat it and threw it in the bin and had a glass of wine to relax.

I believed that if I focused on what I was doing, my mind wouldn't betray me. However, thoughts were like weeds that had their heads cut off but couldn't be removed from the roots and kept springing to life. What Dave had said was true. I couldn't deny it. I'd lost count of how many times I'd peered through the blinds filled with nervous energy. Should I confront Dad? I didn't have the courage. It happened so long ago.

If Dave had said nothing, the past would've stayed buried where it belonged. I found a bottle of whiskey at the back of one of the kitchen cupboards that our parents used for medicinal purposes. Whenever one of us had a cold, they'd make a lemon drink mixed with whiskey, honey, and hot water. I screwed the lid off the bottle and poured some into a glass. I sipped it on the way to my bedroom and finished the rest before getting into bed. Alcohol was the only thing that calmed my nerves and made me sleep.

At the bakery, one of my co-workers was going on holiday. It wasn't until Mrs Mackie asked her if she'd packed her bags that I remembered Mum's suitcase. When I arrived home, I searched for it again in every room but couldn't find it. In the garage, I opened the cupboard against the back wall. I rummaged through old paint tins, carwash, sponges, and a pair of gumboots. I climbed a small ladder to see if I could find it above the cupboard but found oil tins and jars filled with different-sized nails coated in dust and cobwebs instead.

At a charity shop near us, an elderly woman sat behind the counter. No one else was there. I asked her if she had any luggage, and she asked me to wait while she searched the backroom. My feet wouldn't stand still, so I walked around the shop to see if I could find any of Mum's personal effects Dad had disposed of.

The woman held a battered brown bag and placed it on the front counter. I thanked her and said it wasn't what I had in mind. It was like Mum was trying to tell me something and wanted me to find the suitcase and open it. I drove slowly past Dave's house on the way home. His Mum's car sat in the driveway, and I wondered if he was inside.

Two days later, a man phoned and said he was from a Holden dealership where Dad had bought his new car.

'Mr Cooney left a suitcase in the boot of his old car,' he said.

'Dad's away,' I lied. 'I'll come and pick it up for him.'

⁓⧎⁓

The keyholder hanging on the kitchen wall had ten keys dangling from each hook. I left the ones I recognized and took the rest with me into my bedroom. The suitcase sat on my bed. I closed the door and tried each key in the lock, but none of them would open it. I didn't want to phone Nora and ask her if she knew where she'd put the keys. My temples tightened, and I went into the living room and peered through the blinds, half expecting Dad to come home.

Rain drizzled outside, making specks on the window. Mum's bedside table drawers were empty. Dad's drawers had socks in one and jocks in the other. The dressing table drawers proved fruitless. I opened the wardrobe and felt in his trouser pockets, but there was nothing in them. After several attempts to pry the lid open with different-sized knives, I gave up. I hid the suitcase under my bed. I lay on my bedspread and closed my eyes.

'Please show me where the keys are, Mum.'

Brakes screeched, and the sound of voices woke me. The blinds were still open. I peered out the window and noticed our neighbour talking to someone while putting her rubbish bin out. Outside, our bin was sitting at the other end of the nature strip. I thought I was going crazy because I couldn't remember putting it there. The garbage truck was at the other end of the street, and I muttered for them to hurry and waited on the veranda. The ground was cold and wet beneath my feet. A breeze whirled around me, and rain spat on me. I hurried back inside. The bathroom door was closed, and I opened it gently, thinking Dad might be home, but no one was there.

Since Dave had spoken to me, memories kept sweeping in. I tried to think of something else, but they were persistent. When I was five, I spied Nora perving on Dad in the bathroom. The door was ajar, and we saw his naked reflection in the tiles. He had his back to us, and she giggled. He slammed the door shut and yelled at us to go away. I tried to block this untimely recollection and retrieved the suitcase out from under my bed and took it into the kitchen. I dropped it on the linoleum floor to see if it would open. The contents slid back and forth inside, but it remained shut.

In bed, I couldn't stop thinking of Dave's body in his shorts and runners. His hairless abdomen and pecs, the well-defined leg muscles, and the arch in his back. I wanted to see him again. There was something about him that swallowed the loneliness in the pit of my stomach. I lay awake thinking about having sex with him. I rolled onto my side, closed my eyes, and ran my tongue around my lips, imagining kissing him. My hand slipped under my top, and my fingertips gently caressed my chest.

I lifted the sheet and blankets and pulled my jocks down. My hand featherlike caressing my thighs, my breathing heavy. Voices in my head shamed me and heat cursed through my body. A wave of guilt crashed over me, and I tried to think of something else, but all I could see was Dave with his arms around me and I imagined him straddling me and his erect penis trying to find its way into my anus. A shock of static electricity ran over my flesh, and I pulled the covers back and jumped out of bed and went into the kitchen. I opened the cupboard and clutched a glass, filled it with water, drank it, and went back to bed.

In my dreams, Dave and I married on a beach in Fiji. We wore grass skirts, and I had a frangipani lei around my neck. He chased me along the water's edge, picked me up in his arms, and people walked over and congratulated us. I wanted to stay asleep and never wake up. Whenever the alarm clock went off, I'd turn it off, roll over, and try to stay in the dream, unhappy if I couldn't recall the details and put myself back there. Each day in my waking life, I lived in hope one day, my dreams would become a reality.

The rain stopped, and the sun came out, so I went outside and took the bin around the back to the side of the house, and something shone out of the corner of my eye. A metal key lay in a puddle a few feet away. I picked it up, ran inside my bedroom, and tried it in the lock. The suitcase opened. Photos of all sizes were in a large envelope, and I flicked through them and at the back of one of Nora, which read December 1950, Nora, in Mum's handwriting. A young man with black curly hair sat on a motorbike: Giovanni Martinelli, 1947. Another photo of the same man standing next to Mum, both smiling. A note read: My darling Sandra, I can't wait until we elope. Love always, Giovanni xx. A photo of Mum heavily pregnant: June '53. Then a picture of me: Mark's first Christmas Dec '53. A photo of Mum and Dad on their wedding day: April '54.

Mum smiled at a man with blonde hair. He had his arm around her in what looked like someone's front garden. She wore a skirt and a short-sleeved knitted top. Her hair was shoulder-length and curly. On the back read: Peter and me 1944. There were two Valentine Day cards, one from Giovanni and one from Peter. I picked up her wedding garter, and a starched lace handkerchief. Both had turned a creamy colour and had a faint smell of mothballs.

There were several notelets, one of which read: My darling, in 67 days you'll be my bride. Love, Giovanni xxxx. There were no photos of Dad with her except the wedding photo on their dressing table. Dad's name was Russell, not Giovanni. Who was Giovanni? Was he, our father? Did Nora know? I searched through the rest of the photographs. A man sat at a table with a Christmas tree in the background. It had Peter Edwards written on the back of it with no date. Another photo had a man sitting on a motorbike with Giuseppe Martinelli 1950 in Mum's handwriting.

I always resisted conflict; fearful no one would want to know me if I retaliated. Now that Dave was back and living nearby, I felt I could get through anything because we'd reconnected. Usually, I'd avoid ringing Nora. She had family concerns, and I couldn't stand arguing, but I wanted to know if she knew anything about Giovanni, Peter, and Giuseppe.

Her number rang out. I didn't know what time it was in Italy. Ignoring my apprehension, I phoned her again, peering through the Venetians, worried Dad would show up. I held my breath, and my chest tightened when Alfonso answered. He said it was late and to ring again in the morning. I placed the phone back into the receiver and went into Dad's bedroom to look at the photo of him and Mum on their wedding day. I removed the picture from the frame and examined it. In the bathroom, I viewed myself in the mirror. The man staring back at me didn't resemble his parents or his sister. I shaved my face and had a shower. My mind tried to make sense of what I'd seen.

⟡

It was early evening, and I went for a jog around the oval. Outside the clubrooms, I imagined Dad in front of me, and my fists punched the air repeatedly. I'd never hit anyone before.

'Hey, I didn't know you wanted to be a boxer.'

I turned around, startled. It was Dave.

'I don't.'

My arms folded, hiding my hands, embarrassed that he'd seen me in a fit of frustration and anger. We sat on the metal fence, and he leaned forward to do up his shoelaces and laughed.

'It's not funny.'

'Sorry. You just, well, you know.' He raised his arms in the air and pretended he was going to hit me, and we tussled. My body heaved, and I moved away from him.

'Hey, I was only fooling around,' he said, wrapping his arm around my shoulder. 'Is everything alright?'

I turned my head away, unwilling to look at him.

'Don't touch me in public. You never know who's looking,' I whispered under my breath.

He sighed and let go of me. 'You were always so frigid; I can't believe you still are. You need to learn to let go. What's wrong with you, anyway?'

'It's nothing,' I said.

'You're not getting all sooky on me, are you?'

'You should talk after the last time I saw you with your family.'

'What are you doing here?' His expression changed.

I didn't wait for him to reply.

'If you must know, I'm still having trouble processing what you said. I feel overwhelmed. I can't shut it out of my mind. It's like a needle stuck on a record and keeps repeating the same thing,' I said.

'I didn't say it to hurt you. You know that don't you?' He puts his arms around me, and my body tensed. 'Have you spoken to your dad about it?'

'No.'

'Why? What's stopping you? I can be there with you if you like.'

'It's time for me to go. I'll do it when I'm ready.'

My body maneuvered out of his arms.

'You know you can phone me if you need me.'

'But can I? I feel like we're not connected. I want to be with you.'

'I need to think. There's a lot of stuff going on that you don't know about.'

'What? You can tell me.'

'I can't.'

'What are you doing here?'

'I like to go jogging every day. It helps to clear my head.'

'And you?'

'The same. Is everything okay at home now?'

'As good as it ever will be.'

My nose itched, and I rubbed it with my hand. I had the perfect opportunity to say how I felt, but negativity and insecurity held me back.

'You know, Sue talks about you all the time. I think she's had a crush on you for a while now. You have that effect on us.'

Dave leaned forward and kissed me, sending a warm sensation through my body. His hand rested on my thigh. A car entered the car park, and we stood up. Three boys dressed in football jumpers and shorts got out of the back seat and an older man got out of the driver's side, and they walked onto the oval, throwing a football back and forth.

'Come over for dinner. I'm having homemade chicken pie,' I said, trying to entice him, but he said he'd already made other plans. I wondered what they were, but didn't like to ask him.

The lights were on inside our house, and for a moment, I thought someone could burgle us and entered with trepidation.

'Who's there?' said Dad.

'Me. When did you get back?'

'Christ, Mark, you sound like my mother. I don't know. A few minutes ago. Stop asking questions.'

'What've you been doing?'

'Seeing Irene. If you must know.'

'Are you eating here tonight?'

'No, I'm going out.'

I set the kitchen table and placed the pie in the oven. The scent of Dad's aftershave lingered in the room. He never used to wear it because he said it was for sissies. He left the house whistling and closed the front door softly behind him.

⁓≼≽⁓

At the bakery, the morning went by slowly and every person I served seemed to have a grievance about their order. One customer complained I'd sliced the bread too thick. Another said I gave them wholemeal bread instead of white. Mrs Mackie asked me if I was feeling alright, and I said I was fine. She thought I was still grieving over Mum and asked me if I'd like to finish at noon and take the rest of the day off. I said I'd prefer to stay.

As soon as I arrived home, I phoned Nora.

Her voice sounded harried. 'What were you doing ringing so late for the other night? Is everything alright? Don't you look at the time zones, Mark? You had me worried something bad had happened. I've tried ringing you back several times and there's been no answer. I've got enough stress of my own without having to worry about you.'

'Calm down. I found the suitcase you showed me. Did you see all the photos?'

'No, I only saw what I showed you. Why?'

'There's a note from someone named Giovanni that says she'll be his bride in 67 days.'

'Is that all you were ringing me about? They could've broken up.'

'But wait a minute, you were born in 1950, and I was born in 1953, right?'

She sighed heavily. 'Yes.'

'Then why does it say our wedding day, April 1954, on the back of Mum and Dad's wedding photo?'

'She's probably written the wrong date.'

'Come on, you must be kidding. You'd know the date you were married. It's sacred and special, something no woman would forget. It just doesn't add up.'

'That's true. Then what happened? Where's Dad now?'

'I don't know. That's why I'm ringing you.'

'Well, ask him. If you don't, I will. He's probably living with the tart you mentioned.'

'I've gotta go. Dad will bitch about the cost of the call when he gets the bill, and I'm not paying for it,' I said and hung up.

.⟐.

Faces smiled back at me in the snapshots laid out on my bed. The picture of Giovanni appeared familiar, and I couldn't recall why. My hair was light brown like Mum's, not black like his or blonde like Peter's. The man who I chased at the funeral was like an older version of Giovanni.

In the telephone book, I found two listings for Martinelli. I dialled the first one on impulse, unsure of what I'd say. On the fourth ring, a woman answered the phone.

'Hell-o, who is this?' she said in a thick accent like Vince's wife, Loretta.

My hands wouldn't stop shaking.

'I'm looking for Giuseppe and Giovanni Martinelli.'

'Who a wants to know?'

'A friend of theirs. I lost touch with them,' I stammered.

'They a no live a here anymore.'

'Can you tell me where they live now?'

'Giuseppe, you a know he lives a few a blocks from here.'

'And Giovanni?'

She hung up.

I retraced their surname and found another Martinelli with the initials GR next to it and dialled the number. My heart thumped while I waited.

A male voice recited the telephone number and said, 'Hello.'

I couldn't speak after I'd heard his voice. I hung up and sat in the living room, shaking.

❧

The wind tossed leaves over me like confetti as I stepped into my car and contemplated driving to Giovanni's house. My body filled with nervous energy and my palms sweated. I wiped them on my jeans and sat behind the steering wheel and hesitated, before placing the key in the ignition, worried I'd make an idiot of myself if he didn't know Mum. What if he called the police and had me arrested for being a nuisance? If it was him, he might be married with children of his own. I wanted to know what happened to their relationship and why he didn't marry Mum.

I sat in my car in front of an old weatherboard house each day for three weeks, too frightened to knock on the front door. No one entered or exited the house despite my going there at different times. I'd rehearsed what I would say, 'Hi, my name's Mark Cooney. I'm looking for Giovanni Martinelli.' No matter how many times I practiced, I couldn't speak coherently.

Repeating the mantra: no one is home convinced me to step out of my car. An oil stain covered the middle of the concrete under an empty carport. My feet paced up and down the veranda, and I couldn't stop fidgeting with my hands. No one was home. The opened curtains showed my reflection staring back at me. The side gate was locked. I sat back in my car for half an hour, and no one came, so I drove home. I looked through the phone book again, wondering if I had the right house, but something inside me knew it was.

⤜∽⧫∽⤝

Nothing much happened during that time, just me living in an empty house and keeping busy trying new recipes from a cookbook and adding ingredients to enhance the flavour. Concentrating on cooking kept my mind busy, so I wouldn't have to think about anything else. Each night, I prepared something different. Tonight, I made broccoli and cauliflower soup with cheddar cheese and a sprinkle of curry powder for my entrée.

I imagined being in my restaurant and dressed the table with a white tablecloth and matching napkins, set for two with wineglasses and silver cutlery Mum had never used. In one drawer, I found a candle that my parents kept in case of a power failure. I lit it and placed it in a candleholder in the middle of the table before turning the light off. I poured myself a glass of wine from the cask of Riesling in the cupboard, ladled soup into my bowl, and sat in the kitchen.

'Cheers!' I said while thinking of Dave and wishing he were with me. In my imaginary waking life dream, I felt lost. I rose and walked around the room, pretending to wait on tables, answering questions about the different cuisine people were eating. The kitchen staff asked me questions as we prepared the main meal.

Oven-baked trout with lime juice, chilli, coriander, and brown sugar with seasoned vegetables was the main meal. Patrons complained it took too long between the two courses, and I gave them a drink on the house and informed them I only prepared fresh food daily. After I'd finished eating, I washed the dishes. In the living room, I drank another glass of wine while sitting in the dark.

In bed, I daydreamed about my wedding day and the Armani suit I would wear. Brylcreem gave my hair a shiny lustre, and a white rosebud adorned my lapel. Dave dressed in a black suit with a multi-coloured vest. His curly hair framed his face. We stood at the southern end of the Royal Botanical Gardens, just the two of us, with a marriage celebrant. Both of our families were aggrieved by the rotten fruit they'd produced.

Negativity intercepted my story, spoiling my happiness. I wondered if Dave had visited Beth again and saw her child and felt obligated to her. I tried to push the thought out of my mind. There were similarities between Dave and Giovanni - they were both tall and had curly hair. Girls always gravitated towards Dave, and I knew he would never have to worry about having someone to be with. He'd grow tired of me, which I surmised Giovanni had with Mum. I didn't want to settle for someone else and couldn't understand why Mum had either.

A storm diminished around lunchtime, and I drove the mop harder onto the tiled floor, back and forth.

'How many times do you intend to mop the floor?' said Dad.

He startled me, and I slipped and grabbed hold of the washing machine. 'What's wrong with you?' he said, raising his eyebrows.

'I didn't see you.'

A smirk crossed his face.

'It's not funny. You wouldn't like it if someone crept up on you.'

'You look like you're somewhere else,' said Dad.

'I'm fine.'

'Make us a cup of tea. I need to talk to you about something.'

I left the mop against the wall and walked into the kitchen and got out two mugs and lit the stove to boil the kettle. All our family discussions were over a mug of tea or while eating dinner. Dave had invited me out to help celebrate his birthday. I went to my bedroom, opened the wardrobe, and pulled out a pair of jeans, a shirt, jumper, and boots. Through the window, it looked windy, so I sprayed my hair with hairspray before going back into the kitchen. I covered the pot with one of Mum's knitted tea cosies she'd made and opened the kitchen cupboard, took out the biscuit barrel, and put four scotch finger biscuits on a plate, knowing Dad would eat them all.

He came back into the room and sat at the table while I poured the tea. He took the lid off the sugar bowl and put three cubes in his mug. The spoon went around and around the circumference, and he had a meditative stare. Dad picked up a biscuit and dunked it in the hot liquid and bit into it.

'You know I've been dating Irene for a while now.'

I sat at the table with him.

'So?'

'She's coming here for dinner tonight.'

'What are you making her?'

'I thought I'd leave that up to you.'

'I've made other plans.'

'But you don't go anywhere.'

'Well, I am tonight.'

'Jesus, Mark, can't you change it? Do your old man a favour for once.'

I could feel my jawline tighten and my throat constrict. Prickly heat seethed through my torso and up to my face.

My voice sounded raspy, and my body trembled. 'A favour? That's big. I'm always cooking for you. Why can't you do one for me for a change?'

'I swear, you're getting more like that sister of yours every day. You've always had it easy. Other fathers would've kicked you out by now, like David Ogilvy was years ago.'

My eyes rolled around.

'Who is Giovanni Martinelli?'

Dad glared at me. His face was ashen. 'Where did you hear that name?'

'Never mind. Who is he?'

'Hang on a minute. Who's been talking to you? That's private.'

'I want to know who my father is. Is it you?'

'I get it. It's that bloody suitcase. You should know better not to go digging where you're not supposed to.' He let out a sigh and locked his thumbs in his braces. 'Jesus, Mark, I'm not getting into a discussion with you now when I've got Irene coming over. We'll talk about this later.'

'I don't care. I've seen the photos and deserve an answer. To hell with Irene. Nora and I are more important than her. We're family, not her.'

'Listen, you little shit. Don't speak about her like that. She's a good woman.'

'I'll talk about her any way I like.'

'Have it your way. I'm glad you've made other plans. I don't want you here if you're going to be like that.'

'Well, tell me now then. What's stopping you?'

He had a mouthful of his tea.

'I swore to your mum that I wouldn't say anything to either of you. She said she'd tell you when and if she felt like it.'

'Well, I don't think she'd mind now. Do you?'

His face piqued, and a rash rose from his shirt collar up to his face. He pulled at his braces and eyeballed me. 'If you must know, Giovanni's dead. He died when Nora was three, and you'd just been born.'

'How did he die?'

'In a motorbike accident. Your mother was engaged to him. My family knew her family, and I asked her out.'

'Did you love her?'

'What sort of question is that?'

'Well?'

'Never you mind. I could belt your arse for talking to me the way you are. Just remember, you're never too old to strap.'

'Go on, hit me then. See if I care. It won't change anything. Why didn't you or Mum tell us?'

He let out a deep sigh and let go of his braces to pick up another biscuit and bit into it.

'Your mum wanted you to believe I was your father.'

'Why would she want to do a stupid thing like that?'

'So, we could be a family.'

'Does Nora know?'

He shrugged his shoulders and raised an eyebrow. 'I don't know. Your mum could've said something to her.'

'You both lied to us.'

'If that's what you want to believe, go right ahead. We did it for your and Nora's benefit. No one ever asked questions.'

'And that man at the funeral…'

'What man?'

'Didn't you see him leaning against the wall on the other side of the chapel?'

'That was Giovanni's brother, Giuseppe.'

'Why did he come?'

'I don't know.'

'Where does he live?'

'Over the railway line, near where your nan and pop lived. I saved your mother from those spaghetti headed bastards.'

'Did she ever speak to Giuseppe again?'

'Not as far as I'm aware. I hope not. Your sisters like her, always going after those I-talians. I don't know what they see in them. At least Irene's English. I guess you'll see her again some other time.'

Dad drank the rest of his tea, set his mug on the table, and picked up a biscuit. He looked fragile and unsure of himself, although his words portrayed the contrary.

'You're not the easiest person to get along with, Dad. Just because people are from another country doesn't mean you should condemn them. They're just like us, except they talk differently, that's all.'

'Hmm, what would you know?'

'Well, didn't you teach us to show respect? You'd get along better with everyone if you did. I remember Nora telling you the same thing over the years, but you never listened.'

His face darkened, and he glared at me. His thumbs locked around his braces.

'And what makes you or her an authority?'

My voice quivered. 'I'm tired of all the racist remarks. Nora ran away because of you. Besides, it's obvious you were jealous. Even though Mum's gone, you still can't let it go, and it happened years ago.'

His voice raised an octave. 'That's right, blame me for bloody everything.'

I placed my elbows on the table, and my palms clasped my hot cheeks.

'Well, you're the only one who always makes those comments. Mum and I never did.'

He pulled his braces wider.

'You leave your mother out of this and watch your mouth. The way you're speaking to me is appalling.' He stomped his feet up and down. 'If you must know, that's why no one came to visit us. Your mum had both of you when she was single. She'd shamed her family, and they moved away. My parents died in a car accident when you were in primary school. We went to the funeral and left you and your sister at school. You didn't know them anyway, so it didn't make any difference.'

'What about aunts and uncles?'

'I didn't have any siblings. Your mum had a sister. We saw her a few times after we married and lost contact. Once she had her children, her sister moved interstate to be closer to her husband's side of the family from memory. Just as well, you're not here tonight. I don't think Irene would like you. She'd be ashamed to hear you talking to me like that. I guess I'll have to take Irene out for dinner.'

'Why don't you cook for her?'

'Come on now, you know I don't know how to cook. You've upset me. To think you don't want to do your old man a favour for once. I thought I'd never see the day...'

Dad slurped on his tea and dunked another biscuit in it before popping it in his mouth. He pushed his chair back, stood up, and gazed out the kitchen window.

'I know where I'll take her. That new Chinese place in Dandenong.'

'But you don't like Chinese food.'

'I've got a bit of an acquired taste for it now.'

CHAPTER TWELVE

I drove to the oval and waited for Dave to appear. I wanted to avoid him visiting my house while Dad and Irene were there. After Dave's dad's outburst, I didn't want to go to his house. Dave opened the passenger side door, stepped in, and rested his hand on my knee. I asked him where he wanted to go, worried someone would see us.

Tonight reminded me of when I was eighteen and saw a movie with Mr Sinclair. Each time I looked up, his eyes stole a wayward glance at me whenever I served him at the bakery. He made it obvious, and I knew I didn't imagine things. I thought he must've been like that with everyone because occasionally, he'd bring his wife into the shop with him.

Mrs Mackie had said several times after he'd left that he could put his shoes under her bed anytime. He always wore tailored pants, a shirt with a bow tie, and shiny shoes. He had a suave air that made him seem sophisticated compared to everyone else.

When I finished my shift, I walked home a different way and noticed him leaning against the streetlight. He winked, and I turned around to see who he was winking at, but no one was there. My heart stuck in my throat at the thrill of someone being interested. I walked past him, and he strode towards me. He asked in a whisper if I had any plans that evening.

I could tell he was the same as me, despite his wedding ring. I said I'd meet him later near the station and he picked me up and drove me to Dandenong, and we went to the cinema. He insisted we sit a few rows from the back and near an aisle. When the lights faded, he opened his trouser zip and placed my hand on his penis. He undid my zip and did the same. I had to put my handkerchief in my mouth to stifle my moaning.

After the movie, we went to a bar when a tall solid man came toward us from a side street.

'Faggots,' he said.

We were aware of his proximity to us and knew he was moving closer.

'Let's separate and meet back at my car,' whispered Mr Sinclair. He moved away before I could say anything.

'Hey, you,' said someone with a deep voice.

A hand gripped me tightly on my shoulder and turned me around. It was the solid man. A tall skinny man strode towards me and spat in my face.

'You're nothing but a bum boy,' he said and punched me in the face twice before punching me in the chest. A sharp pain ripped through my torso when I fell to the ground.

I vaguely remember hearing tyres crunching on the gravel road and thought it was the person who'd hit me. I pretended to be dead. Mr Sinclair cried out when he saw me, his eyes beseeching, and asked me if I was alright. My lower jaw moved, but no sound came out. My forehead throbbed. Blood trickled over my lips and down my chin, splotching on my shirt. My vision blurred, and I closed my eyes. My body refused to move. He said we had to get out of there and helped me stand up. I wanted to stay where I was and sleep, but he insisted I keep moving.

Mr Sinclair helped me get into his car, and I lay in the back seat while he drove me to the hospital. He pretended to be my father, and we waited in the emergency department for several hours until someone could see me. People whispered when they saw us, but I was too sore to care. I snorted and hyperventilated. My hands searched my trouser pockets for a handkerchief, but I must've left it in the cinema. The doctor scrutinized us both and asked me what happened.

I said I was shopping in the city and a man attacked me, grabbed my bags, and ran off. He said I should report it to the police. After having an x-ray of my face and torso to see if I'd broken anything, the nurse wrapped my fractured nose with bandages. Mr Sinclair paid my medical bill, cussing and swearing under his breath about his wife arriving home and him not being there before her. He appeared eager to get rid of me, muttering something about being caught out and in trouble.

Mr Sinclair helped ease me into his car and stopped a few houses from where I lived. After he'd assisted me out of his car, he drove off in a hurry. My body ached, and my feet shuffled like an old man. It took me a long time to reach the front door. I never saw him at the bakery again and often wondered if his wife knew he was bi-sexual or gay.

Mum was hysterical when she saw me. I lied and relayed the same story. Dad's eyelids flickered, and his eyes moved upwards.

'I hope you weren't doing what I think you were doing.'

'For Chrissake, leave him alone,' said Mum. 'Take him to a police station to make a statement.'

'Christ won't help you or him,' said Dad.

'I'll be fine,' I said. 'I just need to rest.' In my bedroom, I viewed myself in my dressing-table mirror before I lay on my bed. My left eye had swollen shut. Mum insisted on taking me to the doctor in the morning, but I said I felt better and wanted to be left alone. Dad scowled at her and asked her to stop fussing over me, and they argued.

⁕

Now, I looked in the rear vision and side mirrors and couldn't see anyone. I turned the key in the ignition. Dave mentioned a place called Bubbles, in the city. I leaned across him, opened the glove box, and pulled out a small package. I handed it to him before I drove away from the curb. In a city department store, I'd walked around for hours after class, not knowing what to buy him. I waded through shirts but didn't know what size to buy. A display of cufflinks stood before me; I wondered if Dave wore them. I tried on five dress rings but couldn't decide, worried he'd rebuke me if I bought him one. A shop assistant came up to me and asked me if I preferred silver or gold.

'It's for…,' I said and stopped. 'I'll look in the aftershave section.'

The smell of one fragrance blended into another. Still undecided, I let the shop assistant chose for me. Dave tore the wrapping paper off, opened the small box, and sprayed it on the back of his hand. He took an appreciative sniff and thanked me. The aroma of sandalwood filled the cabin.

The vibe at Bubbles was palpable. My body tensed, expecting a police raid and to be taken away in a divvy van to be locked up overnight. A transvestite came towards us with a silver drinks tray, and we had a glass of champagne. Dave spoke to two men sitting near us. I hung back in awe of my surroundings.

For a moment, I felt like I was in another world where only gay people lived. I hoped I wasn't dreaming. If I were dreaming, I didn't want to wake up. Here I felt accepted, and equal, something I'd never experienced before. Everyone had a smile on their face, lost in the realization that they didn't have to pretend to be someone else, wearing a mask to portray that they were heterosexual, so they could fit in with the rest of the world.

It was like having a smorgasbord of men to choose from. As each person walked past me, I couldn't help but catch a glimpse, and they did the same. There was something that defined us that the rest of the community couldn't see. They viewed us like glass, but all I could see were men like me. In one sense, our feelings were the same as a male and female relationship. We each craved the same thing. We were all looking for love and wanted to be loved, but we were hard-wired differently because we chose the same sex and couldn't procreate together.

I left Dave talking and went to find a toilet. I viewed myself in the vanity mirror and a man sidled up beside me and pinched me on my bum. He was older than me. He introduced himself. His name was Barry. He'd been to Bubbles before and was on his own.

'This is the only place I know where I can be me,' he said, reiterating my thoughts earlier. He leaned forward and kissed me on my cheek. His hand touched the side of my face lightly. 'You're such a pretty boy.'

I pulled away from him.

'I'm with someone.'

'Well, if you ever change your mind, you know where to find me.'

Someone else came in whom he knew and wanted to talk to him outside. He touched his lips and blew me a kiss before he left. The scent of his spicy aftershave lingered in the room. I smiled, and my cheeks grew warmer. Intrigued, I went for a walk through the establishment. A door near me was opened. I peered inside and could see men having sex. In other rooms, men were drinking and talking on sofas. Further down the hallway, men stood and smoked while talking to one another.

When I returned, I found Dave still in the same spot where I'd left him talking to two different men than whom I'd left him with.

'Hey, where did you get to?' Dave said.

'I've been having a look around. I never knew so many men were like us. In my mind, I used to think there must be only a handful of gay men.'

Dave laughed. 'There are hundreds of men like us. In Perth, there's a club like this one.'

'How can it stay open with the police the way they are towards gay men?'

'People find out through word of mouth. Nothing is advertised. If it were, it would be shut down, and the clientele would be put in jail.'

I shuddered at the thought of the police raiding Bubbles whilst we were here.

'Tell me that doesn't happen very often,' I said.

'Stop worrying. We'll be fine. Relax and enjoy yourself. Tonight's on me.'

'But it's your birthday, not mine.'

'It doesn't matter.'

The transvestite came over to us and asked us to come with her. I tried to take my clothes off gracefully in the locker room but was clumsy and self-conscious. I fell backwards. Dave helped me up and teased me, saying I'd drunk too much. Wearing our jocks and complimentary bathrobes, we exited through another door, where other men were seated on circular couches. We found a space on one and sat and drank our champagne while we waited for a spa to become available. A man dressed up in drag offered us another glass of champagne.

We each took one and listened to the music. A transvestite with purple eyeshadow, purple curly hair, a matching bra, and a short skirt called out our names. She motioned for us to come with her. She opened the door to a room with a spa bath in the middle of it. We could see her and us in mirrors all around the walls. Two champagne glasses sat on a bench, and another door to the left opened out to a double shower and vanity. She closed the door behind her. Dave turned the taps on and poured a capful of bubble bath into the lukewarm water.

The room was ours for 25 minutes. I felt shy about being alone with him. Dave placed his glass on the bench and removed his bathrobe and jocks, and I did the same. The twinkle in his eyes resembled a beach on a tropical island with sun-dappled water. I wanted to dive into them and see the world as he did.

'What are you waiting for?' said Dave, stepping into the spa. I swallowed some of my drink.

'Just getting in the mood,' I said.

I sat on the side and put my big toe in. Dave turned the jets on, and I stepped in. We kissed and lay back. The foam rose higher, so we couldn't see one another. I got up to get our drinks, and Dave slapped my bum. I half turned to grin at him and handed him his drink. He waved it away.

'Bugger the drink,' he said. 'Someone mentioned to me you've been naughty. If you don't behave, I'll have to spank you again.'

My hands trailed down his arms like I was examining expensive fine bone China. He reached out and put his arms around my waist, pulling me closer to him. His nose barely touched mine, and I could feel the warmth of his breath as his lips caressed my neck, cheek, and forehead. My arms wrapped around his upper back, unwilling to let go. Dave pulled away from me. He downed some of his drink.

He turned the jets off and embraced me once more. His tongue slipped into my mouth. My body came alive with a tingling sensation. I stroked either side of his face and moved my fingers through his thick, curly blonde hair and explored his body. My tongue lingered on his nipples, making them stiff. Dave clasped my buttocks, making them tighten. My penis moved to his touch, sending a pulse through my body. He guided my hand to his erection. I moved my index finger over the tip of his penis, making him grunt with pleasure.

My penis bobbed up and down, and his fingers moved gently down my belly and thighs before turning me around. I bent over the side of the spa, and I felt his lips and tongue over my anus and buttocks before entering me. Dave held his taut body against mine, feeling my erect nipples and gripping my hips, gaining rhythm, moving faster against me. My body moved in momentum, making a smacking sound against his.

I'd waited so long for this to happen, worried I wouldn't know what to do. At home, I always fantasised about Dave while I masturbated in bed or in the bathroom. We came together and fell back against the side of the spa bath, exhausted. He turned the jets on. My skin gleamed with newness. I wanted to know if he'd enjoyed having sex as much as I did. But I didn't ask him. I turned around to face him.

'You look lovely in the pink,' said Dave, examining me up close.

'So, do you,' I said.

I retrieved our champagne glasses and sank back into the foam. We clinked our glasses together before drinking the remaining dregs.

'Happy birthday. Well, I hope it is. It's good to be with you here.'

I lifted my body up out of the spa and opened the minibar. I poured some more champagne into each glass and handed him one before sitting on the edge. My feet dangled in the water, and I clinked his glass.

'Thanks,' he said.

'Hey, why don't you come and live with me? Dad's hardly ever there.'

'That'd be great. But what if he comes home and sees us together?'

'Won't he kick you out?'

'We'll have to think of something in case he does. Don't worry, it'll be fine.'

He let out a small sigh.

'After the way my family reacted, I doubt it,' said Dave.

'Promise me you won't leave again, regardless of whether we live together.'

'I can't. Not after that outburst.'

My stomach tightened.

'Well, let me know where you're going so, I can come too,' I said.

'I'm not sure what I want to do or where I want to go anymore.' There was something in the way he said it. Negativity crept in, and I didn't believe him.

Someone knocked on the door.

'Time's up, gentlemen,' said a deep female voice.

I motioned to stand up. Dave turned the jets off, grabbed my arm, and pulled me back down.

'Not so quick. She doesn't mean right now.' Dave's hand moved down my neck and the front of my body, resting on my groin for a moment before he pushed himself out of the spa with his hands. We showered together in the next room. A memory of Dave flashed through my mind as I washed his body. He was in the shower after football, and I wished I could reach out and touch him. I remember feeling confused when he touched me. I went to change into my clothes, and Dave insisted I stay in my jocks and bathrobe.

'But why can't we change and have a drink somewhere before we go home?'

'I thought we'd do something a little different before we go,' said Dave. 'Come with me.'

We sat on one of the circular couches.

'You know I don't like surprises, Dave. What do you mean by *different*? Not swapping partners, I hope.'

I remembered Barry earlier. It would've been easy to go into a cubicle or another room and get to know him better. Was that what everyone did here: go from room to room to experience everything the Club had on offer?

'Wait and see.'

I gasped with trepidation because I didn't want anyone else to have Dave. He was mine. I'd sulked at the mere suggestion. Dave's head turned towards my shoulder.

He lowered his voice. 'I thought you, of all people, were better than that, Mark. You're embarrassing me. Don't be a child. You're a grown man for Chrissake. Chin up, or you'll cause a scene.' He put his arm around my waist. 'What is it?'

He smirked. 'The look on your face.' He patted my thigh with his other hand and looked me in the face. 'It's nothing to get uptight about. Believe me, it'll be fun. You won't be disappointed.'

I wondered if we'd go into a room to have sex or something civilized, like a drink on the sofa. We didn't smoke, so I couldn't imagine us in amongst a room full of smokers. Drinking together at home would be more intimate than being with a group of strangers.

The music stopped, and the lights went out. Everyone in our immediate vicinity d at one another. I could sense the fear in the room.

'What's going on?' I asked.

The man nearest to us shrugged his shoulders.

'Maybe there's a power failure,' said another man.

The transvestite I'd seen earlier came into the room and put her index finger to her lips.

'The police are outside. Stay quiet, gentlemen, and keep calm. No one is to leave the building.'

'Jesus, what if they come in?' I asked, biting my lip. I was grateful the lights weren't on, so no one could see my eyes glazing over.

'It'll be fine,' whispered Dave. He winked at me and pulled me closer.

I wished I were as confident. We all stood in silence like we were at a surprise party, waiting for the unsuspecting guest to arrive. My feet were rooted in the soft shagpile carpet underfoot and my legs felt like they were going to break. Rampant thoughts went through my mind. Dad had become elusive. Would he answer the phone if I phoned him from the police station? What if I was only allowed one call, and he wasn't home or at work? Would he come and bail me out or pretend not to know me? Suppose the police went to his work and someone overheard the conversation?

'We're sorry, Mr Cooney. We found your son, Mark, at a gay spa.'

He'd say he didn't know who they were talking about. I could imagine him saying he didn't have a son. How would I explain the situation to him? How many days or years would I be put in jail for? Then other thoughts: you're not a child, Mark. It's your life. You can do what you like when you want. Anxiety had its grip on me, and I wanted to hide, but there was nowhere to go.

I refused to look at the fear in each face around me and viewed the carpet. Someone coughed. The sound made my eardrums feel like they were about to burst. I looked up. Dave clasped his wrinkled and sweaty hand in mine. Bile rose in my throat, and I swallowed it back down. A man near us raised his eyebrows.

'It's happened many times before,' he whispered. 'Each time, it's been okay.'

'I hope so,' I said, trying to sound as though I was speaking with conviction.

Dave squeezed my hand tighter. It felt like we'd been standing there for hours, but ten minutes later, the music started, and the lights came back on. A man dressed in drag walked towards us.

'Mark?' He said in a deep husky voice.

I nodded with trepidation. Anyone watching would think I was wanted for questioning down at the police station. His lips pouted and his hips tilted.

'Mmm. You're next, sweetheart. Come with me.'

'I'll meet you at the pub across the road afterwards,' said Dave. 'We can have a drink there before we go home.'

'But I thought it was just going to be you and me.'

More men arrived to have a spa while others left, and I wished I were one of them.

'See you later,' said Dave and waved me goodbye, his smile wide.

I walked through the building with the man. My eyes hovered over the crowd. The buzz was back in the air, and I felt lightheaded. He turned around before opening the door in front of him. A small, mirrored ball hanging from the middle of the ceiling made rainbow sparkles cascade on all the walls.

His lips pursed. 'Take your robe off, sweetheart, and strip off whatever you've got on under there. Someone will be with you shortly.'

He closed the door behind him. A single bed like mine at home sat in the middle of the room. A folded towel sat at the end of the bed. I lay on the bed in my jocks. A few minutes later, someone knocked on the door.

'Can I come in?' said a high-pitched male voice.

My voice sounded barely audible. 'Enter.'

A man came in wearing purple jocks. He smiled when he saw me. A purple bow tie adorned his neck. Black eyeliner enhanced his purple eyelids and blue eyes. His eyelashes had several coats of mascara. He carried a tray with three bottles and placed the tray on a small table beside the bed. He put his hands on his hips.

'I'm glad you're not one of the big boys.'

I didn't understand what he meant. He must've guessed by the look on my face he'd confused me. He put his hands up in front of me.

'These hands take a pounding dahling when they work over gigantic bodies like some gents out there, but you're okay. This is going to be too easy.'

He asked me to sit up and blindfolded me.

'Don't worry,' he said. 'It's nothing devious, dahling. I just want to you take a sniff, and then we'll get to it.'

I put my hands up to take the blindfold off.

'Not so fast, dahling. I haven't let you smell anything yet. You'll have to trust me, okay?'

'But I'm not into drugs...'

He laughed. 'Oh nooo, dahling. Heaven forbid, we don't want to get busted now, do we? I'll place something in front of you, and all you have got to do is take a whiff, then tell me if you like it or not. Okay?'

I didn't have a clue what he was referring to.

'Now, dahling. Do it now.'

The smell of roses, intense, sweet, and suffocating, wafted up to my nose. I sneezed.

'We won't be using that one, will we?' he said, letting out a small laugh.

'I guess not.'

'And again, dahling...'

The pungent smell of limes and lemons shot up my nostrils.

'Any good?'

'It's okay.'

'And last one, dahling.'

The heady spicy-sweet smell of sandalwood and patchouli made me feel relaxed.

'I like that one,' I said.

He took my blindfold off and asked me to lie on the bed face down. Warm oil dripped over the back of my legs and back, and he massaged me, taking all the stress out of my body.

CHAPTER THIRTEEN

At the pub across the road, I sat at the bar and ordered a glass of white wine. The liquid warmed my veins, and I felt lightheaded and heavy-lidded. A waiter found me a seat at a table. Women were non-existent. Some couples were old and young men. My heart twisted when Dave walked in with another man I didn't recognize. Dave rested his hand on the man's back and said something. The man moved to the other end of the bar. I got up off the barstool and waved. Dave noticed me and came over.

'There are so many people here. I didn't know if you were here already. I see you didn't waste any time,' he said. 'Mind if I have a mouthful of your drink?'

I passed it to him, and he swilled it around before taking a swig and sitting down. A waiter came past, and he ordered two more.

'How was it?' said Dave, smirking. 'Did he have an enormous cock?'

'You were right. It was wonderful.'

His face piqued, and for a moment, I thought he was jealous. 'I'm waiting.'

'Huge.'

'What? Bigger than mine?'

'He was a good five inches. A thorough gentleman.'

His eyes widened. 'You can't be serious.'

'Yes, I am. It's obvious you're always trying to get a look at other men's genitalia. Isn't mine big enough?'

A waiter placed a glass of wine in front of Dave. He picked it up and stared at me before he had a swig.

'You were the one who suggested coming here. Let's go to my place,' I said. 'We can talk there.'

I stood up, walked to the bathroom, and could sense him behind me. When we were both inside, I looked around to make sure no one else was in there.

'Who's the jealous little boy? What do you see in them you don't see in me?'

'I guess I get bored,' said Dave. He urinated up the wall like a cougar marking its domain.

I winced and bit my thumbnail. 'Bored? Jesus Christ. Are you seeing someone else?' When we were in the spa, I wanted Dave to tell me he loved me too, but he remained silent.

'What do you think? Do you know what? You need to enjoy yourself and stop worrying so much.'

'Come on, let's go home.'

In the car park, his hand brushed my groin. He moved closer, but someone walked around the corner, and I moved away from him and ran over to my car. My heartbeat pounded.

'Are you alright?' Dave said when he was inside. 'If you don't want me to come, just tell me.'

'I do. It's okay.' I didn't want to tell him about Mr Sinclair.

Neither of us spoke on the way to my house. Dave reached over and put his hand on my thigh. Having sex with a stranger made me feel excited and guilty at the same time.

He stopped at the front door and wrapped his arms around me. His penis pushed against my leg, and I felt my penis moving and pushing against my jocks. His hand brushed over the front of my genitals. I hesitated before I entered my house. I didn't want to see Dad in an awkward or uncompromising position with Irene.

'Beware, Dad's entertaining a woman.'

I scanned Dave, trying to read his facial expression in the moonlight before I opened the front door. I walked inside. Dave raised his eyebrow and opened his mouth to speak, and I motioned for him to be quiet. His penis in his tight jeans reminded me of a fishing rod. He flicked his hair back off his face.

Dad sat on the couch in the living room and looked up when we entered.

'Where's Irene?'

His mouth opened before he spoke. 'She's gone.'

The phone rang, and I answered it.

'Don't touch the phone. It'll be her.'

It was too late. I'd already picked up the receiver and held the phone out towards him.

He waved his hand at me and mouthed that he wasn't here.

'Can I get him to phone you?' I asked. 'He's not here.'

Her voice sounded terse. 'Tell the gutless bastard to speak to me.'

Dad's eyes penetrated mine. 'Hang up,' he mouthed. He stood up, walked out into the kitchen, and poured himself a glass of whiskey with ice blocks. I placed the phone back in its cradle.

His voice quivered. 'If she rings again, don't answer it.' His neck rose with tension, and he winced with irritation. Before I could ask him why, the phone rang again.

'It'll be her. She's relentless.' He sat at the kitchen table and leaned forward, clasped his hands together and moved his thumbs up and down.

'Who?' asked Dave, smirking. He'd snuck up behind me and put his arms around me. I wriggled to get free, frightened Dad would notice.

'Irene,' replied Dad, his eyes focused on his hands.

'Why aren't you talking to her?' I asked.

'She keeps hinting she needs a new fridge and a new washing machine. She thinks I can just open my wallet and pay for whatever she wants. Women!'

'Why don't you tell her how you feel? You've always been open with us.'

His voice rose an octave. 'I already have, but she won't bloody well listen.'

The phone stopped ringing, and a few seconds later, started again.

'You're being silly. What if it's Nora?'

Dad's jawline hardened, and his Adam's apple formed a tight knot. 'It won't be. It's Irene. I'm getting too old to be dating women. They don't have any respect. Everything's changed since I courted your mother.'

He stood up and walked into the hallway, reached for the phone, and threw it on the floor. The receiver dislodged, and he picked up his glass from the table and walked back into the living room. He sat on the couch and skulled the rest of his drink. I picked the phone up and placed it back on the hall table. Soon after, it started ringing again, and I answered it.

'Hello,' I said. I could hear the anger and frustration in Irene's voice when she asked me who was speaking. 'It's Mark Cooney.'

She raised her voice, and I pulled the receiver away from my ear. 'It's Irene. Listen. You tell that father of yours he's an arsehole. We're through. He can piss off and never come back.' She slammed the phone down in my ear.

'What did that bitch have to say?' asked Dad.

'It's over.'

The muscles in his face relaxed.

'I'll just get my keys, and we'll be off,' I said.

'Stay. I'm not doing anything,' said Dad.

'I forgot something,' said Dave. 'Goodnight, Mr Cooney.'

Before I could say anything, Dave was already heading towards the front door.

❧

Dave phoned me and said he'd moved into a unit and invited me over. The unit had one bedroom, a living room, a kitchen, and a bathroom. Everything was tidy. A man in the unit next to Dave's was exiting when I arrived. I knocked on the door to the number Dave gave me, and he opened it and looked this way and that before pulling me inside and closing the door. Dave hugged me, held my hand, and walked me into a bedroom. He started taking his clothes off. It felt unfamiliar in the room. I thought I was imagining the smell of testosterone and other men's body fluids. Afterwards, my chest tightened, and I picked my clothes up off the floor and dressed in a hurry.

'What's wrong with you?' asked Dave.

'Nothing. I've gotta go, that's all.' I wanted to know if anyone else had been there with him but was too frightened to ask him in case he rebuked me.

When I arrived home, I went straight to the bathroom and turned on the taps in the shower. I imagined my skin covered in dirt from ploughing paddocks and scrubbed my body clean.

Each time I visited him; Dave expected me to stay the night. I enjoyed waking up beside him but felt it was too risky. I refused to park my car near the unit and arrived after dark. If a car was turning in or out of the complex, I kept walking and waited a while before seeing Dave. I always knew where my heart was whenever I arrived there. Adrenalin coursed through every part of my body. I was frightened that the police would knock on the front door, or someone would suspect that we were lovers.

Dave woke me early each morning, and we'd have sex. I'd leave before anyone else in the unit was awake. I stayed over four nights of the week, and he stayed at my house the other three nights. The secrecy fuelled our relationship. Doing something the rest of the world was unaware of made it exciting. Whenever I was working or in class, I wanted him. I couldn't stop thinking about him.

Dave had an interview with a recruitment company in the city and said he'd meet me for lunch. I walked to the tram stop. My feet kicked the leaves, and I felt like a child again. I waved to the man in the coffee shop where I sometimes bought a cappuccino, and he nodded. On the tram, I shuffled past people, held onto the corner of someone's seat, and swayed to the gentle motion. It reminded me of sitting on the swings in the park, talking to Dave.

At my stop, everyone around the door moved out of my way, and I disembarked. A driver tooted his car horn at me as I ran across the road without looking and entered a building at the top of Latrobe Street and pressed the button for the first floor. Lately, I'd become engrossed in my lessons but today was different.

Chef made a souffle, and its texture was light when he took it out of the oven. He watched me whisking my egg whites until they formed peaks before moving onto the next student. When I opened the oven door, mine collapsed.

'What is wrong with you?' Chef asked at the end of the lesson. 'Your skills were getting better, and now they're getting worse again.'

I shrugged my shoulders. 'I don't know. At home, everything I cook turns out fine. It only seems to flop when I'm here.'

His eyes narrowed, and I could tell he didn't believe me.

I excused myself and went to the toilet. The window in the bathroom overlooked the cafe where I'd be meeting Dave. For a moment, I watched the people walking along the pavement to see if he was making his way there. A tram stopped, blocking my view, and I waited until it moved on. People walked along the sidewalk, but I couldn't see Dave anywhere. I turned on the cold tap and washed my hands. I pressed my hands over my hair, wishing I had Brylcreem to control my curls because they'd sprung up again.

◦❦◦

The cafe was noisy, and I found Dave seated at a table at the back of the establishment. He looked handsome in a black suit, white shirt, and pale blue tie. I wanted to devour him.

We ordered a pie each, and Dave waited until the waitress disappeared before he spoke.

'I applied for a job involving ordering kitchen equipment from overseas.'

'What sort of equipment?'

'I read a magazine article about a company in France that has crepe machines. A trip there would allow me to see how they operate. If I can find out how much they cost, I might get a loan and buy one and sell it to a restaurant in Australia.'

Dave's voice was full of enthusiasm. He made me feel happy that he'd found something he wanted to do, but disappointed that he'd have to travel overseas.

'Is that Sue?' I asked, taking a brief look at a girl sitting at a table eating a sandwich who kept looking at us.

'No,' replied Dave, nodding in her direction. 'You'd better beware of Sue. It's always Mark this and Mark that.' He moved his head from side to side and made a gesture with his hands and rolled his eyes. 'He's so friendly, handsome, charming, etcetera.'

'At least she has good taste,' I answered, smiling at him.

I ate my chicken and vegetable pie, but there were hardly any pieces of chicken in it. It was mass-produced, as there were more peas and carrots in it than meat, and the sauce was lumpy. My mind mulled over what he'd said, but I'd have to wait until we were alone together before I could say anything to him.

.⁓⊕⁓.

We met at my house after dinner. Dave never used the key I'd given him. He always rang the doorbell in case Dad was home. I greeted him at the front door. His hand moved slowly up my arm, over my shoulder, and lightly around my neck. I turned and looked up at his face, smiling at me. A fuzzy sensation went through my body from all the alcohol I'd consumed whilst I'd been cooking, and I couldn't think straight. Dave's news unnerved me, and the alcohol had curbed my anxiety.

We sat and watched television for a while like an old married couple. He agreed to stay over, and afterwards, we lay in Dad's bed. His lovemaking was meditative, as though his mind was elsewhere.

'You'll be here when I return, won't you?' he asked. 'You're like a faithful war widow waiting for her soldier to return home.'

I rolled over to face him.

'I may not,' I replied, surprising myself.

He grinned and kissed the top of my forehead.

'I don't think you'll ever leave Noble Park.'

I turned on my side away from him.

'What's the matter?'

'Nothing. I want to go to sleep.'

He turned the light out, and I closed my eyes but stayed awake, brooding about the prospect of him travelling. I remembered he hadn't got the job, and after a while, I drifted off to sleep. When I woke up in the morning, he'd already gone.

⁂

My body ached. I wanted Dave to come and live with me permanently because I felt vulnerable visiting him at the unit. Dad slept at home on one night that Dave was supposed to stay. Dad walked inside, and Dave waited in the back garden and left via the side gate.

After that, on the nights Dave slept at my house, we met at the oval, and I'd drive us to the beach. If Dad wasn't home when we returned, Dave stayed. Each morning, he'd leave before sunrise, so no one would see him walk home. We lived on the edge of a fine precipice, and I knew it wouldn't continue forever.

One evening we went to Bubbles, and when we arrived home, Dave kissed me hungrily and pushed me inside up against the door when Dad's car turned into our driveway. We let go of each other. Dad strolled toward us.

'I'd better be going,' said Dave, and turned and waved his hand at Dad before he was level with us.

I hurried inside to the bathroom and tried to urinate. Dad walked towards me when I came out.

'You look like you've been doing something you shouldn't have,' remarked Dad.

'Huh! I didn't expect you. Is everything alright?'

'I didn't know you were keeping a check on me. I need to get some clean clothes, and I'll be off.'

'But I thought you weren't seeing Irene anymore.'

'Never you mind who I'm seeing.'

I waited until his car slipped out of our street into his other life before phoning Dave at a number he'd given me at the unit. I opened a cask of Riesling and sat in the living room until he arrived before pouring two glasses.

'Tell me, what the guy you had was like?' said Dave.

'Roger worked at Bubbles to be around like-minded people and was eager to please.'

Dave's mood became as dark as the sky and the sounds it made.

'Did you fancy him?'

'No. He fulfilled a need, that's all. You're the one who wanted to swap partners whenever we've gone there. Not me. I only did it to appease you.'

Dave sighed and walked out of the living room into the kitchen. My temples pulsated, and I grabbed hold of him and put my hands on his shoulders and massaged them.

'I don't want it to be like this. Why can't we let people know we're lovers? Why do we have to hide all the time? I want everyone to know about us,' said Dave.

'It's impossible. No one will want to know us. We'll be shunned. You've already seen your parents' and my dad's reaction. Come in here and have a drink.'

We went into the living room and sat on the couch together. I didn't want to ask him, but I had to know.

'Did you get Beth pregnant?'

'Why?'

My body tensed with jealousy, and heat rose from my neck up to my cheeks.

'Everyone knew you slept with Laura because she bragged about it.'

'Yes, but I didn't get her pregnant.'

'Mark, why are you doing this? We've already had this conversation before. What if Beth's child is mine? Would it matter? God dammit, it was such a long time ago.'

Dave peeked at his watch and to the floor.

'I don't want a child coming between us.'

'Jesus, Mark. Can't we just forget about the past and concentrate on now? Why complicate things by continually digging up the past?'

I poured both our drinks, and we clinked our glasses.

'Here's to an interesting night,' I said.

'Touché,' said Dave. 'How did you go? What was your partner like? Did he have a big knob?'

'Fine,' I replied.

He laughed, and I could feel my brow frown.

'What's so funny?'

'Your lips are pouted. You look like a sullen schoolboy.' He reached for my hand, but I moved it away.

'Well, I got a newbie,' said Dave.

'Why do you say that?'

'He said I was 'too hot' for him and ejaculated prematurely.'

We both stood up, and he grabbed my shirt collar and pulled me towards him. He pushed me up against the living room wall, his mouth hard against mine. I touched his penis through his jeans and unzipped his fly, opened my eyes, and noticed his eyes were tightly closed. My thumb entered the slit of his jocks and gently rubbed the tip of his penis and made him groan with pleasure. His tongue protruded deeper into my mouth.

We were like two guilty schoolboys enjoying ourselves while our parents were out, which only added to the enthusiasm. I knelt, pulled his jeans off, and put his penis in my mouth. Dave breathed heavily and his body jerked forward. His hands caressed my head. Dave pulled out and sat back in the chair behind him. My penis was rock hard in my pants, and I jerked off in the bathroom. When I walked back into the living room, he said he was going home.

'You can't go home now. Why are you doing this? Dad won't be back. Stay.'

I stood up and grabbed hold of his hands. We walked down the hallway together, arm in arm, towards my parents' bedroom. The front door slammed, and I dressed hurriedly and poked my head outside my parents' bedroom door. It was Irene. I ran my fingers through my hair and half expected Dad to come up behind her into the room.

'Where's Russell?'

'I thought he was with you.'

'I wanted to talk to him face-to-face. It's no good over the phone.'

'He left ages ago.'

'If you see him, tell him I called. I'll let myself out.'

She squeezed my cheeks, and I could smell her chewing gum.

'It's a shame you're wasted,' she said, placing the palms of her hands on either side of my shoulders. She kissed me on my lips.

I wiped the residue of her glossy red lipstick with the back of my hand and waited until I heard the door close and deadlocked it.

'Crikey, what was that all about?' said Dave.

'I hope she doesn't say something to Dad about us.'

'What's there to tell?'

'How long was she standing at the door? She could've been listening.'

CHAPTER FOURTEEN

I drove over to the unit to see Dave. The whole place smelt like testosterone, semen, and body odour. His bed was unmade, like it had just been slept in, and I'm sure someone else had been there with him. He seemed disinterested in me, even though he'd invited me over. Dave wanted to eat out, but I said I'd buy takeaway Chinese and bring it back. He paced up and down in the living room. He appeared melancholy, and I asked him if he was alright.

'Go home. I want to be alone.'

I couldn't handle being rejected. Was he seeing someone else? Was he feeling unwell? He walked with me to the front door and shut it abruptly behind me.

I phoned him when I got home, but he didn't answer. The next evening, I drove over to see him. A male dressed in trousers and nothing on top opened the door, and I walked past him into the kitchen.

'Have a seat,' he said.

'Where's Dave?'

He nodded his head towards the living room. I walked inside and found Dave with a cut on his arm. I viewed him with contempt. He stepped up off the couch and yelled at me to go.

'Why are you doing this? What is wrong with you?'

He walked into his bedroom, and I stood in the doorway, watching him.

'Is that another one of your many lovers?'

'He's just a friend I met at the laundromat.'

'You know I care about you.' I grabbed hold of his arm. 'You need to stop doing this to yourself.'

He pulled it away from me. 'I can't help it.'

'You need to see someone.'

'Not you too. I'll be fine. I don't need anyone. You're just like the rest of them.'

I shook him, trying to make him see sense. The blood trickled in three directions down his forearm and splotched on the carpet.

A heavy sigh escaped him. 'You know what your problem is?'

I leaned against the wall, not wanting to hear what he had to say. The silence ricocheted through my body, and I wanted it to crumble into a thousand tiny pieces. I went to move, but my feet were riveted to the floor.

'You're too fucking possessive. You don't own me.'

My voice quivered. 'I can't help it.'

Dave flinched when I touched his shoulder.

'You've been spying on me, and it's got to stop. I've seen you following me.'

'But I thought you felt the same way as me.'

'Well, you were wrong. You make me feel claustrophobic.'

'So, what? You just fuck me and then move onto the next person who takes your fancy. Is that it?'

Dave didn't want to explain it to me. It made me feel sick, always second-guessing and needing to know. He kept trying to clear his throat. In the kitchen, I filled a glass with water and handed it to him. He drank it all before he finally spoke. He appeared lost in remembering. The anguish showed on his face, making him look older than his years.

'Are you alright?' I asked. A searing pain jarred my chest. I wanted to know what happened and why. I was frightened he'd turn his back on me if I prodded too much. 'One day, you'll cut too deep and that'll be the end of you. Where will you be then? I've already lost my mum. I don't want to lose you as well.'

'Just leave me alone. What's happening doesn't concern you, Mark.'

'Don't you realize what you're doing? People will know something's going on in here if you keep having men visiting you.'

'It's got nothing to do with you. You don't own me, Mark.'

'You know what?' I said, not waiting for him to ask. 'It just occurred to me. I mean nothing to you!'

I yawned involuntarily, worn out from arguing with him. Part of me wanted him to say, 'No, Mark, you're wrong. You mean a lot to me. Please stay.' But I knew that wouldn't happen. I'd been kidding myself since he'd returned. I walked back into the living room, and the man looked at me with his eyebrows arched like I had a problem.

Someone knocked on the front door. I hesitated before opening it. A man stood on the porch dressed in a woollen coat and a hat. He drew back on his cigarette. His eyes moved over my face and the rest of me, and he took his hat off and shook my hand. For a moment, I thought I knew him. I opened the door wider for him to enter and noticed the other man still in the entrance behind me. They nodded, and it was obvious the two of them knew one another.

'Look after Dave,' I said. 'He's fragile.'

It wasn't until I sat in my car that I remembered the man on the porch. He'd entered the pub with Dave after we'd been to Bubbles. We'd had a drink before we went back to my house.

Dave phoned me two days later and said he wanted to see me, but I said I was too busy. I agreed to meet him at the end of the week. Cooking alone at home kept me occupied. I didn't care what Dad was doing.

I had time to think about my future and what I wanted to do. Dave had caused me to spiral downwards in my cooking. Ever since he'd returned, nothing seemed to go right for me. I was better off without him. No matter how much I argued with myself, it wouldn't register. There was a part of me that kept wanting to go back to Dave because he was the only person I wanted to be with. I was like cling wrap, stretching myself to fit in with everyone else's demands.

Men could see through me and knew who I was. I could pretend to be different as much as I liked, but nothing changed. The mask I wore slipped off my face, and the words pansy poofter, faggot and queer became part of my everyday existence. Alcohol helped me fall asleep each night. Otherwise, I would lay awake. Sometimes, I'd have a nightmare about Dad and the past. I'd wake covered in sweat and wouldn't be able to get back to sleep. Traumatized at the thought of going back into the dream and reliving everything all over again.

⁂

Dave strolled towards me at the oval with his arm bandaged. It had been four days since I'd last seen him. I didn't expect to see him again so soon. His body was thin and toned. I pulled my top down over my gut self-consciously. I'd gained weight from drinking wine and felt ugly. 'How long have you been here?' he asked.

'Not long, a few minutes or so.' I waited for an apology, but there was none.

He sat on the seat next to me and picked up a long blade of grass and pulled it into tiny pieces absentmindedly.

'Do you want to do some laps around the oval?'

'No, I've already done mine,' I said.

I wanted to get up and go home, but I wanted him to leave first.

'You're the only person who understands me. I thought about what you'd said. My parents think I should see someone again. They asked me to come home.'

'See who?'

'A psychiatrist.'

'What are you going to do?'

'I've moved back home on the proviso that I don't have to see anyone.'

He stood up and took hold of my hand, lifting me towards him. He wrapped his arms around me. I wasn't expecting his outburst of affection and took it as his way of saying sorry, but it wasn't good enough.

I tried to pull away from him, but he held me tighter and kissed my forehead. My body tensed.

People always displayed affection in public in our suburb, but never the same sex. I'd envied Nora in grade six kissing Dave's brother after school near the supermarket entrance. Mum used to say there was a time and a place for everything, and open displays of affection were vulgar.

'What are you doing? What if someone sees us?' I whispered.

He shrugged his shoulders, and I maneuvered my body further apart from him, feeling self-conscious, and walked a few steps backwards.

'What's the matter? Are you angry about the other night?'

I could feel my brow tighten. 'What do you think?' I waited for him to say something.

He opened his mouth, hesitated, and closed it again.

'I've got to get changed. I'll be late for the bakery.'

His eyes narrowed. 'Fine. Have it your way then.'

We walked back together, and his hand swung back and forth, gently touching mine. I could tell by his face he was teasing. He was insatiable. It was like life was a game, and he didn't care whom he hurt. We separated before we turned the corner onto our street. Dave mentioned he had something to do, even though I didn't ask. If only I had enough guts to ask him who was in his unit, the other night. Instead, I tried to appear nonchalant. I half suspected he'd lie to me and walked up to my driveway without looking back.

When I arrived at the bakery, Mrs Mackie was eating a doughnut and insisted I have one. The jam flowed out of the soft dough; its sugar coating my lips. I used to love jam doughnuts. This one tasted sickly sweet and so I went to the back of the shop, spat the rest of it out into the bin, and had a glass of water. Mr Mackie got the consistency right, and I wanted to know how he did it. There were too many customers to serve, and I didn't have time to ask him. Besides, he'd already made all the doughnuts for the day's takings so I couldn't watch him make them either.

The day before, we'd made jam doughnuts in class. The dough had stuck to my fingers, and Chef said I kneaded it for too long.

'What is wrong? We are making doughnuts, not rock cakes.'

'Nothing.'

'You must decide if you want to be a chef. If you're not prepared to put in the hours required, then you'll have no clientele.'

Cooking didn't fulfil me anymore. I didn't eat everything on my plate. Food always tasted bland and unappetizing, even when I made things I liked to eat.

CHAPTER FIFTEEN

Aweek later, on my way to the oval, I sensed someone was watching me. I turned around and saw Dave's sister Sue walking along the other side of the road. She waved and crossed over towards me.

'Hey, where are you going?' asked Sue.

'For a run around the oval.'

'I'm going to the milk bar,' she said, as though I'd asked her. 'It's such a nice day; I thought I'd walk there. Why don't you come with me? We can get something to eat from the fish and chip shop next door?'

I hesitated. I hadn't seen Dave for several days. What if he saw us together? I surprised myself when I said I'd come. We sat at a table outside the shop and ate potato cakes.

'You know, Dave refers to you as his best mate,' she said.

'He's a good friend.'

She touched the tip of my nose, and I recoiled back.

'It's salt,' she said and laughed. 'Where have you been? We haven't seen you around for a while.'

'I've been taking extra shifts at the bakery and cooking. I haven't had time for much else.'

'It sounds like you need a break. Come out with me tonight. I'm going to a bar in the city with a couple of friends.'

I shrugged my shoulders, wondering if Dave would go too.

'Come, it'll do you good.'

I knocked on Dave's front door with trepidation, worried his dad would open it. I nibbled on one of my fingernails and watched the blood appear on the side of the nail bed. The tip of my index finger throbbed where I'd pulled the cuticle, chewed the nail down low, and made it bleed. Mrs Ogilvy opened the front door. Her face flushed when she saw me. I didn't have to tell her I was there to meet Sue because she yelled out to Sue that I'd arrived.

'Would you like to come in?' she said in a matter-of-fact tone.

She didn't seem happy, and I got the impression it was because I was there and wished that I hadn't come. I couldn't help thinking she didn't want me to have anything to do with her children after the argument at dinner.

Sue came up to us wearing an orange figure-hugging dress and her hair tied in a bun, with tendrils falling on either side of her face.

'Have a good time, sweetheart.'

'We will, Mum.'

I opened the car door for her.

'Thank you,' she said, smiling and blinking. Sue took her patent black leather bag from her shoulder and placed it on her lap. Her mum stood at the front door and waved us goodbye.

We caught a train to the city and stood by the open door in amongst a crowd of commuters. When the train gathered momentum, we swayed against one another. The train jerked to a halt at South Yarra, and she held onto me to brace herself and I could smell her lavender perfume. She asked me what I'd been doing since I'd left her, and I said I went for a jog to lose weight. Sue laughed and said I wasn't fat. She let go of my arms and jerked forward. Her hands landed on either side of my waist.

'It's nice to have someone to hold on to,' said Sue.

'I thought you were dating someone. Who did your mum say, James?'

'He's long gone,' she said, flicking her hair back off her face.

'Where's Dave tonight?'

'Out with his mates. They've gone on a pub crawl.'

I took my jacket off.

'Are you okay?' asked Sue. 'You look like you're all hot and bothered.'

'It's pretty stuffy here with all these people around us.'

I flung my jacket over my arm, grateful when the train stopped so we could disembark. We walked along the street. Sue spoke, and I let her words drift in and out of the public strolling up and down the street. I caught a word every so often–dresses, mum, Madeleine–I didn't know who the latter was and didn't ask. I let her talk, and when she prompted me for an answer, I would shrug or nod politely. Why do women have to talk constantly? Don't they believe in silence? My mind was a jumbled mess without trying to process what she said.

When we arrived at the bar, she went to the toilet, and I ordered us both a glass of white wine and sat staring out the window. I was sure Dave and three other men drifted past. I told myself I imagined it. Everyone wore black like they were going to a funeral. I was the only male dressed in navy trousers with a white open-neck shirt and tan shoes. The men and women appeared younger than me, and for the first time, I felt older.

Sue sat and eyed me while sipping her Riesling. She grinned, glanced at the door, and then back at me.

'The others should be here soon. Did Dave tell you he's going to Canada this month?'

Her question startled me.

'No. When?'

'He leaves on the 17th.'

'Did he get the job?'

'Not that I know of. Why?'

'He mentioned he'd applied for a job sourcing cooking utensils from overseas,' I blurted.

I felt like I'd betrayed a secret.

'He didn't tell me that.'

'How long is he going for?'

'Dad booked him an open ticket. Dave may spend a few months there.'

'That's generous of him, considering the fight they had.'

'Dave has to pay him back. He thinks it will do Dave good to get away for a while. A change of scenery.'

'But he's been away for so long.'

'Yes, but he was living in Perth and working, so it wasn't a holiday.'

I was on my guard and felt like Sue was making excuses for him. She was the keeper of family secrets and would only divulge what she needed to, and it reminded me of the many times I'd asked her when he was coming back. She knew but wouldn't divulge anything about Dave. It was obvious no one else was coming. This night was planned for her to tell me, not Dave. 'Who's he going to Canada with?'

'By himself.'

'Dad wanted him to travel solo to clear his head.'

'But there's nothing wrong with him.'

'I know,' she replied, and I could tell she was exasperated as I was.

She looked through me like she was somewhere else and had forgotten I was here. I ordered another drink. We ate chicken parmigiana with cheese and tomato sauce on top, lots of fried chips, and some carrots and peas. The piece of chicken looked like an overgrown fillet and was dry from being overcooked. Tonight, I didn't care. I ate all of it and felt heavy and bloated not long after I'd finished eating. It was cheap food to make people come in and spend money on drinks, which were always expensive. I disliked the taste of beer and only drank wine or champagne when I was out. If I drank spirits, I'd be bankrupt.

'Why haven't you been around lately?' asked Sue.

'I've been busy.'

She frowned and her eyes narrowed. I could tell she didn't believe me.

'I don't think your dad likes me.'

She hesitated and appeared guarded. 'He has certain views.'

'Does he think I'm to blame for the way Dave behaved?'

'I don't think so. I'm not sure.'

There was a stabbing pain in my chest. I guessed it was Dave that I saw earlier. Having fun before flying away. I couldn't bear to think of him not being around.

'Why didn't he tell me?'

'He's got a lot of things to do before he leaves and asked me to tell you.'

'Right,' I said, downing the rest of my glass of wine. A tight pain ripped through my torso like someone had punched me in the guts. 'Does your dad know that you're out tonight with me?'

'No, only mum does.'

'Are your friends still coming?'

Sue glanced at her watch. 'I guess not.'

'Do you mind if we go?'

'Okay.'

She held onto my hand, and we walked back to the station in silence. My eyes hovered over the people in the street, wanting to see Dave, but I didn't see anyone I knew. On the way home on the train, she laid her head on my shoulder and fell asleep. When we arrived at our stop, I woke her, grateful I didn't have to make conversation. Her news still simmered in my mind. I drove her home, hoping she'd invite me in on the off chance that Dave would be there, but she turned and spoke to me when I pulled up in front of her house.

'I really enjoyed tonight. Hopefully, one day soon, we can do it again,' said Sue.

'It was good,' I lied. 'But I won't be able to because I've got to pre-pare some meals I've made in class, and I've taken on some extra hours at the bakery.'

'Maybe when you're not busy?' She reached forward and kissed me on my cheek before she opened the car door. Her body silhouetted in the streetlight as she walked up her driveway.

When I entered my house, I went into the bathroom and vomited in the toilet. I lay on my bed, fully clothed, and stared at the ceiling. Why didn't he have enough guts to tell me himself?

⁓⦿⁓

Dad opened the front door. His manner was gruff, as always. He spoke to anyone who visited as though they were an intruder. I thought he was talking to Jehovah's Witnesses when I heard him complain about knocking too early. Someone replied, but I couldn't understand what they said. I stopped eating my breakfast and walked out into the hallway. Dave stood in front of me with a sheepish smile.

'This is a surprise. It's nice to see you. Don't just stand there. Come in,' I said.

His voice sounded husky, and his eyes were brighter. If I weren't mistaken, I'd swear he had a pill or something.

'Sorry, I haven't been feeling well; otherwise, I would've come over sooner.'

'I didn't know you were sick.'

'It's just a cold.'

'Are you okay now?'

'I'm fine.'

He stood up against the kitchen door. Dad walked past him and sat back at the kitchen table. He looked Dave up and down, scrutinizing him.

'I've already let him know it's a bit early in the morning to be visiting,' Dad said, looking at me. His head turned towards Dave. 'You did that last time, if I remember rightly.'

I scowled at Dad and stole a glance at Dave, trying to read him. 'Don't listen to him,' I said. 'Have you eaten?'

'Yes, but I'd love a coffee.'

'Coffee it is then. What's been happening?'

'I've been checking out the nightlife and catching up with a few people. You remember Stan and Dillon?'

His arm brushed mine, and he pulled a chair out and sat at the kitchen table. His touch sent tingles through me.

'I'll be off,' said Dad, pushing his plate away from him before standing.

'When will you be back?'

Dad scraped his chair against the floor, stood up, and walked out of the room without answering me. He closed the kitchen door behind him. My eyes met Dave's, and we smirked. I felt lightheaded, delirious. For a moment, fear constricted my throat, but it disappeared just as quickly.

'You look like you've seen a ghost,' said Dave.

I pointed the tips of my fingers into his shoulder.

'I have. You,' I quipped.

'I'm sorry I upset you.'

'Why are you doing this to me? I've done nothing to you. One minute you want to know me, and then you act like I don't exist.'

Dave slid out of his chair and walked out of the room. For a nanosecond, I stopped and watched him go, unable to fathom what to do next. Then I strode down the hall after him.

'Wait up, damn you,' I said. 'I don't have time for this.'

I grabbed hold of his arm, and he pushed me away with his other hand.

'You just don't get it, do you?' he said.

'What?'

'You're the one I was thinking about. We're constantly walking on a tightrope. I don't know how you feel, but I find it exhausting. Why should we have to hide who we are from everyone all the time? I hate it,' said Dave.

'What can we do?'

Dave shrugged his shoulders and screwed his face.

'Have you spoken to your dad about how he treated you?'

My face prickled. My tone sounded sheepish, and I refused to look at Dave. 'I can't remember saying all those things to you,' I said, knowing I was lying.

'You know I didn't bring it up to hurt you. I mentioned it because I care about you.'

I wanted him to tell me he was going to Canada, but he said nothing.

'Can I see you tomorrow night? We'll talk then. I don't want this to come between us. If I don't go home now, I'll be late for an appointment.'

He let himself out, and I didn't stop him.

.~⁓⁎⁓~.

At the bakery, I couldn't concentrate. Someone wanted bread sliced for toast, and I sliced it for sandwiches instead. Another customer ordered a muffin, and I went to place a croissant in a bag for her before she rudely objected. I was sure she'd said the latter. Rattled, I asked Mrs Mackie if she had a pen. She rummaged through her handbag, placing her car keys, lipstick, handkerchief, wallet, address book, and rouge on the bench before producing one so I could scribble what people wanted.

When I arrived home, I wasn't hungry. I sat in the living room and drank the rest of the cask of wine and must've fallen asleep.

Dad said my name in an accusatory tone. 'Mark, wake up!'

He shook me until I opened my eyes.

'Where did you find this?' He held Mum's suitcase out in front of him.

My eyes opened and closed again, and my head throbbed.

'Where did you find that?' I asked.

'In here, behind the couch.'

How could I have been so careless? I remembered getting it out from under my bed and sitting in the living room, going through all the photos again.

'What are you trying to achieve holding onto the past? Your mother's gone, and she's not coming back. It's going in the bin now.'

'No, you can't do that. They're memories of Mum. Destroy them, and there's nothing left.'

He looked at me begrudgingly, holding the suitcase closer to his body.

'It's just sentimental bullshit your mum couldn't let go of.'

'I don't care. It makes me feel close to her.'

He shook his head. 'You're pathetic.'

I sat up and reached out my hands. Dad threw it at me and walked out of the room. I placed it on the coffee table and lay back on the couch again, willing myself to reenter my dream. Dave and I were on our honeymoon in Hawaii, walking along the beach. Dave stripped down to his jocks and went for a swim. Naked, I ran in after him and could taste the saltwater on his lips when we kissed. Afterwards, in our hotel room, I showered and dried my body. I tugged at my shrivelled penis in the bathroom, trying to make it look bigger, and woke to find I'd ejaculated.

CHAPTER SIXTEEN

When I returned home from class, I spent the afternoon preparing the evening meal. I placed a white linen tablecloth on the kitchen table and set the table with Mum's best dinner set and silver cutlery, which I'd polished. The crystal glasses sparkled in the light. I wanted everything to be perfect. The candle in the middle of the table flickered back and forth. I rested the menu I'd written between the salt and pepper and had a bubble bath before Dave arrived. I took my time shaving my face and played with my curls that had grown back and sprayed them.

When we saw one another again at my house, I noticed out of my peripheral that the cut on his arm had healed. I was conscious of his eyes on my face and looked away. I ushered him inside; paranoid Dad would turn up. In the living room, I handed him an apéritif of scotch and soda on ice and made one for me. We clinked glasses. I ran my fingers through my hair, trying to act nonchalant, and hoped that he couldn't see through my facade. I said I'd be back and went to check the oven.

Dave came out into the kitchen. 'We need to talk.'

His whole demeanour had changed. He stood with his chest out, his feet wide apart. His eyebrows arched. His dad had warned me during dinner that Dave could be like this, but I'd never experienced it until now. My heart heaved with panic.

'I promise I'll never cut myself again.'

His eyes searched my face, and he asked me if I believed him. I said I did.

'I don't want to be friends with you anymore,' said Dave.

Anxiety bubbled up inside my stomach and bile rose in my throat. I swallowed it back down again. My body shook and my feet faltered. I held onto the top of the nearest chair, pulled it out, and slid onto it. I gulped some of my drink and put it back on the table before placing both of my hands underneath my bottom to stop them from shaking.

'Will you move to the countryside with me so we can be away from everyone and live together? Be my partner. Well, what do you say?'

My throat felt like it was burning. A heavy sigh escaped me, and I realized I'd been holding my breath.

'Of course. Yes. I thought you already knew. Nothing has ever been more desirable to me. I thought you'd changed your mind about me.'

'Mark, why would you ever think that?' said Dave, looking perplexed.

I finished my glass of whisky and shrugged my shoulders. My body trembled. In the living room, I retrieved a cask of wine and two glasses. I stifled a yawn. All the pent-up emotions I'd held onto made me feel tired. For years I'd envisaged the two of us as a couple but had never imagined it happening like this. I still had to ask him one question.

We sat outside in the back garden, and he clinked his glass against mine. We spoke about opening a cafe. Dave would get a job to help me fund it.

'In time, you can open your restaurant,' he said.

'But what if it doesn't work out? It worries me that no one will like my sandwiches, pies, and cakes. What if I go bankrupt?'

'It'll be fab. I just know it, believe me,' replied Dave.

'How can you be so sure?'

'I've tasted your cooking. There's nothing wrong with it. The cake you made for my party was delicious.'

'You know we don't have to move. You can live with me here.'

'I can't. Besides, what if your dad comes home and finds us in bed? It's too risky. We've already had enough close calls with him and with Irene.' His eyes moved skywards. 'I need my space–with you. My parents think I'm still ten and that they can boss me around. They're always watching me, wanting to know what I'm doing. For Chrissake, I'm a grown man.'

'But isn't that because they care? They're worried about you.' 'Don't you start. That's bullshit, and you know it. I don't need them anymore. When I was on my own, I was fine.'

'If I've upset you, I'm sorry.'

'You're not upsetting me. They aggravate me. Besides, I don't want to live here forever.'

I had a swig of wine.

'What made you come back?'

'Never mind about why I did. It doesn't matter. We'll talk about it at another time. I wanted to see if you'll move in with me. We can start looking for a place to rent this weekend.'

'But I heard you're going on holiday.'

'I asked Sue to see you, so she could tell you.'

'Why would you want to do that?'

'I thought it would be easier.'

'How long are you going for?'

He gave a one-shouldered shrug and wouldn't make eye contact. 'I dunno. I haven't decided.'

'You don't sound happy. What if I save and meet you over there and you can show me around?'

I turned towards Dave and lifted his chin with my fingertips, trying to gauge his facial expression. His skin appeared ghostly white, and for a moment, I thought he might be sick. I waited for him to say something. My heart thundered. I averted my eyes from his face and noticed a fresh wound on his arm that had scabbed.

'You know you can always talk to me about it if you want to,' I said.

'Maybe one day, but not now.'

'You mentioned you would do this again,' I said, pointing to the cut. 'Why did you do it?'

I poured him another glass of wine and he had a mouthful of it and swallowed hard.

'If you must know, years ago, one night after dinner, me and the boys were walking around the streets. It was late, and we went down to the creek. Stan suggested we cut ourselves to show solidarity. I don't like the sight of blood. Fred lit a fire and handed around a bottle of brandy he'd stolen from his old man's cabinet. We took it in turns to carving a 'C' for coterie into each other's forearm. I passed out when Stan did mine. I blamed the alcohol.'

'Didn't it hurt?' I asked.

'The brandy probably masked the pain. I'm not sure. I've always liked males. At church one Sunday, the priest spoke about God condoning same-sex relationships.'

'You ought to thank God, you're not like that, son, said my dad when we were driving home.'

'But I like boys.'

'Not in that way, you don't. No one will want to know you if you do. I'll whip you to heaven and back if you so much as look at another boy. You were made to have a relationship with a girl, get married, and procreate. You hear me?'

'Mum argued with him to leave me alone. She said I'd done nothing wrong. I was only seven. Anyway, does there have to be a reason? He made me feel dirty. At night, I'd wait until everyone was asleep. In the bathroom, I'd close the door, sit on the side of the bath, open the vanity cupboard, use Dad's razor blades, and cut my arm.'

'Is that why your dad sent you away?'

'We'd never got along. After dinner, I mentioned to her I was going to do my homework, and I climbed out of my bedroom window and met the boys at Bob's house. We used to let down people's tyres for fun and steal stuff from the milk bar while the shop owner was serving someone else. We were going to go over to the car crusher's factory on the highway to steal a car seat and put it down by the creek, so we'd have something comfortable to sit on.'

'When I saw my dad coming out of a hotel on the highway with Beth's mum. I hid in the front garden of the house near me. My dad had his arm around her and opened his car door for her, the prick. Tommo hurled me out of the bushes just as dad drove past and he turned in my direction. It was dark, so I didn't know whether he saw me.'

'Is that your dad?' said Dillon.

'I pushed him in the chest. 'Don't be stupid,' I said. 'He's at home with me Mum.' I was grateful he couldn't see my face in the dark. Mum always said I couldn't hide anything from her. She knew if I was lying just by looking at me. 'Come on, let's go,' I said, eager to return home to see if mum had gone to bed. I wanted to ask her where dad was.'

'It's early,' said Dillon. 'Let's go to the fish and chip shop. I've got a dollar. We can get some chips and drinks and perve on Laura through her bedroom window.'

'I said I was going home. We all knew Laura was an exhibitionist. She loved getting undressed with her blinds open no matter the time of day.'

'Come on, Dave,' said Stan.

'Nah, I'm going.'

'It's unlike you not to watch a free matinee.'

"I'm not feeling well. See you tomorrow,' I said. I walked away from them and put my hand up in a salutary wave and didn't look back. Once inside my bedroom window, I changed into my pyjamas and walked into the kitchen. Mum sat where I'd left her reading a book and looked up.'

'Have you finished your homework, love?'

'I nodded. 'Where's dad?' I asked, knuckling my eye and yawning.'

'He's at a meeting.'

'His meetings became more frequent, and the next evening I rode my bike past the hotel and noticed his car in the car park. I wanted to get back at him, but didn't know what to do. Beth kept hanging around our gang and I wondered if she knew. We went to her house one night and her parents weren't home. She said her dad had died in a forklift accident several years ago and her mum had found some guy. I'm quite sure it would've been my dad. At home, I cut my arm deeper, and mum found me in the bathroom. She thought I'd tried to commit suicide.'

'What do you think you're doing, Dave? Are you insane?'

'She ran into my room and came back with one of my t-shirts and wrapped it around my arm. Dad came home just as she'd finished.'

'Where is everyone?' he called out.

'In here,' said mum. 'Dave's cut his arm.'

'Dad had his hat in his hand and looked at us both and said he was leaving. Just like that.'

'What, for Beth's mum?' I asked.

'You little bastard. Come here.'

'I ran out the door and rode my bike down to the creek. Anyway, enough of all that. They sent me to a shrink, and he suggested shock treatment to stop me from cutting. I pleaded with them not to take me there and cut my arms deeper. The psychiatrist said I was mentally unwell, and they had me admitted to a hospital in the countryside.'

He skulled the rest of his wine, and I could tell he was back in the scene while he spoke. His hand touched the marks on his arm. Each vertical line had a slight tilt and a horizontal line running through them like he'd been counting each day he'd been marooned on a desert island.

The timer buzzed in the kitchen. I picked up our glasses and poured us both another drink. He sat at the table while I served us both French onion soup. I pulled my chair back and sat down.

'To us,' said Dave.

I found what he said about the coterie hard to fathom. My eyes focused on him. I could tell he wasn't divulging something. He asked me why I worried so much about my cooking because the soup tasted delicious.

'Wait until you try the main,' I said once we'd finished eating and took our bowls over to the sink.

He picked up the menu, looked at me in surprise, and opened his mouth to speak.

'Shh, just try it.'

I removed the plates from the oven and mashed the potatoes boiling on the stove. Butter drizzled over the steamed beans, and I placed the meat on each plate. I couldn't wait for him to taste it and placed both of our plates on the table.

He tasted the duck with mango and chocolate. His face changed as he ate it.

'I haven't tasted anything like it. I thought you'd gone crazy and mixed the dessert with the main. The meat tastes softer and sweeter, but not like chocolate. It enhances the flavour.'

I bowed. 'Thank you.'

'Seriously, Mark, this is so good you could sell it.'

My face ached from smiling. I couldn't remember when I'd been this excited.

·⥾⥿·

We lay in Dad's bed. I traced Dave's pecs with the flat of my hand and moved my hands along the outline of his shoulders and down either side of his spine. There wasn't an inch of fat on his body. My fingers lingered on his hips, and my lips caressed his lips. Instead of enjoying the moment, I worried it would be the last time we saw one another. He kissed me hungrily, and my lip bled. His finger rested on the cut for a moment, and he licked the blood from it and rolled onto his back. I tried to commit his body to memory, too frightened to close my eyes in case he disappeared.

I must've fallen asleep because the screeching brakes of the garbage truck woke me. It was early: 7 am. I lay in dad's bed, taking comfort in the smell of Dave's aftershave on his pillow. My head ached from drinking too much. The covers were pulled back on the other side of the bed, revealing an indent where Dave had laid. My left leg stretched out and moved over the space. It was still warm. I stepped out of bed and called out to him, but there was no answer. His clothes weren't on the floor where he'd left them. I looked at the side table for a message–anything–but there was nothing.

In the bathroom, a dis-shelved bleary-eyed man stared back at me. I found a packet of painkillers in the overhead cabinet and popped one into my mouth. I turned on the cold tap and cupped my hands with water to wash the tablet down. In the kitchen, I made myself a cup of strong black coffee, and someone knocked on the front door: it was Sue.

She was panting, trying to get her words out. 'Is Dave here?'

She didn't wait for me to answer and pushed past me, looking in each room. Sue stopped at my parents' bedroom and leaned against the door jamb.

'Do you know when he'll be back?'

'I don't know. He was gone when I woke.'

I peeked at my watch without seeing the time.

Sue's brow furrowed, and an anguished look crossed her face.

'Is everything alright?'

'My parents are worried because Dave's stopped taking his medication.'

'What medication?'

'You know, so he doesn't have one of his episodes. Don't worry. He'll tell you about it when he's ready,' she said, staring at the bed. 'I guess I'd better be going. Mum and Dad will wonder where I am. They don't know where he's living, but I thought he'd be with you.'

'I thought he was living at home. Have you tried all his other friends?'

'I've rung all the ones that were at the party. They haven't seen him. We're worried he'll harm himself again. Dad phoned the airline, and his ticket hasn't been used. He thought he might've changed the ticket and flown over there already.'

'Why would he do that? He was here last night but left before I woke. He said nothing about flying early.'

'Dad panicked and thought Dave could've run away.' 'I don't understand.'

She reached out and touched my arm. 'I can tell by the anguish on your face how you feel. We're the same. Hopefully, he'll return. He's got a lot of explaining to do.'

'I'll hang around here for a while longer. He could've gone down the street or something. If I see him, I'll get him to phone you. Otherwise, I'll phone you later if he doesn't show.'

'Thanks.'

Sue leaned forward and kissed me on my cheek.

'You're a good friend.' She let herself out and closed the front door.

Instead of having a shower, I quickly changed into my trousers, t-shirt, and a jumper. I drove to the oval, but no one was there. At the station, a man and a woman got into a taxi. Several minutes later, I paced up and down the empty platform, the wet surface crunching underfoot. I undid the top two buttons on my shirt and loosened my collar. A train approached, and commuters disembarked and walked down the platform, some chatting to one another, heading towards the adjoining car park.

Down the street, tears fell from the sky, and a man walking past popped open his umbrella. I peered through the window of the cafe where I'd had a coffee with Dave. A woman stood at the counter waiting to be served. The rest of the tables were empty.

Back at the oval, people had arrived and were hovering close to the metal fence, waiting for the local football team to begin their warmup.

I moved through the crowd but couldn't see him anywhere. I sat on a swing and took my jumper off. My eyes moved this way and that. There he was! It was Dave, talking to someone and now walking away. His curls moved in the breeze. I strode towards him and shirtfronted a man. He abused me and said to watch where I was going. On the nature strip, Dave turned and walked down the street and headed towards a car parked on the other side of the road. I yelled out to him, but he didn't turn around. I ran up to him as he opened his car door.

'Dave, wait up,' I said, panting.

'Who are you?' he said with a surprised expression.

I walked away from him. The stranger got into a vehicle and drove away. It was cold at the beach, and I put my jumper on when I slid out of the car. A man walked a dog off the lead and threw a stick for him to catch. The wind howled through the bathing boxes and the sand felt like razor blades cutting my face and hands.

The sea turned black, and seagulls hovered in mid-flight. Waves thundered along the shoreline towards my shoes, and I jogged back to my car. At home, I phoned Sue, but there was no answer. I imagined Dave sitting in a bar somewhere, oblivious to all the disruption he'd caused. At Bubbles, I pressed the doorbell. Negative thoughts of Dave with someone else made my stomach lurch, wondering what expletives he'd use if he saw me. The woman dressed in purple remembered me and said she hadn't seen Dave. I vomited on the way back to my car. At home, I couldn't eat and turned on the television and tried to focus on a family sitcom.

No one answered when I knocked on Dave's front door. Music was playing inside. I climbed over the side gate. The music grew louder, and I stopped in front of a large window with a full-length curtain. A halo of light surrounded the circumference of the window. I stole a glimpse of a shadow through the partially opened curtains, unsure whether it was him. I threw a stone at the window, crouched down, and waited. The curtains opened, and his face appeared troubled. Everything else around him was black, making him ghostlike.

'Who's there?'

Dave's head moved this way and that. He saw me and grinned before lifting the sash. 'Come around the back and I'll let you in.' He closed the window and curtains, and a few minutes later, he opened the back door.

'Are your parents' home?'

'No one's home. They've all gone to a church recital in the local hall.' He walked back into his bedroom, and I sat on the edge of his bed.

'When will they be home?'

'Not for a while.'

'Why are you in the dark? Were you sleeping?'

He screwed up his face.

'Not you too. I just needed time to think. Besides, I'm not afraid of lying here in the dark. Everyone's worrying unnecessarily about me. Sorry, I left like that and didn't return. Sue found me and insisted I come home.'

'Where were you?'

He waved his hands in the air.

'Here and there. Never mind, okay. I'm here now. That's the main thing.' Dave put his arm around my shoulder and kissed the tip of my nose. 'Lie down.'

I lay on top of the bed, and he lay beside me.

'Are you okay?' I asked.

Dave's voice caught in his throat. 'Everything's fine. I have to go away for a while, but I'll be back.'

He turned to face me, and I could tell he was lying.

'You worry too much. Don't believe a word they say.'

Dave's eyes searched my face. He pushed himself up and took off his trousers and t-shirt. His body was warm to the touch, and he took off my shoes, unzipped my jeans, and pulled them down. He climaxed within a few seconds. I shivered with a pulsating surge through my body, making me relaxed for the first time since the previous evening. Dave thought I was cold and stood up and pulled back the covers on his side of the bed. We slid in between the sheets, and I felt the warmth of his breath on my face. My fingers stroked the arch in his back and his shoulders, down his arms, over his scars several times.

'What is that?' I asked, moving my fingertips over a long crusty scar on his forearm.

'Nothing.' He pushed my hands away and let go of me.

'Have you been self-harming again?'

He didn't speak.

'I only asked because I'm concerned. I love you.' My words stuck in my throat, and I coughed. No sooner had I spoken than I wished I hadn't.

'You're so sweet. In another lifetime, you and I would've been perfect together.'

I pulled the covers back and got up off his bed.

'What are you doing?'

'I'd better go. Your parents will be home soon.' I picked my clothes up off the floor, put them on, and laced my shoes.

Dave half sat, leaning back on his elbows, watching me. He put the bedside table lamp on and smiled ruefully.

'Don't leave me alone,' he said, reaching out for my hand, and I stayed for a while longer. Nausea swayed through my body, making me want to vomit.

'Why don't you come to my house? No one's home.'

'I wish I could, but I can't. Wait, I'll walk you home.'

'There's no need. I'll be fine.'

I turned around to face him. 'You know what? I don't understand any of this. What's going on?'

'Nothing. Can we talk about something else?'

'Even Dad asked me what's wrong with you. He thinks you're gay.'

What would Dave say if he found out Dad used the word queer? I guess that made me queer, too, even though I felt normal.

'What did you tell him?'

'I said I didn't know.'

'You don't know who you are, Mark. Do you? Did you have a boyfriend or a girlfriend while I was away?'

'Is that what this is about? Your family can't stand you being gay, so they're sending you away again and you want to punish me for it?'

'Well, no one is sending you away. Are they?'

'Don't go. That's what you'd say to me if it was the other way around.'

'I plan to go on holiday. I don't know when I'll be back.'

'I said I can come with you.'

He didn't answer.

'I've got to go. We can talk about it tomorrow.'

The thought of his parents seeing me there sent chills through my body. I turned on the hall light and made my way to the front door, placing one awkward step in front of the other. My nerves jangled, still reeling from what had just happened. When I went to take my shoes off at home, I realised I was wearing Dave's shoes.

CHAPTER SEVENTEEN

I pondered over which recipe to make for my evening meal–chop suey or Beef Wellington–when someone knocked on the door. Dave's dad stood on the veranda with a scowl on his face and wanted to know if Dave was with me.

'No.'

His hand touched the side of the screen door, and I opened it wider.

'See for yourself if you don't believe me.'

He stepped inside and peered into each room as he walked down the hallway into the kitchen with me. He pulled out a chair and sat at the table.

'Would you like a cup of tea?'

He didn't want one, and I slid into a chair.

'When I said to stay away from Dave, I meant it. Goddamit, don't you know he's hurting inside?'

Dave's dad's shoulders hunched over, and his hair stuck up on end. His clothes hung off his body.

I could hear the melancholy in his voice. 'I was hoping Dave would be here. We don't know where he is.'

'He seemed okay the last time I saw him.'

'Dave always appears that way to everyone, but there's another side to him people don't see.'

'I don't understand.'

His tone turned abrupt. 'No, you wouldn't. Nobody does. The boy suffers from depression. He tried to commit suicide several times when he was younger.'

'No, you must be wrong. Dave's not like that. He's always had lots of friends.'

His dad's face turned scarlet.

'Appearances aren't everything. When we arrived home the other night, he'd cut his arm again. Grace caught him in the bathroom doing it. We thought he'd grown out of harming himself, but we were wrong. This morning, he took his overnight bag and left his medication in the bathroom. For all we know, he could be dead somewhere. Sue thought he might be with you.'

'Sue came here the other day looking for him, though I guess you already know that.'

Shame and fear caused a prickling sensation through my body. If I hadn't arrived at his house, none of this would've happened. I tried to understand what his dad was telling me, all the while wondering where Dave had gone.

He shook his head, and snot dribbled onto his upper lip. His hands reached into his trouser pockets, and he pulled out a handkerchief and wiped his nose.

'Have you called the police?'

His look was impenetrable, and his tone wheedling. 'No. If you know where he is, and you're covering for him, tell me now.'

I sat there, not knowing what to say.

'We don't want you to see him anymore because you'll only get hurt.'

'But I haven't.'

His eyebrows lifted. 'Don't lie to me now. Grace found this in his bedroom when she was vacuuming. She reckoned it'd be yours because of the 'M' on it.'

He reached into his other pocket and held my handkerchief with the tips of his fingers. I took it from him and wiped my brow.

My tone sounded like I was accusing, but I didn't care. 'He said you sent him away to an orphanage in Ballarat.'

A tormented look crossed his face. 'We did no such thing. He went to a hospital for aversion therapy and counselling. Then he went to stay with my sister in the countryside. We thought the country air and his treatment would make him understand that his way of thinking was wrong. All we wanted was what was best for our son, just like any other family would want except nothing's changed.'

'What? Punishing him for what he believes in?'

His tone sounded exasperated. 'Don't believe what he says. He's mixed up. That's why we're sending him to Canada. I've booked him in for conversion therapy.'

'Don't you think you're causing him to be missing?'

'And why is that?'

'He doesn't know who he is, and you're trying to change him. Dave doesn't want to go.'

'That's rubbish and you know it.'

His chair scraped the floor, and he stood up. 'I'll let myself out.'

'Isn't everyone entitled to love despite their colour, race, or religion? What if Dave liked a black girl? Would you condone that too?'

'That's a different matter altogether.'

Mr Ogilvy headed towards the front door with his head down. I heard the door close and contemplated ringing his house to see if Dave had returned while his dad was with me. If anyone else answered, I'd hang up. The phone rang. I jumped and picked it up. It was Nora. Before she said anything, I spoke.

'I'm glad you rang. I forgot to tell you Dad's thinking of marrying Irene.'

'You can't be serious. What a bastard. What's she like?'

'Irene's younger than him.'

'That'd be right. When did this happen?'

'Last week.'

She paused and I could hear someone speaking Italian.

'I've got to go,' I said and hung up, fed up with her ringing, asking after Dad all the time.

The streetlights flickered on, and I drove to the local pub and ordered a drink at the bar. I don't know how long I sat there. I woke up in my bed. Splotches of vomit led to the front door. Outside, there was more vomit on the veranda and driveway all the way to my car. I reminisced about my childhood with Dave while I cleaned up my mess.

He was captain of the school football team, and everyone liked him. I used to be envious of him. Dave would never know what it felt like to be awkward, bullied, or picked last on a sports team. He always smiled, laughed, and appeared carefree–that was the Dave I knew and who I thought was still the same. I never understood why he wanted to harm himself when he had everything that other people wanted.

Sue answered when I telephoned. She said they still couldn't find Dave. He usually contacted her, but Sue hadn't heard from Dave. She said he should've made contact by now. The police arrived earlier and were going to put Dave on their missing person list. I busied myself in the kitchen and pre-heated the chop suey for dinner. When it was ready, I left it on the kitchen bench.

The smell made me dry retch, and I went to bed. My body tossed and turned, trying to fathom where Dave could've gone. The clock on my bedside table said it was 8 pm. In the hallway, I opened the phone book to Collinson and searched for Beth's parents. I remembered she lived on the other side of the railway line. My heart pounded, and my palms were slippery. Someone must've been waiting for a phone call because a few seconds after I'd dialled the number, a female voice answered.

'Hello, this is Mark Cooney. I'm an old friend of Beth's and want to contact her.'

The person hesitated. 'I don't remember her mentioning you.'

A man in the background asked her who was on the phone.

'We were in high school together.'

She rattled off the number, and I hung up.

Beth's number rang out. I paced up and down the hallway and phoned her again, but no one answered. In the bathroom, I turned the taps on over the bath and poured some sandalwood bubble bath in. The room fogged, and I lit a candle and placed it on the vanity before I lay in the water.

The smell of sandalwood acted like a sedative, calming my nerves. Whistling interrupted my thoughts, and the bathroom door opened. Dad poked his head in, and my body recoiled.

'Jesus. I didn't know you were there. Why don't you turn the bloody light on?' said Dad. 'What on earth are you doing in the bath, anyway? Baths are for women, not men.'

'Get out!'

'Okay, okay. I've got news for you. I'll tell you when you get your arse out here.' Dad said, closing the door.

'I don't care what your news is,' I said, but I don't think he heard me.

What made Dave leave? Had I upset him? I put my head under the water and came up gasping for air. The bubbles slowly evaporated, and I pulled a towel from the hanger and dried myself.

I put my pyjamas and slippers on and went into the living room to find Dad snoring in a lounge chair with his head back and his mouth open. He smelt of alcohol. I poked his shoulder until he woke up. His eyes squinted.

'There you are,' he said. 'I've decided to marry Irene.'

'Let's celebrate,' I said, forcing a smile onto my face. 'I'll get us a drink.'

My chest tightened, and I walked into the kitchen to retrieve a bottle of Sauvignon Blanc I found hidden in the back of the cupboard and slammed the door shut. I opened the bottle and poured some into two wineglasses. In the living room, I handed one glass to Dad.

'Cheers. Here's to you and your pending nuptials,' I said and sat on the couch.

He smiled and reached across the table, clinking his glass against mine before moving the glass up to his lips and having a drink.

'It's nice to see someone happy for me, unlike that bitch of a sister of yours.'

'Have you let her know?'

'Not yet.'

My throat burned when I swallowed a mouthful of wine. I coughed and had some more, all the while thinking of Dave and hoping it would make me drowsy, so I could sleep. Dad watched me down the rest of my glass and pour another one.

'Come on, drink up,' I said. 'You must be excited.'

'I've already had a few. Irene and I went out for dinner, and I popped the question. It was champagne all around.'

'Oh, well, you've done well then, haven't you, celebrating?'

'What's wrong with you, Mark? You don't sound happy.' Dad had another sip of his wine. 'Why are you so monotone? I hope you're not going to be like your sister. A man has a right to be happy, you know.'

'Dave's missing.'

'Is that all? He'll be back.'

My voice sounded shrill and raspy. 'What do you mean, is that all? It's surreal. I don't know what to think. It's like I'm grieving for Mum and him together. Nothing matters anymore.'

'He's not dead. Besides, you're young, you'll find other people to make friends with.'

'I don't want new friends. It's not as easy as you think. Just because you have wasted no time doesn't mean to say that I should be the same.'

His eyes widened, and his words slurred. 'Jesus, I didn't know you were a poofter.'

'Well, you made me that way.'

'I did no such thing.'

'You did so. When everyone else was asleep, you came into my room. If I told anyone, you said Mum wouldn't want me anymore. You'd deny everything like you are now.'

I topped up my glass and skulled it. My body shook, and my lips trembled. The heaviness in my body lifted. I felt light after confronting Dad.

'Jesus, Mark, that's not true, and you know it.'

'Yes, it is. I remember the first time you opened my bedroom door and woke me. You rushed over to my bedside, and I thought something was wrong. You whispered to me to be quiet before you slid between the sheets. The palm of your hand covered my mouth. You said it was you, Dad, and not to scream. At first, I thought you must've had an argument with Mum and needed somewhere to sleep. I went to step out of bed, and you pulled me back in. Your other hand lingered where it shouldn't. You kissed me and said I was a good boy. My body tensed, and you whispered for me to relax and that you wouldn't hurt me. I can't recall how often you came into my room. I'd lost count after ten.'

'What made you do it? Was it because I wasn't your son? Did you think that marrying Mum gave you the right to do that to me, Dad? What were you thinking? That you owned me and thought that you could do what you liked with me? Is that it? Besides, you couldn't wait until Mum died to start your bloody dalliances. All this bullshit about her being the only one you'll ever love. You've always been full of crap, Dad, since I've known you. If you loved her, you would've taken her out to dinner like all the women you've taken out since she's been gone. Why Mum loved you, I'll never know. You're just like Nora said. You're a selfish prick.'

Dad stood up and swayed towards me. One thumb hooked on his braces. He made a fist with the other one and narrowly missed my face.

His voice raised. 'That's not true, and you know it! Believe me, it hasn't been easy since I lost your mum. She was a good woman, but she was still in love with that I-talian.'

Dad turned side-on, and my fist connected with the side of his face. He leaned forward, clutching both cheeks.

'You bastard, Mark. You'll be sorry you did this.'

Dad lunged at me. He fell forward onto the coffee table and staggered backwards, trying to stand up straight. My body raged like a fire that I had no control over. I needed to put the flames out. I sat on the steps in the back garden. The night was unusually mild for this time of year, and I viewed the stars, imagining that one was Mum and another Dave. My head thumped from drinking too much wine on an empty stomach. My vision blurred. I wiped my face with my pyjama sleeve and wrapped my arms around my torso. My eyes closed. I rocked my body back and forth. Next door's cat circled me purring, and I shooed it away. I had a shower and scrubbed my skin until it felt raw.

In the morning, I waited until I heard Dad leave, unwilling to converse with him. A pile of clothes I'd washed and dried the previous morning sat on Nora's bed, ready to be ironed. I took the ironing board from the laundry cupboard and set it up in the living room. The iron let out a shot of steam, and I ironed each piece of clothing. Afterwards, I lay on the couch and dreamed Beth convinced Dave that her son was his, even though he looked nothing like him. Dave moved in with Beth and her son. They came to my house, and Dave announced he was getting married to Beth in Bali. They were having their honeymoon there and wanted to know if I would mind Beth's son. I said I wouldn't, and he left without saying goodbye.

On my way home from the bakery, Mr Ogilvy called out to me in the street. The grey stubble on his face matched the colour of his hair. His cardigan hung off his body like it was two sizes too big for him, with his torso bent forward. He tottered towards me and a mild sensation of nausea swept through my body, making me want to purge.

He caught up to me and stammered when he spoke. I could hear the melancholy in his voice. 'Didn't Sue tell you?'

'Sue said Dave's missing.'

His face grew more worrisome. 'She was supposed to let you know.'

An emptiness had crept into his eyes. My body froze like a statue cemented to the pavement.

'Is he alright?' I asked, nervous and frightened of his answer, but needed to know. People moved around us, and a man shirtfronted me as he walked past.

'Do you mind if we go somewhere?' asked Mr Ogilvy.

I didn't answer, and we walked into a cafe where a lady sat at a table drinking a cup of tea with shopping bags around her feet. We sat at a table at the back of the room and a girl came over to take our order. As soon as she moved away from us, Mr Ogilvy's lips quivered.

'My son is dead.' His words floated in the air like a dramatic symphony.

I sat staring at the white lace tablecloth, unable to understand the enormity of what he'd just said.

'I'm sorry for your loss,' I said, wanting him to say the same to me too. My hands reached out to hold Mr Ogilvy's hands. His body stiffened, and he sat upright. He blew his nose with his handkerchief.

'It's all my fault. I should've stayed with him when he asked me to, but I went home.'

'Don't blame yourself. None of us knew what was going on inside that boy. If we did, he'd still be here today. I never thought he had it in him to do something like that. It just shows that we didn't know what he was capable of, even though he was our son. We've paid a lot of money trying to get him help.'

I massaged my temples, which were damp with sweat, trying to allow the unwanted news to sink in. My eyes blinked back tears. I swallowed and tried to compose myself.

'When?'

'Last week.'

I looked at him in disbelief and shook my head.

'No. He couldn't have, not Dave.' My eyes hurt. I blinked back tears and wiped them with my sleeve.

'You've seen the lines on his arms. The boy was fraught with problems, so we knew no better than to send him away.'

I nodded, not knowing where his conversation was heading, unwilling to divulge anything about Dave's self-harming. One night at my house, I'd woken to use the bathroom and found Dave sinking the point of a knife along his arm and watched the bathroom tiles turn crimson around him. It wasn't the first time. He said he wouldn't do it again, and I was stupid enough to believe him. He'd cut himself too deep that night and felt faint. I wanted to call an ambulance, but he refused and asked me to leave him alone. Dave's hand gripped the outer edge of the bath. He pulled himself up and wrapped a towel around the wound. He noticed himself in the mirror and looked away.

I smiled at him with reassurance, trying to assuage how Dave was feeling, and made him go back to bed while I lay awake in fear. During the summer when we were teenagers, Dave always played sports wearing a long-sleeved top and wouldn't take it off. A teacher asked him to wear a t-shirt, but he refused and said he wasn't hot. I could tell he was fibbing because beads of sweat formed on his forehead.

'The police found Dave in our investment property on the highway. He hung himself in the master bedroom.'

A shockwave went through my body, and I trembled convulsively. Mr Ogilvy grimaced and wiped his nose with his crumpled handkerchief. His face was clammy and pink. A waitress placed our coffees in front of us. I swallowed some of mine and burnt my mouth and throat.

'I thought he'd moved back home.'

'He did, but he had a duplicate key made to the unit.'

'But he seemed happy.' None of what he was saying made any sense. 'I don't believe you.'

'Mark,' he said, looking at his cappuccino. 'I don't have to explain to you what Dave was.' His eyes met mine with contempt. He picked up the sugar sachet, ripped it open, and held it over his cup. The crystals disappeared into the milky froth, and I wished I could too.

'Grace and I thought we could get it out of him. Our family doctor believed Dave needed to stay in a mental hospital and undergo therapy. He stayed with my sister for a week before going to a hospital in Beechworth. They gave him shock treatment, and he had daily sessions with a psychologist. I couldn't handle it.'

'Grace and I started arguing, so I left her with Sue and John. I blame myself. When Dave finished his treatment, I put him into an orphanage. Grace found it hard enough to cope with Sue and John, and I didn't want Dave. Who wants a poofter for a son? He hid behind a façade, hoping no one would know, but we all did.'

I had a mouthful of my coffee, too frightened to look at him. My body shifted in the chair.

'But you're living with your wife and family now.'

'Bronwyn went back to her husband, so I went back to Grace.' He drank his cappuccino in a hurry, placed the cup back on the saucer, and pushed it away.

My heartbeat was like a time bomb about to explode.

'Why did you send Dave away? Being gay isn't a mental condition.'

Mr Ogilvy's eyes narrowed. 'What would you know? Dave tried to commit suicide at the start of high school, and the doctor recommended he go. He said shock treatment would make Dave better. The doctor prescribed medication for Dave, and it seemed to help, but he thought he was normal and stopped taking his tablets.'

'I never knew.'

A resigned expression crossed his face, and his tone turned bitter. 'Nobody did. We thought it was best not to tell anyone, and he didn't want anyone to know.'

'Where did he go after the orphanage?'

'He worked in a pub in Ballarat and stayed with my sister until he had enough money to move to Freemantle. Something must've happened because Dave phoned us and said he's coming home. He wanted to see us but said he wouldn't be staying long.'

'But Sue said Dave was staying for good.'

'That's what he said to her. Can't you see what I mean? The boy had problems. Everything was fine for the first few weeks when he arrived home. We thought he'd changed for the better. He appeared normal, but then the publican phoned from the local hotel and said a security guard caught Dave in the toilets with another male and kicked them out. The publican advised Dave not to show his face there again, or he'd call the police. Grace booked him in to see a doctor, but he refused to go. It's difficult to get Dave to see a doctor against his will, especially when he thinks there's nothing wrong with him.' Mr Ogilvy exhaled heavily.

'But he always seemed happy.'

'The doctor came to our house to reason with Dave and said if Dave didn't take his medication, he'd have to go back to the hospital. Soon after Dave took them, he seemed like he was normal. It was like we were reliving his childhood all over again. At first, we booked him in to see a psychologist, and Dave said he'd take the pills, and that's it, no psychologist.'

Mr Ogilvy turned side-on to see if anyone was eavesdropping. His eyes narrowed and his brow furrowed. He leaned his body across the table and said in a whisper, 'Did you know the babysitter's husband fondled Dave when he was five years old?'

His voice was so low I thought I hadn't heard him properly.

'No, I didn't,' I said, shaking my head, not trusting him. I felt like a priest in a confessional listening to someone telling me their sins.

His mouth formed a tight line. 'It's true. Grace and I were going to a party. John was at a sleepover, and we took Sue with us. The truth came out when Dave was in the hospital undergoing therapy. The babysitter went to buy her groceries and left Dave with her husband. After it happened, Dave said nothing, so we were none the wiser. We would never have believed such a thing could be true. God only knows what would've happened if we'd let the babysitter mind Sue. Ever since I found out, I've regretted going out that night and blamed myself.'

I blinked, trying to digest what he was telling me, not knowing what to say. The woman at the other table stood up to leave.

'If we didn't go to the party, maybe he wouldn't have turned out the way he did and would still be here today.'

The waitress came towards us to retrieve our empty cups. Mr Ogilvy gave her a stern look, and she walked away.

'It's not your fault he turned out the way he did. It could happen to anyone.'

'But it happened to our son.' Mr Ogilvy ran his fingers through his hair and thumped his palms on the table. 'I was so angry with him. We thought we had three beautiful kids until he started acting up. He ruined everything.'

I was conscious of his voice rising. The door opened, and another woman entered the cafe. Mr Ogilvy sat back and paused as if he was waiting for the woman to be seated. Thankfully, she sat near the front window away from us.

'You know, I tried to talk to him, but he thought he knew everything.'

'You did what any parent would do: seek professional help.'

He raised his voice slightly. 'I don't mean that.'

He leaned his body forward again. His face contorted, making him look sinister.

'Every night, before bed, the children would have a bath. One night, I came home from the pub and found Grace in the living room doing her knitting. I went to get changed and heard water splashing in the bathroom. It was Dave. I leaned down level with him. He thought nothing of it and said, 'Hello'.'

'Tell me you're not a poofter,' I said. 'I must've frightened him because he cowered, and I can still see the fear in his eyes.'

'Noooo,' he said.

'I grabbed him around the neck and dunked his head underwater. He came up gasping, and I asked him again.'

'He coughed and spluttered. 'N...''

'So, I did it again, all the while thinking I could wash away the filth and evil in him. I asked him again. His hands tore at my forearms, but I was too strong for him. He splashed water all over the floor when he came up.'

'What the hell do you think you're doing?' yelled Grace. Her shrill voice cracked, and she slapped me across the back. 'Let go of him. Now.'

'I'm just trying to make the boy see sense.'

'You leave our son alone, you bastard. Get out.'

'She helped Dave out of the bath and placed a towel around him. John and Sue were standing in the doorway. I don't know how long they'd been standing there for, but they had horrified expressions on both of their faces. They ran back to their bedrooms. If Grace hadn't come into the bathroom, I would've probably killed him.'

I squirmed in my seat and peered at the cake display near us, unwilling to look at him. Poor Dave. I wanted to know how old he was when it happened, but didn't ask. I didn't know what to say and stood up to leave. He let out a heavy sigh and signalled for the bill.

'Don't feel ill of Sue for not telling you. She's been trying to see a lot of other people and is aggrieved and saddened, like the rest of us. Sue's a nice girl and I know she's fond of you. You should visit her and take her out sometime.'

The afternoon had slipped away, and it was early evening. The cool air woke me up from the nightmare I'd been having. I pitied the monster, who once held his head up high. He'd always seemed so proud. I offered him a lift home, but he said he'd driven his car as well. Mr Ogilvy placed his hand on my shoulder before he shuffled towards the car park.

I walked away feeling like someone had strapped a ten-pound weight on my legs, making it difficult to move. What I'd just heard felt like a cruel joke. The same mantra played over again in my head since I'd found out he'd died: Dave would come home soon.

CHAPTER EIGHTEEN

Everything after that happened in slow motion. My body ached and my legs hurt when I moved. The next day I donned my gloves and cut the deadwood from a rosebush. The neighbour's cat sat in an upstairs window next door, watching me.

Dad placed a pile of clothes on the back seat of his car and drove off. The grass had sewn its way into the garden bed and the roots were deep. My hands gripped a root.

'Mark,' said a shrill voice.

I fell backwards and noticed Sue's ashen face. I pushed myself up off the ground and strode over to her. A tingling sensation in my head made me dizzy from getting up too fast and I saw dark spots. She nestled into my body, and I put my arms around her.

'What's wrong?' I asked.

'Mum and Dad are arguing about Dave. They're blaming each other for what happened. I can't stay at home.'

'Did someone find Dave before the police got there?'

Her eyes swelled. 'The cleaning lady. I'm sorry you had to hear it from dad.'

She repeated what she'd just said. I looked through her like my body had gone off somewhere else, leaving me behind. My feet were riveted to the ground and a sharp pain surged through me. I flinched.

'What happens now?'

She let go of me. 'We're waiting for the coroner to do a report.'

'Your dad didn't tell me that.'

I couldn't breathe properly. My future was closing around me like quicksand. I felt unsteady on my feet and sat on the ground.

'I wanted to, but we were all in shock and couldn't comprehend what had happened. We still can't. He left something for you. Mum found it in his room.'

Sue searched her pockets. 'Sorry, I must've left it behind.' She grabbed both of my hands and pulled me up. 'Come on.' I hesitated, and she looked at me pleading. 'Don't worry, they're not home.'

Inside her house, the clock in the hallway ticked loudly, and a few minutes later, the melodic chime bellowed the thirteenth hour.

'Wait there,' she said.

A lit candle sat on the sideboard, adorned with photos of Dave. I didn't realize how much my hands were shaking until I picked up a photo of him in primary school and felt numb. His mum used to dress him in grey trousers and a matching jumper like he was going to a private school. A photo of an older lady whom I didn't recognize, with her arm around Dave, sat beside the one I'd picked up.

The front door clicked open, and Mrs Ogilvy made me jump when I saw her. She held me tight, and my vision blurred. I felt like I was suffocating.

'He's gone, Mark,' she said. Her hands rubbed my back.

'It's all my fault,' I said in-between sobs. 'I caused his death. If he hadn't come near me, none of this would've happened. I wished I were with him so we could talk. Maybe I would've been able to make him see sense.'

'It's okay. It's not your fault. No one's blaming you. Are you alright?'

I nodded into her chest, unwilling to let go. Mrs Ogilvy's voice quivered, and she let go of me, her skin moist and puffy from crying. I wiped my face with my tracksuit sleeve.

'I remember how you used to phone and ask after Dave all the time when he didn't show up at school. You said you were Edward, but I knew it was you. I saw you coming up the driveway that day you knocked on the door. I couldn't bear to answer it because Dave had already left. Harry thought he was doing the right thing. And now Dave's gone for good.'

Her body heaved, and she pulled out a handkerchief from her apron pocket and wiped her nose.

I squealed and breathed in gasps.

'Don't worry, you'll make other friends. You're young.'

Sue walked into the living room. 'Mum.' She looked around and her eyes widened. 'Where's dad?'

'Down the street. He dropped me off a few minutes ago.'

My mind kept telling me once again that Dave was on a holiday. Sue handed me an envelope with my name written on the front of it.

'The police opened it,' said Mrs Ogilvy. 'They thought it was a suicide note.'

I didn't know what to say. Sue and her mum stood close, expecting me to read it, but I put it in my tracksuit pocket. They both walked to the front door with me. I stood for a moment and caught my breath.

'We know how you feel,' said Sue. 'We're all the same.' She came over and held onto me. I put my arms around her. Everything closed in on me, and I needed to get out of there. I let go of Sue and said, 'Goodbye.'

The landscape blurred, and my legs moved slowly along the footpath. I jogged around the oval. My mind told me to keep going until I buckled. I sat on a seat, exhausted, and stared at the ground. Why wasn't he still here so I could tell him he'd be, okay? I could fly to Canada, and we could go sightseeing together. The more I thought about him, the more my head ached. What made him end his life? I was the last person to see him, so it had to be me. He believed I was too eager and needy. I wanted to prove to him I wasn't, but it was too late now. I vomited. At home, I lay on my bed and felt like someone had stomped on my chest. My head throbbed. I opened the envelope with trepidation.

Mark,

You deserve better.

Dave.

I pulled back my mattress to retrieve the letter that Dave had sent me and compared them. His letter was straight to the point, like the last one. His first letter had an air of authority to it, each letter of the alphabet well-formed like it was typed. In this note, his writing sloped on, neat, and eloquent.

I put Dave's shoes on and tried to imagine how he saw things. I slammed the front door so hard it made the door knocker reverberate. My feet pounded the concrete, and I wanted it to open and bury me. I thought about Mum and Dad and their relationship. Nora and Issy were too far away. Many times, I'd been chastised and had it drummed into me that if I wanted to be accepted, I must obey society. What is wrong with loving the same sex? In Dave's case, he didn't know who he was. He was mesmerized by the beauty of both sexes. I kept moving until my legs ached and I fell onto someone's nature strip and cradled my head into my knees.

⁓✎⁓

The rest of the week became a blur. My mind refused to conjure up a picture of Dave when I last saw him. He remained elusive. I recalled the younger version of him in the schoolyard. In my wardrobe cupboard, I searched for old school photos, all the while trying to remember what his voice sounded like. Records and books dropped out on the floor in my mad frenzy to find him. An album filled with primary and high school photos sat at the back of the cupboard and I found two pictures of Dave. My finger traced over his face, and I held the photos to my chest, wishing it were him I was holding.

On my bedside table, I propped the photos up against some books, not wanting him to disappear. I kept telling myself the short time we had been together was real and that he had existed. A familiar ache and numbness I had when Mum died came back again to haunt me. Dave had been the only thing that had taken my mind off her dying. I stayed in bed with the blinds drawn. My mind played everything over again from Dave's return until the last time I saw him. Each scene was a piece of the jigsaw puzzle, trying to find signs of what made him do it.

I'd forgotten to ask Sue about the funeral. I phoned her and there was no answer. The morning paper sat on the kitchen table. I searched through the funeral notices and there was nothing. In the laundry, a pile of old papers sat in the corner for burning in the incinerator. I sat on the floor and went through each one. The funeral was two days ago, and his family had a private cremation for him.

CHAPTER NINETEEN

I wanted to die too. Who was going to love me now? Who was I going to love? Cooking and eating didn't interest me. I marked each day off on the kitchen calendar. Today, I had my cooking class. Did I want to go? No. I couldn't remember the last time I'd been to class. I forced my body out from under the covers. No one smiled on the train into the city, which made me feel better. It was like they were all mourning the loss of two people with me who they didn't know.

When I disembarked from the train, everyone hurried, but I plodded. A woman bumped into me, and I heard her mutter for me to move out of her way. The surrounding buildings shadowed the street, and the sun was behind a cloud, giving it a gloomy feeling like my mood. In my class, I watched Chef speak. My body was physically there, but mentally, I was somewhere else. I couldn't recall what we had made. I cursed myself for coming and knew that I should've stayed home. Chef asked me to wait until after class, but I didn't want to talk to anyone. He called out to me, but I kept walking. Instead of waiting for the lift, I used the stairs. I refused to talk to Chef, knowing what he would say. I couldn't be bothered. Not now.

At home, I closed all the blinds and wandered around the house in a dreamlike state. Sunlight looked like fairy dust falling through either side of my window. In bed, I buried my head under the covers. The phone rang several times, but I didn't have the energy to pick up the receiver. I drank my way through the cupboard. The liquid soothed and warmed me. Someone knocked on the front door, but

I didn't answer it. I don't know how many days I stayed in the house. One morning, my bedroom door burst open.

'What the blazes do you think you're doing? Get out of bed,' said Dad.

I rolled over and ignored him. He grabbed my arm, pulled me out of bed backwards and hurled me into the bathroom.

'Don't come out until you've showered and shaved.'

The person staring back at me appeared gaunt, with a makeshift beard. My unkempt curls bounced around my face.

I turned on the tap and stepped into the shower. The cold water burned me. I dried myself off and put my pyjamas back on. I thought Dad had left and was surprised to find him in the kitchen making a pot of tea and cooking toast.

'What are you doing here?' I asked.

'You're a disgrace.'

'You ought to talk.'

'Eat your toast,' he said, placing a plate on the table with two slices. 'You can butter it yourself.'

My stomach grumbled, and I pulled back a chair. Dad poured two mugs of tea and handed me one. He stood at the kitchen bench and stirred his tea, grinding the spoon around the circumference. The sound pierced my eardrums.

'I'm not staying for long. Mrs Mackie said if you don't turn up for work tomorrow, you won't have a job at the bakery anymore. Her husband has been here several times, knocking on the door and ringing the bell, looking for you. When I marry Irene, I might sell this house. I haven't decided yet. Either way, you'll have to find somewhere else to live.'

'When are you getting married?'

'We haven't set the date yet.' He clasped his thumbs around his braces. 'I'm just letting you know so there are no discrepancies when the time comes.' He slurped his tea, his eyes penetrating me.

·✑·

Mrs Mackie reminded me of a squawking hen around her chicks. She made me sit out the back with her. She made me a cup of coffee and handed me two croissants on a plate and wouldn't let me start work until I'd finished eating and drinking. I gagged as I ate. At the front of the shop, customers swelled around me, and I couldn't wait for my shift to end so I could leave.

I forced myself to travel to the city for my cooking class. I arrived just as it started. We made a pavlova and trifle. I loved eating any dessert, but the pavlova was crunchy and sickly sweet. The trifle bland.

'Why did you run away from me last week?' asked Chef.

I shrugged my shoulders.

'You'll have to do better than that.'

'I had an appointment,' I lied.

'You know you are going to fail if you don't change your mood. Cooking is all about mood. If you are shitty, your food will taste the same. You need to be happy, so my advice is to change what is making you angry. Understand? Next week we are learning how to make apricot chicken. Here's the recipe. I want you to surprise me when you cook it.'

I agreed with him for the sake of it so I could leave. Afterwards, I roamed the city streets instead of going home. My belly heaved from all the food I'd eaten, and I threw up in the gutter. At the train station, commuters were lined up on the platform. Like a box of matches, I stood in amongst them feeling hemmed in. They all had their heads held high ready to board the train, and I was the burnt one spurned by Dave.

I waited in amongst them for the train. Other students boarded the same carriage. I turned around, hoping none of them would notice me. I stood in the doorway, hypnotized by the noise and motion of the train as it hurtled along the track, making the scenery blur. Was it wrong to be in love with another man? I didn't want to go to my classes anymore. Would I lead a life of solitude forever? My body felt like it had free-fallen off a cliff into an abyss.

When I arrived at Noble Park, I stopped off at the supermarket on the way home and reached into the freezer compartment for a chicken and overheard two women saying that the Ogilvy's were selling their house.

'It's a shame their son was a poofter. It makes you wonder what happens in one's brain to make them want to be in a relationship with the same sex. How can they love one another?' said one.

'I agree. I don't know either. It's disgusting,' said the other one.

I waited until they'd moved away. The aisle shelving seemed to close in on me and made me feel claustrophobic. I strode over to the cash register, grateful no one else was being served. My heart raced, and I started panting. The girl ringing up the items looked at me with a strange face. I hunched over and said that I wasn't feeling well.

For some reason, I couldn't stop thinking about Mum. Outside, I gasped for air like I was drowning. I walked down the end of the main street into a tattoo parlour and had *Dave* inscribed in small cursive letters on the left side of my pelvis and *Mum* on the right. The intensity of the needles only added to my sorrow.

CHAPTER TWENTY

My fingers searched under the edge of the mattress for my copy of the Women's Weekly. I turned my side light on, lay in bed, and flicked through the pages to an article about making the perfect sponge cake. I heard the key in the front door lock. Dad turned the television on down low and walked into the kitchen. The fridge door opened, making the bottles on the door clink together. The next page had slow-cooked meals for cold winter nights. That's when he knocked.

His voice was barely audible. 'Mark, are you awake?'

My eyes fixed on the picture of lamb cutlets.

His voice sounded distressed. 'Can you come out? I need to speak to you.'

I stifled a yawn. 'Can't it wait until morning? I'm in bed.'

He sounded like a child. 'No.'

'But it's after ten.'

My bedroom door opened slightly. I put the magazine under my pillow and slid down into bed. Dad poked his head in.

'Because I saw your light on under your door, I thought you were awake.'

'I'm just dozing; I'll be out in a minute.'

Dad moved away, and I stepped out of bed, and put on my slippers and dressing gown. I found him sitting in the living room, waiting for me. He turned the television off and put his head in his hands.

'Irene said she doesn't want to marry me.'

'Why are you telling me for?'

'Well, I need to talk to someone.'

'Is she English?'

'Yes, I've already mentioned that. Irene's father is English, and her mother is Romanian.'

'I thought you hated other nationalities. If Irene were a dog, she'd be a Pomeranian,' I said and couldn't help smirking.

'That'll be enough out of you. It's nothing to laugh about. Irene's an excellent cook and a homemaker. What did you think when you met her?'

'I don't know. It was a while ago. Slim thighs, drunk, wasn't she? Besides, I only saw her a few times. Why do you want to rush to get married, anyway? Why can't you live together?'

'She said she's not sure. She wants children and isn't convinced I'd be okay with a baby because I've got two grown children. I don't know what to do.'

'But Mum's only been gone a couple of months.'

He spoke like a child wanting reassurance from his mother. 'Don't bring her into it.'

'Phone Nora. She's better at these things than I am.'

He looked at me in disbelief. I hadn't bothered telling him she was pregnant.

My cheeks prickled and my voice sounded strangled. 'Do you love Irene?'

He put his hand in his pocket, pulled out a handkerchief, and wiped his eyes before he blew his nose. I'd never seen him so perplexed.

'I'm not sure.'

'What does your gut say?'

'Gut? Bugger my gut.'

'Well, it's not for me to decide.'

He left before I had time to discuss it further. I mulled over, ringing Nora to let her know, and decided against it. In my bedroom, I opened Mum's suitcase, looked at a photo of her sitting on a picnic rug, and asked her what she'd do. I remembered her telling me once to mind my own business. Knowing Dad, he would let Nora know when he was ready–an uncomfortable conversation for her, but not for him. She'd never accepted me as a trusted confidant. Our conversations had been more of a formality–civil–on a need-to-know basis. She'd always been the secretive one but wanted to know everyone else's business.

I removed my dressing gown and slippers and read a magazine article about the Queen, hoping it would send me to sleep.

CHAPTER TWENTY-ONE

After breakfast, I washed the dishes thinking about Giuseppe. I tried the second number and after several rings, a man answered, breathing heavily into the receiver.

'Hello, is that Giuseppe?'

'Yes.'

'This is Mark Cooney, Sandra's son.'

'You've got the wrong number,' he said and hung up.

In Giuseppe's street, I parked several houses away and waited. A car reversed from under his carport, and I followed it onto the highway. My heart fluttered. Different scenarios played out in my mind about what would happen when I approached him. I wound down the window to let in some fresh air, wondering where they were heading. My car weaved in and out of the traffic, trying to keep up with them, but I didn't want the driver to know I was pursuing them. The car pulled up in the last parking spot a block from the market. I double-parked further down the street and watched a man carrying a caged chicken run to his car in the rain. A woman and three girls stepped out of the cabin. The woman pulled an umbrella out of her bag and put it up. They all linked arms and ran towards the Dandenong market.

I did a U-turn, and my sweaty palms slid down the steering wheel. A car tooted. The driver made a fist and yelled abuse at me as I swerved past him and headed back to Giuseppe's house. I parked further up the street and stepped out of my car. My knuckles made fists deep in my pockets, and my armpits smelt of perspiration despite using deodorant. I pressed the doorbell, and my feet moved up and down. I bit the quick of my thumb and sucked it to stop it from bleeding. The man I'd seen on the other side of the chapel leaning against the wall opened the front door. I pulled my thumb out of my mouth, hoping he hadn't seen me and thought I was an idiot.

'Is your brother my father?' I stammered.

My foot stuck in the doorway, frightened he'd closed the door in my face. He gave me a cursory glance and shook his head.

Resentful frustration could be heard in his tone. 'You'd better come in.'

In the living room, photos of younger versions of the three girls I'd seen earlier adorned the wallpapered wall. A figurine of Jesus on the Cross hung on the opposite wall. Giuseppe motioned for me to sit in a lounge chair. He picked up a box of cigarettes and held them out in my direction. I shook my head.

Ever since Nora had opened the suitcase, I'd lain awake thinking about what to say to Giuseppe, and now my mind went blank. He placed a cigarette between his pursed lips before lighting it with a match.

Giuseppe exhaled and ran his other hand through his hair.

'What'd you say your name was?'

'I... I... I didn't. It... it... it's Mm...mark.'

It was strange being in a room with a man who resembled me. He was the same height, with curly black hair and brown eyes. Giuseppe had the same frown and laughter lines that were on my face. The person staring back at me was an older version of me. He exhaled and brushed away the shock of curls that had fallen across his forehead. He was the same height as me, whereas Dad dwarfed me. Dad had straight hair and pale blue eyes. I often believed I was adopted because I looked nothing like him or Mum.

'You know about Giovanni?' He drew back on the cigarette and blew the match out.

'I know he's dead.'

'We were twins and used to play jokes on people, but one day, it went too far. Giovanni went away for a few days with our mother to a funeral in the country, and I stayed home and pretended to be him.'

'Didn't Giovanni tell my mum that he was going away?'

'He didn't have time. Our mother made him leave straight away. I invited Sandra out for dinner, and we shared a bottle of wine. I mentioned Giuseppe and our mother were away for the weekend. My mother was a strict lady. She only liked our nationality and wanted Giovanni to marry what she called 'A nice Italian girl.' She would never allow Sandra to sleep at our house. Our mother was away, so I encouraged Sandra to stay.'

'Didn't Giovanni phone Mum to tell her where he was?'

'No, why would he do that? My mother would've kept him busy chauffeuring her around to see relatives. He drove my car, so I had his motorbike to ride around on.'

'Surely Mum would've known you weren't Giovanni?'

He crossed his chest with one hand and drew back on his cigarette with the other.

'I swear on my father's grave she couldn't. We were identical twins.' Smoke blew out of his mouth, and he coughed.

'But what if she got pregnant?'

He shrugged his shoulders and crossed his legs.

'According to Sandra, she was pregnant, but I still don't believe it was mine. Look, it was lust, alright. We didn't discuss protection. She'd been in a relationship for two years with Giovanni. They would've discussed contraception when they first started going out together.'

He raised an eyebrow, and his foot jiggled up and down.

'Giovanni said he usually used a condom whenever they had sex, but after they'd had a few drinks... Well, you know how it is. Besides, they were getting married, and she played along with him.'

'Did you tell Giovanni?'

His eyes glazed over. 'No, but Sandra must've talked to him about the night, and he realized what had happened. I was eating dinner with my mother, and he strode towards me at the kitchen table. Giovanni lifted me out of the chair and punched me in the face twice. He said he never wanted to speak to me again. My mother was hysterical. She yelled at Giovanni to calm down, but he was furious. He swore at her, slammed the door, and rode off on his bike.'

Giuseppe spoke perfect English, but it felt like he was talking another language.

'A month later, Giovanni died in a motorcycle accident.' Giuseppe's eyes glazed over, and he viewed the ceiling. He made the sign of the cross on his chest and flicked his cigarette ash in the ashtray.

'Did he come back the night he left?'

'Giovanni came back when we were in bed. He still stayed at home, but he refused to speak to me no matter how many times my mother asked him. I was invisible to him. He went out a lot and wouldn't tell her where he was going. My mother used to sit in the living room holding onto her rosary beads, worried something bad was going to happen. She blamed Sandra. She said if he hadn't met Sandra, none of this would have happened. My mother didn't want Giovanni to marry Sandra because she already had a daughter, but Giovanni wouldn't listen.'

'Nora,' I said.

'That's right, a cute little girl with dimples.'

'But why didn't you marry Mum?'

His brow furrowed, and his eyes locked onto mine.

'It's not as easy as that, alright. She thought I was Giovanni. We didn't love each other. Your mum was a loose woman, okay? What my mother called a putana–a slut–because Sandra slept around.'

'Hey, watch what you're saying. That's my mum you're talking about, not just anyone. Besides, how do you know she slept around?'

'Well, Sandra had your sister, didn't she?'

I couldn't imagine Mum as he'd described her. It sounded like he was talking about someone else.

'She came over to our house after Giovanni died and let us know she was pregnant and that the baby was Giovanni's, but there was no evidence to prove it.'

'But you had sex with her.'

He shook his head.

'Sandra had sex with Giovanni as well, don't forget. It could've been his child. She wanted my mother to pay maintenance, otherwise Sandra said my mother would never see the baby again.'

I couldn't imagine Mum being like that with anyone.

'She asked me to marry her, but I couldn't love her. There was no chemistry between us, you understand?'

'I don't believe you. Mum would never ask someone to marry her. She was too timid. You must be confusing her with someone else.'

Giuseppe ruminated for a while before he spoke. He had another drag on his cigarette and uncrossed his legs.

'Sandra was desperate, alright. Think about it. She had Nora and was pregnant with you. She needed someone to support her. The people in the community would look down on her if she didn't have a husband. Sandra asked me to have a coffee with her. She didn't want one in our house because my mother was always there. When I met Sandra in a cafe, I asked her to have an abortion. If you looked at her, you couldn't tell she was pregnant.'

'My mother said to me that Sandra could try to force me to marry her. Mum believed Sandra wasn't pregnant and wanted a father for Nora. Mum insisted Sandra was trying to trick me into marrying her. I told Sandra if she booked into the hospital, I would drive her there and pick her up afterwards. She said she couldn't do it because her parents were Catholics like us. Sandra said her dad would never allow it. I asked her if she'd said anything to them, and she told her mum she felt nauseous. Her mum asked Sandra to visit the doctor and said she'd come with her. That's when they found out she was pregnant.'

'How could you use Mum up like that? Was it because you were jealous of Giovanni's relationship with her?'

He scratched his head and eyeballed me. 'I know I did the wrong thing, okay?'

'The baby could've been yours.'

'That is something we'll never know.'

'Giovanni knew how to act around women, while I was more reserved and waited for women to approach me. It was a silly idea, alright? I tried to find out what he saw in Sandra to make him want to marry her. She kept coming over here after Giovanni died, and I tried to get to know her to see if I could love her, but she spoke to me as if I was Giovanni. It was weird. Sandra made me feel sad talking to me like I was him. Mum warned Sandra that she wasn't welcome anymore.'

He drew back on his cigarette and stood up. I felt awkward, not knowing what to believe. He stubbed his cigarette son an ashtray on the mantlepiece and blew smoke towards the ceiling.

'Was she happy, your mum?'

'She was until she got sick.'

'I know I saw the death notice in the paper.'

'Was it you I saw at mum's funeral? I called out to you but looked again and couldn't find you in the crowd.'

He hesitated. 'It was me.'

'Why did you come then if you had no feelings for her?'

'I don't know. Memories, I guess.'

'She asked me to meet her again. She said she needed to tell me something and wanted my opinion. I thought she was going to change her mind and have an abortion, so I agreed to see her. She said her dad had invited a man who used to work with him for lunch. The man had never married before. His parents died in a car accident and left him with everything. When he met Sandra, she said he agreed to marry her.'

'What prearranged? I don't believe you.'

'It's true. Your dad had his parents' house and a car, and he liked Nora. At first, Sandra was unhappy because she was still grieving for Giovanni and didn't know what to do. Her mum pleaded with her to marry the man for the sake of Nora and the baby–you–but she wasn't convinced and wanted my opinion.'

'Why would she ask you? Why not a girlfriend, anyone?'

'I don't know. I think Sandra hoped I'd say that I'd marry her, but I couldn't because I didn't love her. My mother said she'd disown me if I didn't marry an Italian. Sandra would bring shame to our name. My mother believed Sandra was lying about the man. She thought Sandra was trying to trick me into feeling sorry for her so I would marry her.'

'Mum always denied it if anyone said anything untoward about us and is still the same way about me today. Giovanni was a bit of a rebel. He didn't care what our mother wanted. He thought of himself; but I'm different. I wanted Sandra to take her time. It's an enormous commitment. If he's a nice man, she should consider it. She never spoke to me again after that. I used to see her walking along the shopping strip and in the supermarket, but after our last conversation, she pretended I wasn't there.'

Giuseppe sat on the couch and crossed his legs.

Dad's behaviour towards Nora and me made sense. He accepted us when we were younger, but when we were teenagers, he wasn't interested in us anymore. He always seemed unhappy, and I could never understand why. The factory closed, and he took a while to find another job. He became argumentative with us, and we were the same with him. Dad must have felt like he was looking at Mum's other lovers each time he saw us, which explained why he was racist. Whenever we argued with him, Mum seldom agreed with our point of view and always said we should sort it out amongst ourselves. Nora was like a younger version of Mum: petite, same hair, eye colour, facial shape, lips, and they both had the same laugh.

'Nothing in life is perfect. You'll find that out as you get older.'

'Can I see you again?'

'I've got my family to worry about. Besides, it would only complicate things if you know what I mean.' He opened the cigarette box, pulled out another cigarette, placed it between his lips and lit it.

'You'll have to go.'

'How can you turn me away like this? It's obvious you're my real dad.' He uncrossed his legs and started fidgeting again.

'It doesn't matter what you think. You'll have to leave now. The girls will be back soon.' He pushed himself out of his chair, escorted me to the front door, and walked me to my car.

He was unwilling to look me in the face; his wet brown eyes scanned the streetscape before relaxing toward the ground.

'You know what your problem is, don't you?' he asked.

I stood frozen like a snowman, not wanting to hear what he had to say.

'You need to get a life and move on. Forget all this. It's not important.'

I drove around the corner into an adjoining street. A deep sadness consumed me, and my vision blurred. I pulled over, struggling to breathe, and wiped my face with my jumper sleeve. Pain ripped through my chest. I bent forward and rested my forehead on the steering wheel. I was glad I'd finally met Giovanni, albeit to be disowned. Why hadn't Mum married someone who enjoyed the things she did, eating out and going to the theatre, who was attentive and kind? Other men liked Mum: the baker I worked for, Dave's dad and her boss. They always greeted her and had a conversation with her. Mr Mackie always insisted on giving her a doughnut, croissant, or something sweet. I couldn't fathom why she married Dad. She should've waited to find someone else to fall in love with, even if she was pregnant.

CHAPTER TWENTY-TWO

Irene wanted children of her own. She couldn't handle having two adult children a few years younger than herself. Dad pleaded with her, but she refused to change her mind. He started dating an Italian woman named Francesca. They met at the pub two weeks later. He seemed relaxed and more accepting of everything and not as cranky since he'd met her. She brought a playful side to him I'd never seen before. I wanted to meet her, but Dad always returned home alone, frightened Francesca would run away if she met me because of what Irene had said. I asked him why he was dating an Italian after all the years he'd cursed them and every other nationality. He said he didn't know. It just happened. When I mentioned it to Nora, she couldn't believe me.

'The old bastard must have forgiveness in his heart after all,' she said.

'He's getting married.'

'You can't be serious. I thought Dad was marrying the Irish woman.'

'It's off. Irene's not interested in us; she wants to have children with him.'

'What's wrong with us? I'd love to meet her.'

'Who cares? What does it matter anyway? We won't be seeing her again. Last week, a man from a clothing company in Dandenong phoned and left a message for Dad. The man wanted me to tell Dad they had a safari suit in his size for his wedding Friday fortnight if he'd like to come in and try it on.'

'The sneaky bastard. Just wait until I see him.'

'What? Are you going to come out here again? But you've just been...'

'Don't you want to see me?'

'Of course I do.'

'I'll think about it. Why didn't Dad mention it to us? We are his family, whether he likes it or not. Even if he marries her or someone else, he has a right to tell us. We've got nothing to be ashamed of. We're not drug addicts or murderers. And after all the shit I've put up with over the years about Italians. He's got more front than the variety store in Bourke Street in the city. Men!'

'If I find anything else, I'll let you know.'

.⚬⁂⚬.

A week later, Nora stood on the doorstep with a small suitcase at her feet. I expected Alfonso and Issy, but they didn't come.

'Well, don't just stand there. Aren't you going to let me in?'

I opened the door wider, and she waddled in.

'Who is it?' asked Dad.

'It's me, Dad.'

'What are you doing here?'

'Mark phoned and said you were getting married next week.'

'Did he now?' He turned around from the kitchen bench and hooked his thumbs in his braces, stretching them outwards.

I felt my face growing hotter.

His eyes narrowed. 'What the hell happened to you? You've been eating too much pasta, or you're...'

'I can see things haven't changed since I left last time. You're still as rude. I'm pregnant.'

'That'd be bloody right. Why didn't you tell us you were having another one?'

'You never asked.'

He pulled his braces in and out. Disdain crossed his face. 'When are you due?'

'In six months.'

'Will we get to see it?'

'That depends on whether you're nice to me. It's not cheap flying back and forth. Maybe if you pay for the airfare, I'll come back again.'

'You should tell that husband of yours to change jobs, so he earns more money.'

'He's doing alright, but soon there'll be four mouths to feed instead of three, and things aren't cheap in Italy.'

'Where are Alfonso and Issy? I thought he'd at least like to meet my future wife.'

'Don't be ridiculous. Alfonso's busy with work, and Issy's in school. I'm grateful my work gave me time off. Otherwise, I wouldn't be here either. You may as well know I won't be staying long.'

He pulled his braces in, and we sat at the kitchen table.

'What happened to your hair?' asked Nora. 'Did Francesca meet you with the salt and pepper version or the new you?'

'Steady on. I'm only just trying to keep up with the times.'

'Who's doing your hair for you?'

'I do it myself.'

'Oh, so you're a closet colourer.' Nora stood behind him and flicked her hand through his hair. 'At least you've covered all the greys. If you decide to leave your job, you might get a job as a hairdresser.'

He burst out laughing. 'Thanks for the compliment.'

'You'd better go easy on your colour, though.'

He put his hand up and patted the top of his head. 'What der ya mean?'

'Last time I was here, you were brown with grey streaks. Now it's jet black. It makes you look like a ghost with that pallid complexion of yours.'

.⊷⧉⊶.

Francesca arrived with three trays of food. Nora and I all helped her bring them inside. We didn't know Francesca was 20 years younger than Dad. We expected a woman Mum's age, not the tall, thin woman wearing patent black stilettos and a low-cut dress showing her cleavage that approached us. Thick foundation covered her face, and her lips were scarlet. She towered over Dad and leaned forward to kiss him on both sides of his face, knowing we were watching. Her hair tied in a bun showed a soft jawline and loose tendrils softened her high cheekbones. Her eyelashes fluttered over her big brown eyes. Dad introduced us to her and excused himself to put the food in the oven. Her head darted from me to Nora.

She pulled me close and kissed me on either side of my face before doing the same to Nora. We moved into the living room, and she sat on the couch. We sat on the lounge chairs. Her hands folded in her lap to reveal a diamond ring twice the size of Mum's engagement ring. Nora sat up straight in her chair and was confident, asking Francesca one question after the other. Francesca said she hadn't been in the country long and would like to bring her parents here.

'Russell, very nice, very generous.'

'Have you been married before?' asked Nora.

I coughed when I heard Dad approaching. Francesca's eyes widened, and she looked at Nora quizzically.

He walked over to her and sat beside her, patting her knee.

'How's everyone getting along?' asked Dad. 'I hope the kids are being nice to you.'

Francesca smiled at him and nuzzled his cheek. He reached for her hand and clasped it in his. Her gaze met ours and drifted to his. A pink rash travelled down her neck to meet her breasts. The entire display of affection sickened me. It was amazing how little I knew him.

It made me think of the things he'd said about Italian people. Is that what people did: say something without meaning it? Did they do it to get their way or because it felt good at the time and the right thing to do when they didn't care? Or was it jealousy? Love was complex. I knew Dave had fooled me.

Dad had a softer side that he'd never displayed in public until now. Nora gave Francesca a long, appraising look and said something in Italian. Francesca had a surprised expression on her face.

Francesca moved closer to Dad and whispered in his ear. He glanced at me for a moment, and I shifted in my chair and turned to face Nora so I wouldn't have to look at them. Dad announced they were going dancing tomorrow night, and Francesca stood up and motioned her body back and forth, making her breasts wobble.

Nora let out a shrill laugh. 'But Dad doesn't dance.'

Francesca made a poker face at her. 'Russell, wonderful dancer.'

'Don't you insult your mother or me,' said Dad.

Nora looked down at the mouth. 'She's not our mother and never will be. She's old enough to be my sister.'

'Oh, yes, she is. We're already married,' said Dad.

Nora's eyes bulged. 'Well, there will only ever be one Mum for me, and mine's dead. Isn't that right, Mark?'

I coughed, unwilling to comment. Francesca went into the kitchen to check the oven.

Nora scowled at me and raised her eyebrows. 'Mark! Why didn't you tell me? You could've saved me a trip.'

I shrugged my shoulders.

'Don't look at me. I didn't know.'

'What's going on, Dad?' Nora sat back in her chair, her face scarlet. 'So you're already married? When did that happen?'

Dad looked at her with a smirk on his face.

'We were married yesterday afternoon at the Registry Office.'

'You'll have to excuse me,' said Nora. 'I'm not hungry. Vince and Loretta want me to stay with them. I'll let myself out.'

'Have it your way. You're missing out on some good tucker.'

'It won't be anything I haven't eaten before.'

I walked with Nora to the front door and asked her if I could stay with them too, but she said, 'No.'

'Are you sure you didn't know they were married?'

'No, he told me nothing,' I said.

'How can you stand living here under the same roof?' she whispered.

'Houses to rent aren't cheap, but I have been looking for a flat to rent.'

'Good on you. You need to get out of here.'

'Aren't you pleased he's married to an Italian?'

Her jawline tightened. 'Pleased! Are you kidding me, after all the bullshit he's dished out over the years? He's nothing but a fucking liar and a hypocrite. I'll leave you to the two lovebirds.'

I sat on my bed and placed my head in my hands. Why did I say anything to Nora? I should've kept my mouth shut.

'Mark, are you still here?' Dad called out.

He looked up when I entered the kitchen.

'Take a seat, son. You don't want your food to get cold.'

Dad ate the spaghetti bolognese Francesca had made, splashing it down the front of his shirt and on the sides of his mouth. She patted the front of him with her serviette like a mother would do to a child. He smiled affectionately at her.

'Thank you, darling.'

'Munjare,' said Francesca, handing me a bowl of spaghetti bolognese.

I held onto my fork and stabbed the air with it.

'What made you decide to get married yesterday? I thought you said in a couple of weeks. Why didn't you want Nora and me at the wedding?'

'Why does there have to be a reason? We married when we wanted.'

'Why hurry? You've just met one another.'

'Russell loves me. I love Russell,' said Francesca as though it was that simple.

'I'm glad you're both happy,' I replied under my breath. 'You'll have to excuse me. I'm not feeling well.' I pushed my plate aside.

In my bedroom, I read a chapter of Great Expectations. I'd borrowed the book from the local library. Later, I went into the kitchen to get a drink of water, hoping they'd gone. I wanted to be alone. The light was on in the living room. Dad was seated lengthways on the couch, and Francesca massaged his feet. I slipped back to my bedroom, unnoticed. The words in the book blurred, and I closed my eyes.

.⚬⚬⚬.

All my life, I'd looked up at Nora. I waited to see her reaction to something and would copy her. She acted demure but provoked boys with little or no effort. From what I could tell, she was happily married. Dad and Nora had both changed, but I had stayed the same. Mum's death had set Dad free. The shine had gone off his wedding band like it had in his relationship with Mum long before she'd died.

Nothing seemed real anymore. My life continued the same as before. Everyone avoided me in my cooking class like they always did, concentrating on what meal they were creating and then leaving straight after the lesson finished. The house was empty when I arrived home, and I didn't know what to do. I lay in my bed and stared at the ceiling.

I thought about Dave and Mum, and a surge of grief welled up inside of me for them both, and I blinked away my tears. When Mum died, Dad functioned as if nothing had happened. He never showed emotion. I know it sounds cliché, but he used to say tears were a sign of weakness, and only women cried. Dad believed a person had to be stoic if they wanted to survive. Outward appearances never showed how he felt inside.

I spent an inordinate amount of time in the kitchen, wondering what I was doing there. It was like I'd forgotten what I desired. As soon as I left, I was back there again in a daze. My subconscious knew I had to eat, but the thought of food was far from my mind. The bathroom door slammed, jolting me back to reality. I went to investigate. No one was in there. I shut the window, sat on the floor, and remembered when I'd found Dave self-harming. The amount of blood on the tiles had shocked me into believing he'd done something worse than cutting his arm. I opened the drawer, pulled out a razor blade, held it in my hand for a while, and put it away. Nothing could make me feel worse than I already felt.

·⁕·

In the morning, I walked through the house, entering each room immobilized for the longest time before moving on to the next. My eyes were sore from lack of sleep. My Dad's bed remained untouched. In the living room, I switched on the television for background noise and sat down.

I can't remember when or how I found myself outside. My actions were like a windup toy as I made my way to the mailbox.

'Mark.'

Startled, I turned around. It was our next-door neighbour, Mrs Thomlinson.

'I'm sorry for your loss,' she said, leaning forward on her walking stick.

Mrs Thomlinson was ninety-two, and we hardly ever saw her. She stayed inside and had people bring her food. A cleaning company arrived once a month to clean her house. Mum used to groan when she saw the cleaning van, wishing that she could afford such a luxury. Mrs Thomlinson's comment was like a punch in the face, making everything real. Her eyes widened, and I knew I was a window she could see straight through.

'Are you alright? Come and have a cuppa with me. You look like you could do with some company.'

I was surprised by her kind gesture.

'I'm okay,' I said, feeling uncomfortable, and gave her a feeble smile. She shook her head to one side. 'Alright then, but mind how you go. When I lost Albert ten years ago, the only thing that kept me sane was a strong cup of tea and putting one foot in front of the other.

I had to keep doing what I was doing before he died. It hurt, and not because of this stick,' she said, poking it in the air. 'Being lonely isn't good for you. Everybody needs someone. You learn to adjust and live with it.'

'But Mum won't be part of it.' Neither would Dave, but I didn't mention him.

'One day, you'll have your own family and memories of your mum you can take with you. You can teach your children what she taught you.'

I could understand what she was saying, but I knew her words would never apply to me. From this point on, I considered myself a single man. The mailbox was full of mail. I opened the latch and pulled it all out. I couldn't remember the last time I'd been to retrieve it.

'Anyway, the offer's still there if you need someone to listen. I can still hear with these bloody things.' She pointed to her hearing aids and turned around to go inside.

'Thank you,' I said.

I opened the envelopes in the kitchen, leaving the biggest one until last. It was a sympathy card from Laura about Dave. My whole body felt numb.

'But he's coming back,' I said, as though Laura was in the room with me. 'Don't you know he's on holiday? And then: no, he's not silly. He's dead.'

On the television, I watched Tarzan swinging from the trees with his monkey. I didn't go to class or to work at the bakery and rang in sick. The party replayed in my mind. It was the last time I'd seen Mum. Everything appeared vague. Why hadn't the specialist detected the haemorrhage earlier? Dave was a mystery.

My mind wouldn't stop going through each encounter I'd had with him, trying to work out what made him take his life. The only time I'd seen him unhappy was when he cut his arm with a razor blade. Other than that, he seemed happy. I couldn't understand the pain and sorrow he must've been feeling behind the happy façade that he showed the world.

I pulled out my school photos again and looked at Dave. Although we were all small in our group shot, I could still see his smile and dimples. His hair was still the same. The tip of my finger covered his face, and I imagined touching him. I pulled the suitcase out from under my bed and opened it. Mum smiled at me, standing in her bikini on the beach. I placed the photo of her on my bedside table alongside the photo of Dave.

In my dreams, they had a conversation with me. Mum said she knew my secret and just wanted me to be happy. Dave said he'd wait for me, and we would get married. I'd found Dave's white t-shirt under the bed when I dressed after sleeping with him. Dave went into the bathroom, and I noticed it when I looked for my socks. I never washed it. Since he'd died, I wore it under my shirt every day. The smell of his sweat mixed with mine was intoxicating. Wearing his clothes made me feel closer to him and kept him alive in my waking life.

His quirky smile used to drive me crazy, and the way he tilted his head when he spoke. His husky voice I found irresistible. He was an alchemist and made everything appear beautiful, especially him. I berated myself for not asking him more questions about his past. Hearing it from him would've been more believable than from his dad. Part of me thought Dave had led me on, but our first kiss in the schoolyard, him touching me in the shower, and his letter all sustained me until we met again. Yesterday, I'd stubbed my toe on the pavement and felt nothing. My whole body still felt numb.

Dave's death was too big to grasp. It still amazed me how he appeared as the model child in his family while wrestling with his internal worries. I hated myself because Dave didn't reach out to me for help, and I couldn't read him better. I'd failed him. Everyone else knew the character he played on stage, but no one came close enough to know Dave, only what he wanted us to see. I regretted not having enough guts to tell Dave how I felt about him. There were many missed opportunities to let him know. Why had I felt so embarrassed when I said I loved him?

My parents had never said they loved me, and I had never said it to them. I'd only ever heard a male actor in a movie say it to a female actress or vice versa, and then they'd kiss. The loneliness made me feel hollow. I needed to find somewhere else to live. The walls appeared closer and darker. Overwhelming thoughts of never-ending blame consumed me. No matter how high I turned the volume on the radio or television, my self-loathing about my life and what had happened was louder.

I went for a walk down the street. I didn't look at the lights and stepped off the curb. A car beeped its horn at me. A female pedestrian in the rush hour traffic pulled me backwards. For a moment, I stood rooted to the spot. I kept walking, unaware of where I was going. I still couldn't fathom why Dave committed suicide. He said he found it easy to talk to me. Why didn't he tell me how he was feeling? I went to the bottle shop and bought a cask of Riesling.

Unable to sleep, I sat in the living room and drank several glasses of wine while looking at old photos of my family and Dave. My bedroom appeared lopsided. I flopped on my bed, fully clothed, and fell asleep. The alarm clock woke me, and I forced my body out of bed. My head thumped. In the bathroom, I nicked myself, shaving, undressed, and showered in cold water to fully wake me.

In the kitchen cupboard, I found a loaf of stale bread, toasted two slices, and ate it. I made myself a pot of tea and took two painkillers. I threw my bloodstained handkerchief from the cut on my chin into the troughs and walked to the bakery.

It was a winter's day, and the sun pierced my retinas, making me close my eyes. I went home and put on my sunglasses. My whole body hurt, and I felt singed to the core with guilt. No one was on our street or the adjoining streets until I turned onto the main road and bent my head, not wanting to see anyone I knew. When I arrived at the bakery, I was sweating and uncomfortable. I wished I'd never come.

'Mark, look at you,' said Mrs Mackie. 'You look like you haven't slept. Should you be here?'

My voice sounded strained. 'I'm fine. It's just a cold.'

'Well, let us know if you want to leave early.'

The last time I worked, she gave me a loaf of bread to take home and said to keep my strength up. Each customer who entered the bakery appeared infuriatingly more cheerful with the sun out. The day felt like torture. Mrs Mackie made me a cup of coffee and gave me an iced doughnut for morning tea.

'You need to eat something. The coffee will make your throat feel more lucid.'

Her kindness made me feel guilty for all the days I didn't go to work. She fussed over me like I was her son. I said I'd be fine and went back into the shop. A customer wanted a loaf of white bread sliced for toast. I thought about Dave and when I'd see him again. Then I told myself: 'Get it right. He's dead.' And 'I'm sorry, Mum. Please forgive me for not grieving for you.'

❧

The synapses in my brain were branches of a tree twisting and turning in the wind. Dad was out when I returned home. After three hours of fidgeting without sleep, I got out of bed, went to the vanity cupboard, and took drowsy medication for cold and flu even though I didn't have either. Dave's voice was like a tape recorder I couldn't turn off. He kept telling me to take better care of myself. I fell asleep. I woke with an aching jaw from grinding my teeth. My clothes were on the floor, and I picked them up and put them on. I made myself a cup of coffee and ate an old apple sitting in the fruit basket in the middle of the kitchen table before leaving the house.

It was overcast on the way to the station. People were reading the morning paper. The wind blew the top off a garbage bin and made it hurtle down the road, but no one seemed to notice. I sat next to a window in the train and peered into people's backyards.

On my walk to class, everything grew as dark as my mood. Rain pelted, but I didn't care about getting wet. Pedestrians scurried to cafes for their morning coffee and into office buildings. In the class-room, I donned my apron and hair net while I waited for the other students to arrive. Since childhood, Mum had kept me insulated, living in a cosy bubble. I put my apron on and tried to take comfort in preparing the food. Today's menu was minestrone and pork pie. My temple throbbed. I could sense Chef watching me from the front of the room. The soup gave me acid, and I overcooked the meat.

'Your soup is the right consistency, but you should have diced the ingredients into smaller pieces, not chunks. As for the pie, you'll need to make it at home again. Your pastry is too flaky,' he said.

CHAPTER TWENTY-THREE

After breakfast, I packed my clothes and photos of Mum and Dave in my overnight bag. There was no point in staying in Noble Park any longer. I went for one last walk through the house and took my bank book and $200 cash out of a glass jar I found hidden in the back of the kitchen cupboard before getting into my car.

In Yass, I bought petrol and walked down the main street to stretch my legs. A good-looking man dressed in jeans and an open-neck shirt stepped out of a car and waved at me. I smiled at him and sheepishly waved back, only to see a blank expression on his face. I turned around. A girl crossed the road behind me and waved to him.

He walked towards her, and when he was level with me, he whispered, 'Faggot.'

A prickly sensation of shame coursed through my body, and I reminded myself that just because I was somewhere else, it didn't mean that men would be more accepting of me. My head hung low, and I hurried to my car—my haven—and drove until I reached Sydney.

I found a room at the YMCA to stay in overnight and flung my bag on the floor. I took my jeans and jumper off, eager to get into bed. My body eased between the heavy ice-cold covers, and I fell into a deep sleep. The next day, I moved into a boarding house in Balmain. My room was small, with a single bed, wardrobe, and a chest of drawers. A window overlooked the courtyard at the back of the property. I had become accustomed to the solitude of our house, and in the morning, the noise of doors opening and closing woke me.

The smell of bacon and eggs cooking wafted through my room. Two men, older than me, were seated at a table in a room next to the kitchen. I scraped a chair back on the linoleum floor and sat at the other end. No one spoke, so I didn't either. A man with a long grey beard and long hair tied into a ponytail came in, rattling a cereal box. He took several bowls from a cupboard with a wooden framed glass door and set them on the table.

'Help yerself,' he said, sliding the box in my direction before sitting.

I filled my bowl with cereal and poured milk over it from a ceramic jug he placed in front of me after he'd used it.

'The name's Roger,' he said. 'And you are?'

I felt like I'd committed a crime and was at the police station. The other two men stopped eating, waiting for me to speak. Roger said I looked too young to be there. He wanted to know where I had come from, why I was here, and what I did for a living. I cringed when Roger asked me if I'd ever been inside. Disbelief crossed his face, and I'm sure he thought I was lying.

The owner offered me a job cooking the meals and cleaning up afterwards. We had one thing in common. We were outsiders, making our way into life as best we could. My new life started early in the morning at the market, buying meat and vegetables before everyone else had woken. Each night, I sat in the living room reading a well-worn copy of One Flew Over the Cuckoo's Nest and browsed through old car magazines I'd found in a small built-in bookcase.

No one else sat in the living room after dinner. I felt like I was back home again until someone opened the front door. I lay in bed awake, listening to the street noise competing with the ticking of my alarm clock. My mind played a movie of me walking to the oval searching for Dave, and when I returned home, he was there waiting for me, asking me where I'd been.

Three months later, I wrote a letter to Nora explaining where I was in case; she needed to find me. When a letter arrived from Italy, I didn't recognize the handwriting and wondered who it was from until I opened it. The last time I'd seen Nora's writing was in high school. The tone of her letter sounded informative about her, Alfonso, and Issy. Nora had stopped working. She said she was getting ready for the birth of her baby and took Issy to and from school. She'd heard from Dad. Francesca was pregnant, and they were thinking of travelling to Italy for a holiday to visit Francesca's parents. My family had become distant relatives I didn't associate with anymore. I tore the letter into tiny pieces and threw it in the bin.

I sold my car because I was within walking distance of everything. After dinner each night, I walked around the neighbourhood to get my bearings. I envied people sitting in cafes and couples walking together, laughing, and talking. One night, on my way back to the boarding house, several people walked out of a building opposite the fire station.

I didn't see a man in cream trousers and an open-neck shirt behind them. I bumped into him and cowered back, waiting for him to yell something obscene at me. Instead, he apologized. Under the streetlight, I noticed the sincerity in his eyeliner, accentuated hazel eyes. He handed me a leaflet before striding away. My heart raced. There was a gay rally in Kings Cross the next day.

After Yass, my habitual fear resurfaced when I arrived at the rally, but a man named John introduced himself to me. We marched along George Street together. Another man came over to us and shook my hand. He said his name was Tony. My stomach fluttered. I was in awe of how many men there were like me. I held my head high, watching everyone and smiling for the first time in a long while. We all went to the building I'd seen them coming out of the previous evening. Inside, drinks and finger food were on trestle tables.

I waited in the queue and took a glass of Riesling. An overwhelming sense of belonging hit me for the first time since being at Bubbles with Dave. I didn't have to hide my feelings and wished he could be there, too. I was free to express myself and be me. John and Tony were partners and lived in Sydney. They said that everyone got together at The Club on Thursday night. My mind buzzed with happiness at the prospect of going there each week.

When I arrived at the boarding house, someone had left a message marked 'urgent' for me in my room to phone Nora. Even though I'd written to her and given her my details, I never expected to hear from her again. I considered her part of my old life and was enjoying my new one without her, but I knew Nora wouldn't phone me for the sake of it.

I imagined Dad had arrived in Italy with Francesca and Nora, wanting to air her grievances about them. After dinner, I took my time clearing the tables. I placed the dishes in the sink and washed and dried them. Afterwards, I walked down the street, looking for a payphone.

'Dad's in hospital. He said he had a fall and broke his hip. You need to see him. It's too hard for me to get there from here. He needs someone with him,' said Nora.

I breathed heavily into the receiver. 'But I thought Dad and Francesca were visiting you in Italy.'

'They did, but they're back home now.'

'What about Francesca? Why can't she visit him?'

'I knew that bitch was only after his money. She flirted with one of Alfonso's relatives when they came over here, fluttering those eyelashes of hers. She's left, Dad.'

'When?'

'A couple of weeks ago.' 'Where did she go?'

'How should I know?'

'What if I can't come?'

'You'll just have to.'

'And how is Dad?'

'The silly bastard's still pining for her.'

I wanted to tell her Dave had died. Nora would remember him, but my news stayed in my head. I was too frightened to let it go. Instead,

I listened to her ramble about Dad and said I had to go. I mulled over our conversation on my way to the boarding house. In the kitchen, I opened a bottle of scotch I found in the cupboard and poured a glass. I sat on the sofa in the living room and held it out.

'Cheers to you, Dave,' I said and had a mouthful. It burned as it went down my throat. My mind whispered that I'd imagined him.

Bill, the owner of the boarding house, interrupted me.

'I could do with one of those,' he said.

Bill put his hand out for the bottle. I drank the rest of my glass before telling him about Dad.

'Take as much time as you need off,' he said.

Suddenly, I remembered I'd forgotten to ask Nora whether she'd had her baby.

CHAPTER TWENTY-FOUR

Back in Melbourne, I stood in a tram squashed against office workers on my way to the hospital to visit Dad. When I entered the hospital, the familiar smell of disinfectant greeted me and reminded me of Mum.

Dad's unkempt dyed hair had greyish-yellow regrowth, and his bushy eyebrows looked unruly. His face appeared smaller. A set of dentures sat on top of the drawers beside his bed. His eyes narrowed when he saw me.

He spoke with a stridency, spitting slightly. 'What are you doin' here?'

'What do you think?'

He tried to sit up in bed and winced. His pallid face grew scarlet.

'I don't need you or anyone else. I'll be fine on my own. Get out! You bloody piss off without telling me where you'd gone.'

'You ought to talk.'

A nurse came over to us.

'I'm sorry you'll have to leave. Mr Cooney needs rest,' she said, pulling the surrounding curtain.

The sun shone through the train window on the way to Noble Park, and I dozed off for a while. I walked past Dave's house, and my mind played tricks on me, telling me he still lived there. The front door opened, and a woman came out carrying a child.

Our house repulsed me with its overgrown lawn and garden beds covered in weeds. Flower petals flew around the front yard in the wind. I searched under a rock near the veranda for the house key I'd put there the day I'd left. Inside, a framed print of Jesus with a halo and shining red heart hung in the entrance.

In the kitchen, the tap dripped over a sink full of dishes and condiments sat on the bench. Dad's unmade bed had clothes strewn across the top of it. A wedding photo of Francesca and him sat on the sideboard in the living room. Apart from that, there was no trace of Francesca. The laundry basket was overflowing onto the floor. The fridge and pantry were empty.

Clothes, shoes, and other possessions I left in my bedroom were gone. In its place was a small table with a sewing machine. My wardrobe had an assortment of materials stacked on one shelf. It was like I'd never lived here. The house no longer looked or smelt familiar, and I felt like an intruder in someone else's home. Nora's bed was gone from her room, and a knitted baby booty lay on the carpet.

Outside in the back garden, small green apples with specks on their unripe skin were around the trunk of one of the fruit trees. I peered through the garage window and saw Dad's car parked with a scrape on the passenger side. Down the street, I bought some groceries at the supermarket. It was like time had stopped because people seemed the same as before I'd left.

When I arrived home, I opened all the windows to air the stale cooking smell in the house and hung out a load of washing I'd put on earlier. I squeezed into a pair of Dad's overalls, and after I'd cleaned the house, I mowed the lawns, trying to keep busy so I wouldn't have to think. The letterbox was full of junk mail and envelopes. I left the envelopes on the kitchen bench for Dad to open and phoned the hospital. The nurse said he was sleeping, and they were operating on him early in the morning.

I soaked in a bubble bath. Nora phoned before I left the house. She wanted me to put the house on the market and stay for a while longer to put Dad into a nursing home. At first, I was against the idea, but after seeing the house, I changed my mind.

'The whole place is a mess. All I've done is clean the bloody joint. I'll have to convince him to go into care. I won't be coming back. He can't look after himself.'

'Mark, you, and I know you'll never get him to agree. I've already had that conversation with him, and he hung up. You'll have to speak to his doctor and explain the situation.'

'I'm leaving as soon as I know he's okay.'

'How was he when you saw him?'

'He said he doesn't need anyone and wanted me to go.'

'He's nothing but a stubborn, ungrateful old bastard.'

I ate my dinner at a new Chinese restaurant in Noble Park. It was already dark when I arrived home. I searched the bathroom and laundry cupboards for sleeping tablets. There were none. A bottle of red wine and a glass were in the living room cabinet. I poured myself a drink and sat outside on the back step, annoyed that I'd come here. The Merlot tasted acrid, sliding down my throat.

I poured another glass and thought about my new life. The men in the boarding house would eat the dinner I'd pre-prepared for them now. If I were there, I would clean up after them and get everything ready for breakfast before exploring one of the many bars. We respected one another's space, and there was no disdain. I unpegged the washing, folded it in the basket, and brought it inside. In the living room, I drank another glass of wine. I lay on the couch and fell into a dreamless sleep.

Dad had his eyes closed and a mask over his nose and mouth. His eyes opened at the sound of my footsteps approaching.

His words sounded muffled. 'I've got pneumonia. They can't operate until it clears up. Don't just stand there, sit down.'

He appeared upset, took the oxygen mask off, and tried to say something else, but it came out hacking wet and inaudible. His eyes closed, his breathing fast and shallow. Watching him made me uneasy. I tried to put the mask back on his face. His eyes opened wide like he'd seen something. Dad brushed my hand away and took the mask off his face. His face crumpled, and tears pooled. He gazed at the wall opposite, clawed my arm and tried to sit up—his skin like sandpaper.

'Stay.'

Dad pulled his mask off and coughed. He spat into a tissue and eyeballed me. I could tell he wanted to say something.

'What is it?'

Saliva floated around Dad's gaping mouth and burbled down his chin. I released his grip, and he fell back against the pillows. I clasped the apparatus back onto his face. He flicked my hands away, closed his eyes, and opened them again.

His voice sounded irritable. 'What are you doin' here, anyway? Where's Sandra gone?'

I clasped his limp hand in mine.

'Mum's coming,' I said, trying to soothe him.

Dad seemed happy with my reply and appeared calmer.

'You'll be fine,' I said, not believing the words as they left my mouth. 'You just need to rest.'

He said something else, his voice raspy against the machine. I couldn't understand him and didn't ask him to repeat himself.

Dad's eyes closed, and I moved closer and glanced at him. The life he'd led pitied and repulsed me. What would it be like having to marry someone you didn't love because it was your sense of duty? Had Mum and Dad grown in love over time? I waited a while and pried his hand away from mine before leaving.

Two days later, Dad died. Disbelief washed over me. I looked around the ward, expecting him to appear from the shower or toilet. I placed his belongings in his overnight bag and brought them home.

Nora arrived four days later to help me arrange his funeral. She was breastfeeding and had her son, Ricardo, with her. In the evening, we ate takeaway Chinese and shared a bottle of red wine. The phone rang when we sat in the kitchen to eat, and Nora answered it and spoke fluent Italian. I thought she was talking to Alfonso or Issy, but when she hung up, she said it was Francesca.

'What did you say?'

'He's dead. The funeral's next Wednesday. You'll have to look in the paper for the details.'

'You didn't have to be so harsh.'

'Nonsense, you've seen nothing yet.'

Francesca must've seen the funeral notice because she arrived at the chapel heavily pregnant, wearing a black lace dress and a black silk headscarf. She was with another woman who I didn't know. At the entrance, Nora nodded her head at Francesca, but they didn't speak. Despite Nora's misgivings, I walked over to Francesca, kissed both sides of her face, and said I was sorry for her loss. Her hands dropped to her sides. Her skin, usually covered in makeup, now lacked its healthy glow.

'Your father no good.' She touched her bum and said something to her friend in Italian. They both sniggered before turning to walk inside the chapel and sat in the front pew while Nora and I greeted the other mourners.

There was nowhere for Nora to sleep at our house, so she stayed with Vince and Loretta. Nora arrived after breakfast. We started in the kitchen and removed all the dishes, mugs, cups, and saucers from the cupboards. We placed them into empty boxes I'd taken from the supermarket earlier that morning. The cutlery drawer tilted open, and

I took the knives out and put a rubber band around them, the forks, spoons, and teaspoons. The Tupperware containers tumbled out of a cupboard. A Fowlers Vacola set with ten glass jars that Mum preserved fruit was at the back of the pantry.

Lace tablecloths she had hand-embroidered were piled high in the linen cupboard, and matching napkins sat beside them. They were all used for best and never used. Nora placed them in a new suitcase she'd bought down the street. Presents they'd received from friends at their anniversary party: a cheeseboard and knife, a tarnished silver tray, and a matching sugar bowl and creamer sat on the sideboard beside the cabinet in the living room.

'Remember these,' she said, holding a pair of silver wine goblets. 'That was what they drank out of when they cheered on their twentieth wedding anniversary, and Dad made a speech. They had a barbecue and invited all their friends. He said there would only be one woman for him. I used to think he was romantic with Mum when I was younger.' She let out a sigh. 'Why do men say such things?'

'Maybe we should leave something for Francesca,' I said.

'Are you kidding me? It's all going to charity. Mum would've wanted it that way. It's a shame I don't live close because I could take everything. It's too expensive to get a container shipped home.'

'Wouldn't Dad want Francesca to have something?'

'To hell with what he would've wanted. Besides, it's all Mum's stuff, not hers.'

I picked up my favourite baking dish and left her in the living room. In Dad's bedroom, I opened the wardrobe and found an old bag to put the dish in. The pockets of all his trousers and jackets had nothing in them.

When we'd finished filling the boxes and taking some of them to charity, Nora contacted only the furniture remained. Later that evening, I poured a capful of bubble bath into the bath before stepping in. I lay back and relaxed, reflecting on the events of the past couple of days.

Vince and Loretta invited me over to their house for dinner. Nora insisted I come, even though I preferred to be alone. Loretta greeted me at the door, kissed me on both sides of my face, and hugged me. She chastised me for not visiting them after Nora and Alfonso had moved to Italy.

'We a missed a you,' she said.

I was overcome with emotion and didn't know what to say. Vince greeted me with a glass of one of his famous wines and placed his other hand on my back. We sat at the dining room table, and they spoke Italian. Talking didn't interest me, and I sat and listened while I ate my lasagne. My stomach bloated after I'd finished it.

'Sorry,' said Nora. 'I forgot you don't speak Italian.'

I shrugged my shoulders. 'It doesn't matter. I don't feel well. Would you mind if I go?'

Nora said something to Vince and Loretta.

Loretta made a face. 'Si, Si. It's a okay,' she said.

⚬◦⟋⟍◦⚬

Nora found me asleep on the couch at home and woke me. We travelled into the city by train. At Spencer Street Station, she picked up her handbag beside her, stood up, and shouldered it to go. I carried her two suitcases to the taxi rank. She gazed at me with an apologetic cringe while she waited for a taxi to take her to the airport.

'You're all I've got left here now,' Nora said. 'Promise you'll come to visit.'

'Yeah, yeah,' I said to appease her. I took Ricardo out of her arms and kissed him, wondering if I'd ever see him again.

A taxi pulled up. I put Nora's luggage in the boot and hugged her and Ricardo. She pulled back and searched my face before kissing me on both cheeks. I waited for the taxi to pull away from the curb before I walked to the bus depot to catch the bus back to Sydney. The dim light in the bus flickered, and a woman sitting in the aisle opposite me eyed me suspiciously. The door closed, and the light went out. I sat on my own in the back and watched the city lights disappear.

The landscape turned dark. The moon and streetlights made the odd tree and farmhouse appear burnt. Inside, a mother pulled a small blanket out, placed it over her daughter's knees, and whispered for her to sleep. The man sitting next to me had his eyes closed. His lips moved back and forth like he was talking, but no sound came out. I read some of Nora's well-worn copy of The Great Gatsby in the weak light.

At some point, I slept, then woke up and read some more. At 5 am, we arrived in Sydney just as Tom was having an affair and was furious because he thought his wife could be unfaithful to him. The morning sun was breaking through the clouds, and the air was crisp. I looked forward to going to the Club on Thursday night.

The door to my cage opened, and I flew out. Free.

ABOUT THE AUTHOR

M.A. Quigley was born and raised in Victoria, Australia. She has an Associate Degree in Professional Writing and Editing from RMIT University in Melbourne, Australia. Her work has been published in anthologies in America, Australia, India, and the Philippines.

If you enjoyed reading this book, please review it.